*Blood and
Water*

Lucy McCarraher

Blood and Water

MACMILLAN NEW WRITING

First published 2006 by Macmillan New Writing,
an imprint of Macmillan Publishers Ltd
Brunel Road, Basingstoke RG21 6XS
Associated companies throughout the world
www.macmillannewwriting.com

ISBN-13: 978–0230–00186–2 hardback
ISBN-10: 0230–00186–6 hardback
ISBN-13: 978–0230–00734–5 paperback
ISBN-10: 0230–00734–1 paperback

9 8 7 6 5 4 3 2 1

A CIP catalogue record for this book is available from
the British Library.

Typeset by Heronwood Press
Printed and bound in China

*For Richard, who has enabled
me to do what I always wanted*

*"Uncertainty and expectation are the joys of life.
Security is an insipid thing."*
WILLIAM CONGREVE

Acknowledgements

This book's publication was set in motion by Maya Elliott, who encouraged me to submit an abandoned fragment to the Richard and Judy 'How To Get Published' competition; and made possible by Lizzi Becker, who had saved a hard copy when all electronic files had long since self-destructed. When Mike Barnard of Macmillan New Writing asked to see the full novel, I turned to Verity Ridgman for editorial support as I wrote the rest of the story. Her linguistic incisiveness and structural insights were invaluable as she read, re-read and helped revise my infelicities. Jackee Holder's coaching sessions kept me focused, and Mike Elliston was, as ever, my right-hand man and the first to make me think I might have written something worthwhile. My sons, James and Christopher Page, read drafts and gave constructive feedback, as did their father, Rob Page, who allowed me to turn his excellent real-life proposition, UR M8, into the fictitious TXT M8 service. Sister writer Jo Holloway was always there when I needed her, and Ros Ali and Sue Reynolds read and commented throughout. My book group discussed the final draft for one of our meetings; thanks especially to Ann Carrington, Aileen Cook and Helen Lycett for their helpful contributions. The McCarraher and Wagner families have been sources of inspiration and, as always, totally supportive.

Main Characters

The family
Mary Patterson – also known as *Mo Mozart* (her maiden name), a "social issues" researcher
Jack Patterson – her husband, a GP
Lily – Mo and Jack's four-year-old daughter
Mark – Mo's student son
Zoe – Mark's girlfriend
Jess – Mo's eighteen-year-old daughter
Paul – Mo's ex-husband, father of Mark and Jess

Mo's family
Athene Mozart – Mo's mother
Anthony Mozart – Mo's younger brother, an art dealer
Sally Mozart – Anthony's wife, an interior designer

Jack's family
Julia Patterson – Jack's twin sister
Danny – Julia's eight-year-old son
Betty Patterson – Jack and Julia's adoptive mother
Colin Patterson – Jack and Julia's adoptive father

Next door
Mel – Mo's childminder for Lily
Andrew – Mel's husband
Bethany – Mel and Andrew's four-year-old daughter
Noah – Mel and Andrew's two-year-old son

The search
Peggy Finch – a local vagrant also known as *Old Peggy*
Caitlin Doyle – Jack and Julia's birth mother
Niamh O'Connor – a post-adoption counsellor

The friends
Venetia – a senior civil servant in the Department of
    Information
Aurora – Venetia's daughter, an artist
Ros – a child psychotherapist
Joe – Ros's partner, an actor
Suzy – a campaigner for disabled children
Duncan – Suzy's husband, a solicitor
Olly – Suzy and Duncan's eighteen-year-old Down's Syndrome
    son
Martin – Suzy and Duncan's younger son
Miranda – a pharmaceutical scientist
Si(mon) – Miranda's husband, friend of Mo from student days
Naomi – Miranda and Simon's fifteen-year-old daughter
Lola – Miranda and Simon's younger daughter
Nick – Mo's ex-boyfriend, a political lobbyist
Dennis Reid – a local historian

Work
Erica Beamish – a "social issues" journalist
David – MD of Generation Productions
Jane – producer of the sex education project at Generation
    Productions
Peter Braithwaite – a media sex-expert
Ellie – receptionist of Generation Productions
Maxwell Robards MP – a right-wing politician
Kathleen Robards – his wife, supporter of children's charities
Ruby Wadilove – a secretary

Chapter One

The tunnel between Gipsy Hill and Crystal Palace always disorientated me. Stretching almost the whole distance between the two stations, its curving length of dismal brickwork made it hard to gauge the right time to stand up, gather my belongings and move towards the doors so as to step out onto the platform without a last-minute rush.

This evening, though, I timed it perfectly, packing my book away, gathering my long coat from under my feet, hitching my bags onto my shoulder and reaching the doors exactly as they snickered unevenly open to release me onto the rain-swept platform.

A tiny example of good timing, but the cumulative effect of such minor successes was increasing my sense of being in control of my life.

The rain turned into driving sleet as I walked home down Auckland Road. I put my umbrella down and turned up my face for an abrasive, but all natural, facial and hair treatment.

Passing the church hall where my weekly yoga classes were held, I reflected on my progress during the year since I had started going. Not only had I regained some suppleness, learned to quell my anxiety with breathing techniques and release stress through relaxation, but I had finally made contact with what I thought must be a spiritual power. After weeks of fruitless meditation, the Universal Spirit, the Source, Life Force, Energy Flow, Spirit – I shied away from the word God – had made herself known to me. Not through words, images or bolts of lightening, but with such a strong sense of presence that I now actively tried to invoke her in every aspect of my life.

Using my walk to smooth the transition between work and home hadn't quite had the effect I'd been hoping for. I looked in the hall mirror as the wind blew me and a swirl of dead leaves through the front door: my glowing nose and dripping curls failed to portray the healthy, well-balanced working wife and mother I was almost managing to be.

"Hello, I'm home …" I called, draping my soaking coat and scarf on the radiator and running upstairs. There was laughter and splashing from the bathroom on the half-landing and Jack appeared in the doorway, behind a tousled Lily wrapped up in a towel.

"Hello, Mummy. Do you want my towel?" asked my youngest daughter, helpfully.

"Oh, Mo! Did you forget your umbrella? You should have rung and we'd have come and collected you," added my husband, unhelpfully.

"No, you know I like walking in the rain. It was a nice way to chill out," I said.

Jack's smile looked unconvinced. He had spent the seven years we'd been together trying, as he saw it, to sort my life out, get me grounded and working to the principles he prized so highly – rationality, logic, scepticism and good planning. I, on the other hand, had made few attempts to convert him to my cherished values of intuition, creativity, empathy and responsiveness, but wished he would respect that these made me the person he had fallen in love with.

It was true that he'd taken on a fistful of problems when he committed himself to me and mine: an older, divorced partner with an unstructured, single-parent lifestyle, two self-willed teenagers, a 'portfolio' career, debts and an opinionated mother-in-law. By contrast I had gained a stable, supportive husband with a good job as a GP in a thriving local surgery, savings and a plan for life. While most of my friends had told me how lucky I was to get Jack, some of his told me how good I was for him, making him less uptight, more relaxed and able to have fun, more like the person they had known in their student days. Myself, I thought our differences made for an exciting tension in our relationship, which complemented a deep commitment to each other and our life together – although perhaps I was expected to conform more to his wishes than he to mine.

Lily's bedroom was chaotic – I'd left early this morning and whilst I couldn't fault Jack on doing his share of the childcare, tidying up was never something he saw as falling into his domestic remit. I couldn't find her favourite pink butterfly pyjamas anywhere and, now she had both of us in attendance, Lily was winding up to pre-bedtime hyper-activity, when crossing her could result in a major tantrum. "Peace and calm," I repeated in my head as I exhaled. "I am relaxed and in control, relaxed and in control …" Jack was diverting Lily from the pyjama issue by spinning her round until she was dizzy; inevitably she fell over and banged her head – not badly but enough to trigger tears.

"Mummy kiss it better," prescribed the doctor, depositing our daughter in my arms, and made good his escape to catch the start of his football match on TV. I persuaded her to wear the blue pyjamas instead and have her hair dried in our bedroom, trying to turn the few moments I'd spend with Lily today into quality time. People said we looked alike, and in the mirror I could see similar curly, coffee-coloured hair – though my tint was synthetic and hers a temporary shade on the way from baby blonde to dark – and she had inherited my large, dark brown eyes. I scrunch-dried her hair and mine, and dabbed a bit of powder at the healthy glow my nose was still sporting. As she scrambled off my knee, I turned the dimmer switch down a little, smiled my jaw-line taut and thought that for forty-five my complexion didn't look too bad, provided it wasn't directly compared to Lily's peachy, four-year old skin.

Jack was watching football with a can of lager and a family bag of dry-roasted peanuts when I went into the living room with a glass of sparkling water.

"This is my exercise for the day," I said, cuddling up to him on the sofa. "Did you know that the calories in a glass of wine take fifteen minutes on the treadmill to walk off?" He put his arm round me without taking his eyes off the screen. "Do you want something to eat before I go to yoga?" I asked, getting to my feet.

"Oh, it's not tonight, for heaven's sake!" Jack left the match and followed me into the kitchen. It wasn't great timing, my one full working day out of the house coinciding with my yoga evening, but then I wasn't supposed to complain when Jack was out on call at night after a full day at the surgery. He justified it on the grounds that nights paid double time; I claimed yoga gave me back double the time I spent there.

"Yep, sorry. It'll have to be tuna pasta. I don't think I'll eat before I go – potential flatulence in the child position ..." I rummaged in the cupboard for *penne*, a jar of pasta sauce and a tin of tuna. At least there was some fresh basil and a dry hunk of parmesan in the fridge.

"Leave it, Mo. I'll get a pizza. I thought we'd have a chance to talk this evening." That sounded slightly ominous. Not that Jack was often confrontational, but I could guess what was coming and tried to pretend I hadn't.

"Work wasn't that interesting. I only interviewed the couples. Dr Braithwaite and Jane were going to do the 'auditions' later – I refused to be in on that. I mean I'm not prudish, but I wasn't going to work late for the privilege of operating the video while they checked out which of the couples could really cope with having sex on camera."

"My wife the pornographer," snorted Jack, taking the bait. Better to argue about the nature of my work than whether I should be doing it at all.

"It is going into schools now; the Education Department said today that they'd back the project, so it's all very socially responsible. Teenagers need information."

"Shit, I wouldn't sit through your programme with a room-ful of fifteen-year-olds – not for a teacher's pay, anyway!"

"Well I'm just pleased to be working on an important project that could have a real effect on unwanted teenage pregnancy and sexually transmitted diseases," I replied, trying to sound above reproach. Then hearing the crowd roar fortuitously from the TV, "Sounds like a goal!"

As Jack ran back to the living room to see if his team had scored, I escaped upstairs to change.

After pulling on my tracksuit, I checked on Lily, who was sleeping soundly, thumb in mouth, and revelled in this vision of pure tranquillity and undiluted innocence which my older children, Mark and Jess, had long outgrown. I gathered yoga blocks, mat and rug into my peasant-woven basket and slipped back down to the hall. I was searching silently for where Jack had left the car keys when the phone rang. "Don't let it be for me," I fired off a request to the Universal Spirit, "you know I need my meditation to stay in touch with you ..." But clearly the Life Force had other plans for me that night. I didn't know that they would affect so much more than that one evening when Jack shouted, "Mo! It's Julia, she's upset – you'll have to take it," and thrust the phone into my hand before disappearing back into the sitting room.

"Hi, Jules, what's the prob?" I asked breezily. "Just rushing out to yoga, can I call you later?" I located the car keys under the day's unopened post, still hoping to make a quick getaway. At the other end, quiet snuffling noises told me Julia's inability to form words through tears wasn't going to make this a short, or even postponable, conversation. I put the keys down again and sat on the stairs. "OK, Jules. In your own time. Take a breath, feel the calm … Is it your mum?"

"How did you know that, Mo?" Julia seemed shocked into speech. "How do you do that mind-reading thing? Yes, of course it is. I've got to find her, I've got to make contact, it's the only way I'll find myself."

It was true, there were times when I could be intuitive to the point of telepathic, but strangely this was not one of them. I had guessed, in part rightly, that Julia had had another row with Betty, her and Jack's mother, but this was not what she wanted my advice about. Instead, the latest *contretemps* concerning Julia's somewhat unconventional lifestyle had goaded her into saying what she had always denied any interest in before: that she wanted to find her birth mother.

I let Julia maintain her belief in my powers of perception by saying nothing as she unravelled the story. I could imagine how intense the argument between mother and daughter must have been for Julia to have unleashed this lethal weapon. Betty, who had always proclaimed herself entirely open to the twins getting in touch with their biological parents, nevertheless took a transparent pride in their hitherto united stance that she and Colin were the only parents they wanted or needed, and that their genetic inheritance was of no interest to them. This about-face from Julia must have cut Betty to the quick and I was keen to ring her, offer sympathy and hear her side of the story. Jules, though, was unstoppable in her efforts to recruit me to her scheme.

"You're a researcher, Mo. You know about social issues and this is a social issue, isn't it? I've got the right to look for my real mother, find my roots, haven't I? I'm sure that's what's missing in my life, it's the answer to all my problems. Once I know where I come from I'll be able to fill my emotional gaps. There's nothing wrong with me, but how can anyone expect me to be totally stable and, like, rooted, when I don't know who I am? And Danny has the right to know who his real grandparents are. I got my file from Social Services a couple of years ago, but I don't even know where to start looking. You could help me, Mo. You could. Please say yes."

When I could get a word in edgeways, I told Julia that she had every right to search for her birth mother, but tried to point out that there were a few pitfalls in her plan.

"You can't look on it as a panacea, you just don't know what you might find, Jules. To be blunt, what if you find she's dead, or some down-and-out junkie, or just someone you don't really like? What if she doesn't want to know you – that would be double rejection?"

But Julia had made her mind up. "It doesn't matter. At least I'd know, and maybe she'd have family I would like and who'd love me and Dan, and I'd feel part of them – like I don't with my own, I mean my adopted, family."

I didn't take her up on this, confront her with the fact that, as I saw it, she'd always been the spoiled one, cosseted because she was the 'delicate' twin, pandered to by her adopted parents and her biological brother because she had 'problems'.

"And if I did help, what about Jack?" I asked her.

"What *about* Jack? He's never going to help me".

"Exactly, Julia, because *he doesn't want to know*. And you've always said that you didn't either, and now you're asking me to help you find your mother when you know Jack won't have a bar of it. How do you expect me to square that one?"

To be fair, Julia shut up for a few moments and perhaps considered her brother's feelings and my dilemma. But she was soon back with an answer.

"Easy. We won't tell him. He doesn't have to know anything about it."

I told her I wouldn't lie to him or have secrets from him, and nor should she. Not about something so fundamental as this.

"Alright then, tell him we're looking but we won't tell him anything about what we find. Come on, Mo, you're the only person I know who can do this. You're, like, such a brilliant researcher and you're so sensitive about people and all that. You could even handle Mum and Dad on this one – though we don't have to say anything to them yet."

Julia's appeal to my expertise and people-handling skills was spot on, though I was aware of her own speciality in flattery and manipulation. Betty and Colin did think their son had made a good marriage even though he had picked a single mother of two, six years older than him. But I told her I'd have to think about it, talk to Jack and get back to her. She seemed pretty sure her blandishments had had the desired effect as she didn't bother with any more persuasion tactics and rung off with a chirpy, "Thanks, Mo, you're a star. Talk to you tomorrow, yeah? Byee."

I sat on the stairs a while longer. Yoga suddenly didn't seem as important as having a serious talk with my patient, stable (despite having the same background as Julia), kind husband. He was a tolerant man and never one to shy away from other people's problems, especially his beloved, if irritating, twin sister's. But once his mind was made up on some issues, there was no changing it. This might be one of them.

"No, Mo! You are not to do this! It's none of your fucking business and I don't want you helping her. It's a whim, she's just being emotional. She'll get over it."

Jack's particular choice of words was a red rag to me. First, I never liked being told what I could and could not do. Second, how dare he tell me that the identity of his birth mother and Lily's grandmother was not my business? And third, though I agreed that Julia was a creature of caprice and crazes, I felt instant sisterly solidarity in the face of this male attack on emotion.

So we had a row.

Not a loud airing of disparate views arcing into a bit of personal abuse and subsiding into grudging acceptance of each other's point of view, but a shouting, vituperative exchange where our faces grew flushed and ugly, we slashed at each other's Achilles' heels with any weapon to hand, then left each other alone, bleeding and bruised, me in the bedroom, Jack in his study, with an impenetrable atmosphere of freezing fog between the two.

"Bugger! I should have gone to yoga and ignored Julia's

tears," I thought. "He's right, she'll probably give up on it if she doesn't get a result straight away, and then there'll be this rift between us for no reason."

But I couldn't surrender, go and say sorry and that I'd refuse to get involved. It was more than Julia's request for help or her need to know; my fundamental allegiance to Jack couldn't be shaken by his sister's wheedling. It was more than idle curiosity, the nosy parker in me refusing to stand away from the net curtains; and beyond professional pride in my ability to get a result from such a challenge. It had touched my own deep-rooted concerns with the Chi of parent/child relationships. The absence of their own father had worried me as I brought up my first two children alone and, even when Jack became a loving and dependable stepfather, I wondered what they had missed and whether it was retrievable. Now I had the chance to see at close quarters the restoration of a biological parent to an adult (or two, if Jack participated) who had grown up without knowing them.

I had to find this woman; the quest had already become my own. And I had to make it right with Jack.

Tearful and shaken by our clash, I sat on the floor in the Sukhasana position and did my Pranayama Complete Breath: inhale down to the belly, fill the ribcage, top up to the throat, hold; exhale from the diaphragm, empty the thorax, clear the trachea. Peace and calm, peace and calm, peace, calm … Jack's words kept floating into my head, but I pushed them back out into the void. I cleared my mind, asked the Ultimate Source for advice, and waited. There was no explicit message for me – there hardly ever was – but I could tell when she was there: a kind of floating feeling, detached but intense awareness and a slight fizzing in my veins – that was how the connection worked for me. And then not so much specific knowledge, but a sense of clarity, reassurance. I had to do this, it was the right choice.

All would be well and all manner of things would be well.

It got me to sleep and I didn't hear Jack come to bed, but I woke up early with the old anxiety pulsing behind my eyes. The fact that it hadn't bothered me for months, perhaps over a year now, made it particularly noticeable. The only cure was to get up and get going, and when Jack came downstairs to find his breakfast on a properly laid table, he seemed calm and friendly. He accepted scrambled eggs with a surprised smile, poured us both coffee from the cafetiere and teased Lily into finishing her cereal. Though neither of us apologised, he showed no signs of nursing a grudge.

As he opened the front door to start his five-minute walk up to the surgery on Sylvan Hill, Jack turned back to me and said, "I know you'll do what you have to do and I can't stop you, Mo. Just two things: make the right choice and, whatever it is, you'll have to live with it yourself. I want to know nothing, *nothing*, about it at all. OK?"

"OK," I said, "but—"

"No, that's it. End of discussion. Bye, Li'l Girl." He swung Lily up, kissed her and she hugged him with relish.

"Bye bye, Daddy. See you tonight."

"Bye, baby. Bye honey," he kissed me affectionately and left me to puzzle over his decision. Was it a gesture of generosity, of reluctant acceptance, or a poisoned chalice?

Lily bounced up the path to next door's house, tugging on my hand to pull me along faster and laughing in delight when Mel opened the door with Bethany and Noah around her legs. She had known Melanie and Beth from the day she came home with me from King's College Hospital, a tiny, four-weeks-premature scrap, so viewed them and Noah, born a year later, unreservedly as her extended family. It had seemed the perfect arrangement when Mel had told me she was registering as a child-minder and asked if I'd like Lily to be her first charge.

Mel and Andrew were archetypal good parents: relaxed, warm and child-focused in a traditional Caribbean way. I had taken this as a sign that I should go back to work, and persuaded a slightly reluctant Jack that it would be good for Lily to have a range of secure environments and carers. Four years later she was as happy in their comfortable, toy-filled home as in our side of the Victorian semi-detached – perhaps more so, I sometimes thought. She often pleaded to go and see Beth outside child-minding hours and our frequent social visits didn't seem to bother Mel and Andrew, although they didn't make the return trip up our front path nearly so often.

"You got a lot of work on, girl?" asked Mel, as the children scampered off down the hall behind her. "She's come out of her-self so much lately, you must miss her when you're off working all day. She was fine yesterday, no need to worry about her. Happy all day long – but pleased to see her Daddy at teatime," she added, tactfully.

"Yeah, I do miss her, but I'm too old to give up work completely this time round, Mel. I'd never get back in again. And I enjoy what I do, as well as needing the money."

"Sure you do, clever woman like you. What you doing today – more of that crazy TV business? You can leave her as long as you like, I'll take them to soft play in South Norwood after dinner."

It was a tempting offer, and one that Lily would have leaped at, but as I was going to meet friends this morning, rather than doing real work, I felt too guilty to accept. I never liked to ask, either, whether Mel was suggesting an extension of paid child-minding hours or a switch to a social kids' outing.

"No, that's fine, thanks, Mel. I'll finish this bit of research by lunchtime. We might meet you at the Leisure Centre, or go swimming there anyway this afternoon. Fancy the toddlers' pool after soft play?"

"Well, maybe, Mo. I'll see how Noah's cold's going on. See you later, girl. Get some good work time in. Make it worth your while!" She smiled and closed the door, cutting me off from the cheerful yells of the children.

As I started up Auckland Road, it struck me that, in a sense, I was going to use the morning for my work – my support net-work was an essential part of my work-life balance. "I am always in the right place at the right time," I reminded myself. And I could ask Miranda and Venetia to be case studies for the mother/daughter relationships article I was researching for Erica Beamish. Erica was a high-profile writer on social issues who often paid me to do background research for her newspaper articles. She always wanted me to find case studies who would agree to be photographed, as well as quoted, for her pieces and I usually had to persuade friends to do this. The people with real problems I tracked down would normally only talk if they could remain anonymous, and Erica could not seem to grasp that a black and white mug-shot in a major daily paper was not the ideal way of preserving their privacy.

The walk back up the hill was somewhat more tranquil than last night's walk down. The storm had blown itself out, and only a reedy wind was still blowing through the skeletal trees. There was little warmth from the thin, winter sunshine and I could see why the Victorian developers had marketed the new Crystal

Palace neighbourhood as the Fresh Air Suburb. Though the alpine motifs – steeply raked gables, half-timbered facades and Swiss chalet-type roof carvings – on otherwise bog-standard London terraces might have taken their theme a little too far. I decided to turn left just before the top and walk up Fox Hill, but despite the yoga breathing practice, my lungs started to regret it about halfway up the steep incline. I concentrated on trying to visualise the road in its earlier, rural incarnation, basing my mental picture on the reproductions of Pissarro's watercolours we had bought from the local art shop.

It was a relief to regain the flat pavement of Church Road, historically the grottiest street in the Upper Norwood Triangle. I tried to lose focus and see through the facades of the second-hand shops and ungentrified cafés, like a magic eye picture into the past, when St Aubin's School had housed abandoned pauper infants on this site. That was until shareholders in the Crystal Palace Company had forced out the insalubrious little neighbours of their newly installed exhibition hall. I liked to picture the spirits of these long dead, unloved children skipping gleefully at night through the ruined grandeur of the once glittering pleasure dome that had been the raison d'être of our local park.

As luck would have it, Venetia and Miranda were the first two arrivals at Café St Germain, or the French café as we always called it, on Crystal Palace Parade. We'd been meeting regularly for the best part of twenty years, since Venetia, Suzy and I had hung out at the swings and the now defunct children's zoo when our kids were small. We had originally staked out our coffee mornings as child-free time where we could be women as well as mothers; now we dedicated time out from work to touch base on our personal lives. At twenty-four Venetia's daughter, Aurora, was the eldest of all our children, while at fifteen and thirteen, Miranda's were the youngest – apart from Lily. They both agreed to give me a verbal snapshot of their mother/daughter relationships, and Miranda said that Naomi and Lola would get a buzz from being in the paper, and she could do with some new photos of them in any case.

Work done, we ordered our usual cappuccino (me), herbal tea (Miranda), espresso with cream cakes (Venetia) and waited for the others to turn up.

Venetia was incensed by the slack attitude of the new team she had been put in charge of at the Department of Information. "The problem is," she fulminated, "they've got it all sewn up between them. Whatever I say, whatever line I take to get them working harder or faster, they manage to make me look like a tight-assed, middle-class spinster and I feel totally alienated." It was true that, though her Chanel suit came from Oxfam and she had discreetly slept her way through the upper echelons of the Department, Venetia had morphed in appearance from ultimate wild child to senior career civil servant.

"Do you want me to drop into your office and start reminiscing about the old days?" I asked. "I could tell them about the bad trip where you sat in the bath eating chocolate biscuits till you threw up over yourself, or about the orgies in your room that stopped everyone else from sleeping …?"

"Thanks for the offer, Mo, but I'd like to keep my job," she replied, smiling at the student memories. "On the other hand, it might be time to show them I'm not just a suit – but with a touch more subtlety. Not such a bad idea." She looked over half moon specs, tucked a strand of faded blonde hair into her slide and smiled her private smile. I wondered what revelation from her multifaceted experience she thought would shock her staff into action.

"And how's things with you and Si?" she asked, turning her steely blue gaze to Miranda.

"Oh, Simon's totally preoccupied with his doctorate, but he should be through by summer," Miranda replied, a trifle defensively.

I had never been sure whether Si had been one of Venetia's lovers at university, but suspected that Miranda might know and resent the past. Venetia and my eyes flickered together for a millisecond. Si was notoriously late for everything and had been writing his famous PhD thesis since we'd all three graduated together. He was still only halfway through when he returned from a university lectureship in the States twelve years ago, accompanied by Miranda and their two small children. Even now, she maintained a wifely belief in the completion of his oeuvre against what we considered long odds.

"That's great," I responded quickly, before Venetia could get in a wry comment. "But it must be a bit tough on you and the girls if he's lecturing all day and writing all night."

She made a face. "Naomi's fine, she's like me, knows what she has to do and gets on with it. Lola's just so – so rebellious. About schoolwork, domestic chores, family commitments, anything we want her to do. I just cannot get her to do her homework on time, keep her room tidy – in fact I can't get through to her at all, and right now Simon's leaving all that to me."

"So she's inherited Si's attitude to deadlines, then!" laughed Venetia, turning to welcome Suzy and Ros who were scraping chairs out from under the table and noisily apologising for their lateness. She didn't hear Miranda mutter, "If only it was that simple."

Our traditional routine involved each of us sharing a problem we were facing and a success we'd achieved during the week, either from work or home. Miranda and Venetia expanded on the subjects they'd already raised and we all chipped in with advice. Miranda, an ambitious pharmaceutical scientist, had also reached a breakthrough in her research on a new drug, while Venetia revealed that she'd notched up a record six months with her current boyfriend, a nearly-divorced MP with a junior ministerial post in the Foreign Office, and was still hot for him.

"Is it all that sex that keeps you so skinny?" moaned Suzy. "I've probably put on five pounds just by watching you eat that cream cake. Yesterday at Weightwatchers I'd put on weight, not lost it. That's my problem for the week."

"Suze, you are what you're meant to be. You and I will never have Venetia's figure, no matter how much we diet, never have had, never will do. You're a fantastic, flamboyant, substantial woman and Duncan adores you, so why put yourself through all this?" I rolled out my personal mantra to her, drawing comfort at the same time from the fact that Suzy was, and always had been, much fatter than me and that Jack didn't fancy Venetia's stick-thin frame.

"That's so sweet, Mo – do you think that's what I am, girls? A substantial person in the spiritual sense?" Suzy cocked her head with its jaunty cloche hat to one side and adjusted the matching pashmina over her ample cashmere coat. Then before anyone could answer, she burst into self-deprecatory laughter that raised every head in the café. "Well, if I am, Olly's helped me get there. I think I've got him into the special needs college in Redhill I've had my eye on. It's residential, but we can have him back at weekends. We've already been down to look at it and there are several other Down's Syndrome children there. They teach them independent life skills and there's lots of opportunity for art activities – especially drama and dance, which Olly will adore. Persistence pays off with Lambeth Education Authority."

"That's brilliant, Suzy. You've done really well there, I do admire you." Ros's rich, deep voice stroked the air. And I admired Ros. She listened to and advised the rest of us on our endless problems with our children, while we feigned a polite interest in her Dalmatians, Phoebe and Silvius. "I feel bad enough that we're having to put the dogs into kennels next week – Joe's gone up to Stratford for the repertory season, and I've got a child psychologists' conference in Manchester – not quite so glamorous. I hate not being around for Joe when he's out of town, he likes at least to know I'm there to phone when the show ends, and you can't avoid the evening networking at conferences."

"And some of those new RSC actresses are just so young and gorgeous," sniped Venetia. "Don't you ever worry when Joe's on tour?"

Ros just smiled and, as ever, looked cool and collected. At nearly six foot she was an imposing figure, her stunning long legs, without an atom of cellulite, were balanced by a strong-featured face and glossy black hair. Today it was newly cut into sharp, swinging layers and she wore just enough make-up for her dark eyes to look particularly large and lustrous. She had the kind of perfect relationship with Joe – long-term commitment combined with undying romance – that brought out the bitchy comments in those less well partnered. Ros's profession, and her empathy with children, would have made her a wonderful mother, but she would never be drawn on why she and Joe had not had children.

"Look, I've got a really serious dilemma, and I'd appreciate all your advice," I told them, truthfully, but at the same time diverting Venetia from pursuing Ros any further.

The smell of Old Peggy reached me before I looked up from the pavement and saw her trundling her Morrisons trolley, piled with ancient plastic bags, towards me as I walked home down Anerley Hill. I smiled at her as I tried to speed-walk past her, breathing through my cappuccino-tasting mouth, but she shot out a claw-like hand and grabbed my wrist.

"Give Peggy a hand to the park, lovely. Can't breathe too good today."

That was the understatement of the year. Peggy's emphysemic breathing, no doubt self-inflicted by the perpetual, flattened fag-end in the corner of her mouth, was painful to hear. She must have been well over seventy. The Universal Energy nudged me with a sudden prompt – *whatever you wish for yourself, give to another* – and I felt a pang of guilt that I could so easily be deterred from making good karma by the stench of old clothes and stale piss. I turned back.

"Of course I will, Peggy. Here, let me push, you hold onto the side," I told her, seeing that the shopping trolley combined as her suitcase and her Zimmer frame. We moved slowly up the hill and I wondered how she ever managed to push the heavy structure herself, with its stiff and wonky wheels. "Couldn't you swap this for a newer one at Morrisons, with straighter steering?" I asked her.

"Peggy ain't welcome at Morrisons no more. New manager don't like her sleeping in the car-park, but some of the younger ones give us past-its-sell-by-date food. Nice buns they do there."

We had to stop while she caught her breath after this little speech, so I didn't attempt to make any more conversation until we got to the park gates, beyond which the wide drive ran down at a slight incline.

"Thank you, lovely," she gasped. "Peggy can manage now." She grasped my hand again as I moved aside from the trolley handle. "Peggy helps those who help her," she wheezed, turning up my palm and staring at it. "Oooh, lovely, you got a hard choice, ain't ya?" She looked into my eyes and held my gaze. Her greasy black fringe and bony, wizened face with its hooked nose and pointed chin, seemed to melt away around worlds contained in her deep, black eyes. "Love says go, fear says no." Old Peggy stared another second after this pronouncement and turned back to her trolley. "Go on, lovely. She's waiting for you, even if she don't know it."

I was still disturbed when I arrived back home. An old woman's pathetic pretence at fortune telling couldn't be taken seriously and of course rated as nothing beside my friends' thoughtful advice. And yet they had been equally divided. *You got a hard choice here …* Suzy and Ros had been all for my helping Julia find her birth mother: Suzy because she believed in the responsibility of genetic parents for their offspring and, anyway, loved the prospect of some intrigue; Ros because she felt Jack did want to know about his mother, but was afraid of looking himself. Telling me to go ahead, but not to let him know about it was, she had inferred as a professional psychologist, the only way he could deal with it. *Love says go …* Venetia, on the other hand, was habitually dismissive of Julia's antics and thought biological relationships much over-rated; and I still couldn't figure out Miranda's uncharacteristically emotional response to the whole issue, what terrible revelations she thought I might uncover, or rifts it might engender. *Fear says no …*

Go on, she's waiting for you ... Lily, I had assumed she meant. Peggy had seen me about the Palace with her and knew I'd have to be getting back to my little daughter. *Even if she don't know it ...* Of course Lily wouldn't know when I was due to pick her up, so wouldn't know she was waiting for me. But could she have meant someone else? Ridiculous. Peggy knew nothing about my life and, like horoscopes, she had only made the most sweeping statements that anyone could have found some relevance in.

I had to clear my mind of the whole episode and make a logical decision. It was ten past twelve and I had twenty minutes before I was due to collect Lily. I piled up my yoga blocks and sat, back straight, legs crossed, in a half-lotus position – I couldn't quite manage both feet up with comfort, yet. I did fast Kapalabhati breathing from the diaphragm, exhaling all thoughts of Old Peggy and decisions to be made. As I settled into regular breathing, my headspace seemed to expand – but not into the usual state of slightly altered awareness I managed in most meditation now.

The inside of my head suddenly filled with an image of startling clarity, as if a three-dimensional film had started to play around me. I seemed to be standing in a river, the water was icy-cold and the river wide and deep, with a strong current. It was a beautiful summer day, early afternoon I guessed, as the sun was still high in the sky. It illuminated an idyllic landscape of green fields rising towards the horizon on one side of the river, while the other bank rose up into woods whose trees were thickly covered with rich and variegated leaves. I felt an intense happiness and an awareness of someone else on the bank. As I turned to call to them, the image faded and I snapped out of my meditative state with a start.

This disquieting experience, which seemed to have taken me

into another world, a life other than my own, had diverted me from Peggy's words and thoughts of adoption, but didn't make me feel any more grounded. I must have been seriously stressed, I concluded, for my mind to play such a bizarre trick. What I needed was a simple session with Lily in the swimming pool, book-ended by the practicalities of managing a small child in a communal changing room. I stood up creakily from my cross-legged position and went next door to Mel's.

Chapter Two

I gave Jack a few days to raise the Julia business again, but he said nothing. He stayed cheerful, said no more about my work and made an effort to finish surgery earlier and be home for Lily's bedtime. It was disconcerting, but I decided to enjoy it and hope that Ros had been right: this was his way of giving me permission to do what he could not, perhaps out of fear, perhaps out of loyalty to Colin and Betty. The Source was quiet on the subject as well. She thrilled through my veins and buzzed in my ears when I meditated, but offered no further visions, words or signs. It seemed I was on my own.

"Hello, Erica, it's Mo Mozart. I was just—" ringing to ask whether she wanted the mothers and daughters case studies emailed or faxed through to her.

"Can you email the words and give me the phone number of the woman who's going to do the pics then I can send the photographer round this morning."

"Sure, but I don't think she'll be—"

I knew Miranda wouldn't be home till the girls were back from school, but Erica expected the subjects of her articles to be available at her, rather than their, convenience.

"Good, Pete can call her when he's on the way. Now listen, Mary, are you available for some heavy-duty research this week?

It's not your usual and I wouldn't normally take a commission from the tabloids, but this is an important issue and it may be the best way to tackle it. I'd do it myself, but I've got my book deadline looming – and of course having a well-known name isn't a help for this sort of investigation. Someone more anonymous like you may be able to get in under the defences."

Gee, thanks, Erica, I thought. Get a nobody like me to do your dirty work and then take all the plaudits. What was this tabloid commission about?

"I presume you've heard about Robards' call for a clamp-down on teenage sex and abortions? Of course he's imported the campaign wholesale from the States."

Luckily I had heard something that morning on the news, about Maxwell Robards MP, and his ultra-conservative, evangelical Christian group. They were demanding that contraception of all kinds be made unavailable to unmarried teenagers under eighteen, withdrawal of the morning-after pill in chemists and surgeries, and penalties for young, single mothers such as reductions in benefits and council housing. Apparently the government felt they had to take him seriously, and Robards had been given a surprisingly easy ride by the interviewer.

"I can get all the stats together for you – poverty, social exclusion and poor education leading to under-age sex and STDs; compare the UK and USA's attitudes and high teenage-pregnancy rates to the more enlightened approach of the Northern European countries," I offered.

"Well, that won't hurt, but it's not going to cut much ice the way Robards is going on. What the editor wants is more personal stuff: extra-marital sex, dodgy business-deals, family background. I know it's not the way we'd like to do it, but these self-righteous fanatics aren't interested in the facts, or rational debate. It's all based on personal values and that's where we have to undermine them. All in a good cause, and I've got a decent budget, Mary. Can you do it?"

I hesitated. I'd never been into tabloid journalism and, anonymous as I might be, I had a reputation as a thorough, knowledgeable researcher. Digging this sort of dirt didn't sound like good karma, either. Erica's brusque voice cut through my reservations.

"Mary, make a decision please or I'll have to find someone else. I can pay you more than the usual," and she named an hourly rate more than twice what I was earning anywhere else. "I may even be able to include your name as 'additional material from ….'"

I decided to take the plunge. "OK, Erica, I'll do it. What's the deadline?"

"Good. A couple of weeks at most, but feed me stuff as you get it, then I can decide what direction to take and when to run with it." She hung up with as little ceremony as she had opened with.

I felt slightly queasy as I put the phone down. Sex education, tabloid revelations, was this the research into important social issues I was making the justification for continuing to have a career? I didn't look forward to telling Jack about my latest assignment. Perhaps I didn't have to, and I could ask Erica not to use my name in print. He didn't tell me everything about his work, indeed patient confidentiality made it impossible. Maybe I had a duty of confidentiality in this very personal area as well.

Later that afternoon I took Lily up to the Library on Westow Hill so we could return her books and puzzles at the Children's Library upstairs and I could look up some basic information about Maxwell Robards on the ground floor.

We turned the corner from Auckland Road into Sylvan Hill, and walked past the surgery. The ground floor of the big old Victorian house made a pleasant working environment for Jack and his partners, and still held a special place in my heart. It was where I had repeatedly brought an eleven-year-old Jess with agonising sore throats and swollen glands, only to be told by our elderly doctor, now retired, that it was only a viral infection. At yet another emergency appointment, I had to see the new, young GP and he had diagnosed acute tonsillitis and booked her into Mayday Hospital to have them removed. On one of several post-operative home visits, Dr Patterson had asked me if I would, in future, see one of his colleagues at the surgery, rather than him. I had felt a massive pang of disappointment; we all felt safe in the good-looking young doctor's hands and I had secretly started enjoying our consultations for more than medical reasons. Jack had smiled, reassured me that I had done nothing wrong as a patient, and explained that he wanted to ask me out to dinner without breaching his professional code of conduct. A year later, we were married and, having both sold our small flats for much more than we had paid for them, moved into our own, spacious house conveniently close to the surgery.

Another six years on, his little daughter always wanted to go via Sylvan Hill when we walked up to the Triangle, so she could see him through the blinds of his office window as we passed. This time we could make out the silhouette of a woman, rather an attractive woman, in the patient's chair.

"Is Daddy giving that lady some pills?" asked Lily, but I was prevented from answering her by the ring of my mobile phone and the problem of locating it in my junk-filled basket. Extracting it just in time, and seeing "Julia" on the screen, I pressed the button with a pang of guilt, simultaneously glimpsing Jack come over to the window to gallantly help his patient out of the chair. The woman turned towards him and I saw it was Miranda.

"Yes, Jules," I almost snapped.

"Mo. Hey! Where've you been? I thought you were going to ring me. You sound really out of breath, are you OK?"

I didn't waste time answering her question, but told her that after much thought and talking to Jack, I would help her search for her birth mother. She had to agree, though, to say nothing at any time to Jack, and nothing, for the moment, to Betty and Colin. The search might lead nowhere and I didn't want to upset them unnecessarily, nor did I want Betty to view me as siding with Julia against Jack or offer any opportunities for wedges to be driven between us.

"Deal, Mo," she responded instantly. "I don't want them knowing anyway, this is my business, not theirs. So what do we do first?"

I told Julia I'd email her later and rang off. I thought for a moment of waiting outside the surgery for Miranda to emerge so I could warn her of the photographer's impending visit, but decided she might not want anyone to know she had been to see Jack on a professional basis, whether her visit had been for something serious or just a regular check-up. I pushed aside sudden, unwanted images of my husband taking a cervical smear or doing a breast test on Miranda's toned, brown body.

I sat down to check my email while Lily played with her new, borrowed toys. My computer rose like an island from the ocean of paper on my sizeable, battered old desk, with the screen perched on the cliffs of a couple of out-of-date Yellow Pages and the keyboard lapped by mouse-mat, wrist-rest and desk diary. I clicked into my inbox and found half a dozen new messages waiting for me. Two were junk mail: unwanted financial advice and a cheap wine offer. Delete. One was from our accountant asking if we'd received a refund for fifty-four pounds and thirty-two pence from the Inland Revenue for Jack. Not that I'd seen, but we never opened each other's mail. Forward to Jack. Ellie, Generation Productions's PA/receptionist, asked me to email the interviews with the couples that I'd written up. Damn, I'd forgotten to send them through yesterday when they were due. Reply, attach files, type a lie that I'd sent them yesterday and copy the lot to Jane, the producer on the sex education project, and Dr Braithwaite, the sex expert. One from my mother:

Hello Darling,

I don't seem to have seen you or little Lily for too long. Why don't you bring her over for tea. I'm marking papers at home this week. Hope all's well with you and Jack, Mark and Jess as well. Lots of news to tell you so hope to see you soon.

Love Ma xx

I'd saved the best till last. An email from Jess, who was away on her gap year between school and university, teaching children in a village in Nepal:

Hi Mumma

Hows it going. Sorry its been so long since the last email but weve been too busy to get into Kathmandu lately.

Ive really settled into life in Pulimarang, just had the coolest couple of weeks. The schools just had its sports day and for the fortnight before they practiced sports day every day after school. The sports were weird, the girls did a walking race with spoons in their mouths and balanced marbles on the spoons while others played musical chairs! The music was drums and the boys ran relay races and did a strange simon says game. It was freaky sitting around in the sun in the playground eating grapefruit in January. The skies are perfectly blue in Pulimarang at the moment and the mountains are so clear that you can see them by moonlight. We are helping with the harvest which is literally back breaking work, we drive the buffaloes to flatten the straw and carry huge bales of straw with the strap on our heads, it's a killer up the steep paddy fields. On Saturday we beat the familys millet, the whole village helps out with everyone elses work and they work so hard. My hands are covered in unpopped blisters and my neck and arms are pure agony. The novelty wore off very very quickly but the community spirit was wicked. I really feel like part of the family dressing Osmita for school washing the dishes and making tea. Youd hardly recognise me! Miss you all of course and home comforts but this is an amazing experience.

Love to Jack and hugs and kisses to Lily. Hope shes missing her big sister.

Luvyamuch Jess xxxxxxxxxx

Her missive brought me mixed feelings. Involuntary annoyance at her poor punctuation was subsumed in pride and delight that Jess was doing so well and getting so much out of her travelling and voluntary work. Then came a twinge of sadness that she could give to, and feel so much part of, a community and family where she had no roots and no long-term relationship. I had empathised with Miranda's description of Lola's behaviour. Jess had been similarly hard to live with during her last years at school; we had continually clashed about everything from the state of her bedroom and failure to help around the house to her unsuitable boyfriends, frenetic social life and lack of interest in her school work. I didn't consider myself an authoritarian or out-of-touch parent; unless she asked, I left her to her own devices as far as more major questions like sex and drugs were concerned.

After all my nagging, I had had to eat my words when her excellent A level results came through, but when she left the confines of home three months ago my relief was almost equal to her obvious delight. Ignoring my worries, she had wheedled money out of my mother to fund her on a nine month placement doing voluntary work in one of the world's least safe areas for young British girls.

She had had, I supposed, classic grounds for her behaviour: a single mother upbringing in insecure circumstances, a stepfather to deal with, and competition from a new sibling – yet her brother was so different. At that moment, as if telepathically, my mobile beeped with a message from Mark:

> Yo ma! heading for big smoke with zoe
> soon 4 wkend. will stay night 4 takeaway
> & chatting. luv u mark xx

My blues instantly banished, I texted back:

> Gr8 news! Indian or pizza? Let me know
> date asap. Mum xx

I sometimes felt that Mark, at twenty-one, was more mature and better-adjusted than I would ever be, and balanced the loss of no longer having him at home with the gain of an adult whose sensitive and sensible support I valued enormously. I quickly rang my mother to say that Lily and I would be over for tea this afternoon and began to ransack my battered filing cabinet for the research on adoption I had once done for Erica. Eventually I found the file I wanted, bent and out of order, between "Alimony" and "Arguing in front of the children". Erica had covered all sorts in her time. There wasn't a lot in there, but the little booklet I recalled, *Tracing Records of Births Marriages and Deaths*, was full of useful addresses. I emailed Julia some instructions about where she could start:

Hi Jules,

Your starting point is going to be your birth certificate, on which your mother should have put her own permanent address, rather than a temporary one. Have you got your own birth certificate in your original name? If not, you need to send off for one from: The Superintendent Registrar, The Registry Office, Chelsea Old Town Hall, Kings Road, London SW3 5EE. If that doesn't have an address on it, then the next step is to write off for your mother's birth certificate, which would have her original family address on it. At least we know her name and d.o.b. from your and Jack's adoption records, and that she came from Belfast. The address for the Northern Ireland Reg Office is: The Registrar General, Oxford House, 49/55 Chichester Street, Belfast BT1 4HL. Probably worth phoning them first and you could also ask them whether they can do a search for your mother's marriage certificate – though we don't know if or when she got married later. They might agree to look within a five year span or something. The point is, that would have the most recent addresses for her, her parents, her husband and his parents, which would give us lots of leads. Should probably try and get hold of all these documents.

Let me know what you get. Talk soon. Remember, you can't talk to anyone else about this in case it gets back – and that includes Danny. You know what children are like.

Love, Mo xx

* * *

I told my mother about the quest for Jack and Julia's birth mother as she helped Lily with a jigsaw puzzle that I and my brother Anthony, then Mark and Jess had, in different decades, pieced together with her at the same kitchen table. I could trust her not to say anything to Jack and I thought with her academic viewpoint she might have some insight into the situation.

"It's interesting," she reflected. "It seems it's always the mother that adopted people want to find, rarely the father. Mostly, once they find their mother, it's enough, they feel rooted."

"Well that's how Julia's thinking at the moment. She's never mentioned their father and I've never heard that there's any information about him."

"I think it's to do with the deep-seated, often sub-conscious, feeling of abandonment they have. They tend to feel it's their mother who's abandoned them – some experts think pregnancy is a psycho-physiological bond and that a baby taken from its mother can never truly recover. Adoptees seem to find, though, that if they can hear from their mother about why she did it, and especially that she didn't want to lose them, but felt it was in their best interests, it puts their mind at rest." My mother bent her white head close to her granddaughter's curly brown one, wisps escaping from the bun she always pinned her still long hair into. "There, Lily, if you put that last piece in there …" She placed her wrinkled, but still elegant, hand over Lily's little plump one to guide it. "It's finished. Clever girl."

Mum got up to take the whistling kettle off the old gas hob as Lily slid off her knee in search of other amusement. Despite being in her mid-seventies, Emeritus Professor Athene Mozart still assessed doctoral theses at the London School of Social Sciences and could be relied on to be well informed about most subjects remotely within her area of expertise.

"Mum, if Julia finds an address for her mother, what's the best way of getting in touch with her?" I asked, hastily removing a Staffordshire shepherdess from Lily's grasp and substituting it with a tiny pewter tea-set from the ottoman. "Here, Lily, you make a cup of tea for the dollies like Granny's doing."

My mother poured weak Lapsang Souchong into delicate, tannin-stained china cups from a tarnished silver teapot. "Well, certainly a letter in the first instance – no unannounced visits or phone calls. Far too confrontational and you don't know who around them knows about the adoption. It might even be better if it came from you, or another intermediary to begin with."

"From me?" I hadn't anticipated any personal involvement in the search itself. That would make the position with Jack even more complicated. I took a bite of the shortbread biscuit she offered, and tried not to wince at its powdery staleness.

"Well, it's less shocking, darling. It gives the woman a bit more space to deal with the situation without feeling so directly confronted. You don't know what it can be like for these birth mothers from the 1960s, hearing from their lost children. You see, up until 1976, adopted people weren't allowed access to their records, so the natural parents believed they would never be traceable, and lots of them never told their families or friends. It's a great joy for many mothers, but for some it's not a revelation they welcome."

I didn't think Julia would want me, or anyone else, to act as an intermediary. Her first instinct would be to pick up the phone as soon as she got hold of any contact details, but my mother had sensible advice on this.

"I should suggest this modus operandi before she gets the chance to take matters into her own hands. She might see sense in it – Julia's not stupid, just rather highly-strung and impulsive. Why don't we sit in the drawing room while Lily's occupied with the dolls? I can show you the photos of Anthony and Sally's holiday, if I can lay my hands on them."

I poked some horse hair stuffing back into the Queen Anne chair before sitting in it, and looked around at the eclectic assortment of art that filled almost every inch of wall in the tall, thin Pimlico house. Beside one of my father's oil landscapes and below a leather *commedia* mask, the original Mary Wilhelmina Mozart smiled coquettishly at me, with brown eyes and dark ringlets above an ample cleavage swelled by a Victorian bodice. Perhaps because she was my namesake, I'd always felt a certain affinity with her, and she was certainly the most engaging of my otherwise dour-faced relatives.

"Here we are." My mother returned with a packet of photos. "I must show you the ones of the children snow-boarding down this great high mountain – aren't they wonderful? But then they've been skiing every Christmas for years now, so they should be pretty good."

She proceeded to regale me with the latest achievements of my brother's three children in the way that always made me feel defensive for Mark, Jess and even Lily. Anthony's successful art gallery and Sally's still more lucrative interior design business paid for a live-in nanny, private schooling and frequent luxury holidays. I felt there was no way their kids could slip through the safety net, while life for me and mine had, until Jack's arrival and steadying influence, seemed like a constant precarious high wire walk.

"Oh, and I wanted to tell you, Mary, that I've decided to leave

all the Mozart portraits to Anthony. That was what Daddy
wanted because Anthony knows about art and their house is big
enough to hold them all. You've never liked the old ancestors
much, have you, darling?"

"But Mary Wilhelmina's mine, Mum, you named me after
her. You always said you'd leave her to me. And Jess thinks she's
getting her when I die!" I was surprised to find that I felt almost
tearful.

"Oh, darling, it's much more practical to keep the family
paintings together, and I've tried to help you more in other
ways. Anyway, Mary, you're not a Mozart any more, you're a
Patterson."

Only the truly brave, of which I was not one, argued with my
mother, so I didn't insist that I still used my own name for work,
thought of myself as more Mozart than Patterson and would
have hyphenated Lily's name if Mozart-Patterson hadn't
sounded so bathetic. Nor did I point out that in the past my
mother had been highly critical of the male-line inheritance
tradition that had cut her out of her own family's wealth.

Instead I told her how well Jess was doing in Thailand and
that Mark was likely to get a first, and we were so mutually
indignant about the outrageous Maxwell Robards and his retro-
grade social policies that she offered to check on her intellectu-
als' grapevine for any information that Erica could use against
him.

"Honey, it's just a painting, dried, coloured oils on canvas. You'll
be able to go and see it at Anthony's place any time – and anyway, your mother's not dead yet, nor likely to be for some time."

Jack's inevitably rational approach could be either refresh-

ingly restful or deeply frustrating. He got up from our battered
pine kitchen table, filled the water filter without complaining
that I'd left it empty and got out the cafetiere and mugs.

"I know, but they named me after her, I feel a bond with her.
She's the only Mozart I've ever liked – probably because she was
supposed to be a gypsy maid who married the master. And anyway, why should Anthony have them all because he's got a bigger house? The family stuff should be divided equally between
us."

Jack laughed. "Aye, there's the rub! Isn't this more about you
resenting your brother again, feeling he's the favourite? It's rubbish you know, you're much closer to Athene than he'll ever be."

That was reassuring. Perhaps I was a little paranoid about
my successful brother and his perfect family with their splendid
house and swimming pool next to Bushey Park and their *petit
chateau* in the Loire Valley. I told Jack about the skiing photos
and our niece and nephews' latest sporting and academic
achievements; he predicted late teenage rebellion and latent
political angst, saying that Mark and even Jess were, on the
whole, level-headed and open-minded because they had been
fed no false expectations and I'd given them nothing major to
rebel against.

"Can I take that as a compliment?" I asked. He smiled his old
smile; the skin around his blue eyes crinkled and a dimple
appeared at the left-hand corner of his mouth. As he turned to
pour the filtered water into the kettle, I noticed how his auburn
hair had begun to curl down the back of his neck, as it did when
he needed a haircut.

"You know that being a mum is one of the many things
you're great at, hon. Lily's not doing so bad either, is she?"

"You mean in spite of—" I paused, wishing I hadn't started

what I had been going to say – the fact that I don't spend enough time with her – and cast around for an alternative ending. "... having a pornographer for a mother? Oh, we must watch this!" Maxwell Robards had conveniently appeared on the television news in a dark, expensive suit, his silver grey-hair sharply cut, exuding statesman-like empathy for "the benighted youth of today".

A wholesome, articulate sixteen-year-old with 'VIRGIN SOLDIER' on her t-shirt and a gold cross round her neck explained how she felt sorry for her sexually active peers and was proud to be waiting for marriage. She was followed by a stringy-haired girl with a snotty-nosed baby, who claimed she had got herself pregnant to qualify for a single mother's council flat and allowances.

"These girls," intoned Robards, "are being led astray by ill-thought out, liberal policies. Sex education in schools is encouraging this kind of promiscuous behaviour. They must be protected for their own moral welfare."

A respected but untelegenic colleague of my mother's from the LSSS, was wheeled on to explain that the UK's pregnancy rate among under-eighteen-year-olds was seven times that of the Netherlands, four times that of France and twice that of Germany, where access to information and contraception was far greater. Robards dismissed her as "part of the wishy-washy, politically correct, socialist mafia", and with that they moved on to the next news item.

Jack railed against Robards as he poured the coffee, so I took the risk and told him about Erica's strategy to discredit him and my role as digger of dirt.

"Mo, I know you won't agree," he said gently, "and maybe I'm partly to blame for nagging you, but I do wonder if you're ... trying to make too much of a point, taking on projects that aren't your thing. I don't want you not to work, honey, but parenting's a hard job and you're very good at that, as well. I really do think Lily's a huge achievement, for both of us, but especially you, as the primary carer."

"An achievement? Is that how you think of your daughter?" I snapped.

"No, of course I didn't mean that," he back-tracked, genuine embarrassment flushing his face. "Sorry that came out wrong."

His sudden vulnerable look almost made me ask Jack what he thought of my mother's advice about first contact with Julia's mother. But an instant reminder from The Source that this was also his mother, about whom we had an agreement not to speak, made me shut my mouth before I'd fully opened it. Jack looked enquiringly at me, so I smiled, put my arms around his neck and stroked the curls on his neck.

"OK, I'll think about it. Maybe I'll be more selective about what projects I take on after these, but I can't back out of the Robards stuff, or the sex education, now."

He held my face and gave me a tender look before turning me round to massage my shoulders.

"Thanks, honey. You are tense, you know. How about we try out some of those tips from the programme upstairs, maybe?" I would just as happily have relaxed in bed with the *New Statesman* and a cup of tea, but I smiled and followed him upstairs to the bedroom.

As we lay in the dark, satisfied and sleepy, I snapped alert to the image of Miranda in the surgery this morning.

"Miranda seemed a bit tense at the café this week. Have you

seen Si lately, did he say anything was wrong?" I asked, sitting up and putting the light on.

"Turn it off, Mo, I was just dropping off. No, Simon hasn't said anything to me. I haven't seen him, he's trying to get his thesis finished."

"She was supposed to be having her photo taken for one of Erica's articles this morning – I wonder if she remembered to stay in for the photographer," I fished.

No response. I tried another tack. "If one of my friends, our friends, was really ill, would you give me a hint, you know, subtly, not breaking patient confidentiality or anything?"

"Mo, give me a break, I'm on early in the morning. No, no of course I wouldn't. A subtle hint would be breaking confidentiality as much as if I told you details. And I don't want any subtle hints either, if that's what you're getting at, OK? Now for God's sake go to sleep."

But I lay awake for some time, regretting the no-go areas between us, re-running the sight of Jack taking Miranda's arm in his office, unreasonably resenting both Julia and Erica, and fearing that I might have made not one, but two wrong choices in a short space of time.

Chapter Three

I was getting nowhere fast in my efforts to track down anything dubious about Maxwell Robards. I'd tried the usual sources. The MP's Register of Interests showed he had a couple of company directorships, but Companies House records revealed these businesses to be perfectly above-board and he had declared openly what they paid him in fees and expenses. There were no conflicts of interest with his constituency or parliamentary work and he had been ensconced in a safe seat in East Anglia for nearly twenty years, after resigning from a profitable career as a management consultant with a well-known international firm.

Maxwell Robards listed himself as a founder and trustee of the Family Fellowship, the charitable trust which promoted hard-line, Christian values about marriage and the family, and was providing "research" and back-up for his current political campaign. The Fellowship's records with the Charities Commission presented nothing out of the ordinary; it was informally connected with one of Washington's largest right-wing think-tanks and must have had wealthy backers and/or excellent fund-raisers as the organisation had a massive bank balance. Its accounts, though, were in order and Robards apparently donated all his time for free. He was in his early sixties, married, though childless, and his wife, Kathleen, had been a teacher and now spent her time on committee work for a number of children's charities.

Nothing obvious, then, to interest Erica and her tabloid masters, so I would have to seek out other sources of information. I searched through my ancient Filofax, drew a deep breath and phoned the number of a powerful Westminster lobbying company, PPR. An old boyfriend, Nick, with whom I'd had no contact for ten years, had started the venture after working as a parliamentary researcher, struck gold with some major clients and made himself millions. He came on the line quickly when his PA told him who was calling, and I was flattered that I could still be the recipient of his time and charm. I briefly filled Nick in on my marriage to Jack and the birth of Lily, told him I was working on an Education Department project and asked if I could take him to lunch for the privilege of picking his brains. Nice man that he still was, he laughed and asked me what I wanted to know.

"My world's all about back-scratching, Mo," he reassured me. "I'm always happy to help with anything I can tell you, and I'll be back to you for a return favour at some point, but you don't have to waste your time or money on a lunch!"

Nick didn't think there was anything dodgy doing the rounds about "Missionary Max" – an insider nickname at least that I could pass on – but he'd ask some questions in the right places and get back to me. If he found anything really juicy, he said, I could take him for a drink in repayment.

I swivelled my chair around from my desk to look out of the French windows onto our garden and South Norwood Lakes Park beyond. Closing my eyes and breathing deep, I sent out a call to the Universal Spirit to plug me into the connections and the information I needed. But when I rang her, my mother told me that though the Family Fellowship's research sources were considered dubious in the academic world, and mainly based on American data from similar Christian, pro-life organisations, she'd heard nothing personal to discredit Robards.

So that was my moan to the group at the French café, followed by a request for any leads they could dredge up between them.

"If he's tried to cover his tracks with a libel case anywhere, Duncan will know," offered Suzy. Her husband was a senior libel partner with one of the "Magic Circle" City legal firms and would have been horrified to know how much celebrity gossip he provided, via Suzy, for the edification of our coffee mornings.

Ros said she'd come across Kathleen Robards in some of her child therapy work for voluntary organisations. "But she's always come across as a nice enough woman; quiet, sincere, well-informed about children's and family issues. I've never got the impression she's at all hard-line about marriage. She's quite beautiful, actually, in a faded, pre-Raphaelite sort of way."

"Oh, the fragrant Kathleen," Venetia chipped in acerbically. She was dressed to kill, in a severe but sexy black dress and jacket, and I couldn't help noticing a push-up bra was making the most of her small breasts. Ros sighed quietly without bothering to answer, as Venetia continued. "She's a good little MP's wife, does the charity stuff with kids – probably because she hasn't any of her own"– I kicked Venetia under the table at this tactless barb and hoped Ros hadn't taken it personally – "and totally under his thumb. Not the way I'll play it if Charlie decides to make an honest woman of me ..." She waited for the inevitable exclamations before continuing airily. "No need to buy your hats yet, girls, but it's not impossible that we might go public when his divorce is done and dusted. I'll ask him to keep an ear out for dirt on either of the Robards – it's often the ones who look as if butter wouldn't melt who have the noisiest skeletons to rattle. Which reminds me, how's Joe getting on at Stratford?"

Ros gave a resigned smile. I sometimes wondered why we were all so fond of Venetia when she took such blatant pleasure in rubbing salt in our emotional wounds, but her malice was only skin deep and she had proved herself a good friend to all of us over the years.

"Full houses and raves from the critics. I've been in Manchester listening to research papers all day and Joe's been on stage all night, so there hasn't been a lot of communication." Miranda put a small, tanned and French-manicured hand on Ros's arm.

"I know the feeling, and Simon and I are in the same house. Sometimes you've just got to take a break, follow your own path for a bit." I looked up at Miranda sharply. Her skin looked even tauter than usual over her wide cheekbones and her almond-shaped eyes seemed over-bright.

"Are you OK, Miranda? Nothing really wrong is there?" I asked, concern in my voice. "You look a bit pale – perhaps you should have a check-up at the surgery. You know Jack would always find an appointment for you." She smiled and shook her head.

"Geez no, there's nothing wrong with me. My body is a temple!" She laughed and stretched like a cat, as if to make a point. "Lola's still hard work and Simon and I are not seeing eye to eye at the moment, but, hey, that's life. By the way, Mo, the girls and I did that photo for your friend. Nice guy, the photographer. He had to reschedule till I could get away from work, and he did some extra ones of the four of us, as Simon was home early that afternoon. You know, happy family shots?" Miranda had an edge in her voice that only I seemed to notice.

As I walked along Westow Hill with Venetia, stopping to pick up some fresh olives from Sergio's Delicatessen, I asked her whether she thought anything was up with Miranda. She shook her head.

"Nah, no more than usual. Americans are always a bit up-tight, and living with Si would stress anyone, let alone a control freak like Miranda. Especially while he's finishing his thesis – yet again! Thank god I escaped that fate." I raised an eyebrow at her – as far as I knew no long-term relationship between Venetia and Simon had ever been on the cards – and she laughed, teasingly. "No, of course not. Darling Si would have bored me rigid within weeks and I'd have gone off with the first man who looked at me. Perhaps that's what's happened to Miranda – maybe she's just got a bit of a sparkle in her eye." I didn't have time to react before she continued, "And talking of which, thanks for the idea about shocking my staff into action. It's worked like a treat. Haven't you noticed …?" Venetia pulled out the comb pinning her hair back and shook her head, allowing freshly-trimmed, straightened and highlighted locks to tumble onto her shoulders.

"I had a change of style and over the last couple of weeks I've got an old friend to 'pop in' to the office and take me out to lunch or a drink every day. Last week two cabinet ministers, a high-powered civil servant, a lesbian TV presenter – yes, you know who," she grinned slyly, "and a spin doctor obliged, and today I've got Stephen coming in, hence the new outfit. Who would have guessed he'd get so famous after such a slow start?"

"Venetia!" I was quite shocked by her audacity, let alone her connections. "And has it worked – have they stopped treating you like a dried up old spinster?"

"You would not believe it," she replied, smirking. "They're so shallow, so easily impressed. They've started coming in on time, working late, and competing to be in my good-books. A couple of the young guys have even started flirting with me and I know they're running a book on how soon I'll have a lunch date with the PM. I'm working on that one!" She roared with laughter and I wasn't sure how seriously to take her.

Venetia turned right to go down Gipsy Hill to catch the train into Victoria as I turned left into Westow Street to walk back home and attempt to put together something for Erica on Maxwell Robards. As I passed the cream stucco frontage of what used to be the Queen's Hotel – once the hostelry of choice for such wealthy and eminent visitors to the new Crystal Palace as the German Emperor Frederick III – my phone beeped with an incoming text message. Julia again:

> hey mo hope u r all ok. guess what? think
> I ve found my mum! now have folks address
> & fone no. how exciting! call me soon.

I speeded up my pace and walked by the surgery without casting a glance in the direction of Jack's window, hoping that Julia wouldn't have tried to phone her unsuspecting birth mother before I could warn her not to.

"Mo, I might have found her! I got your email and rang up the Registrar General in Belfast to ask him how much the birth certificate would cost – it's seven pounds – and whether they'd be able to search for the marriage certificate." Julia was bubbling with excitement and unstoppable at the end of the phone. "He was really nice, really helpful. He said they'd definitely have the birth certificate as they've got all the records since eighteen something, and he looked it up on his computer straight away and Caitlin Mairhe Doyle was born in Belfast on September the 23rd, 1947 – the same date as Caitlin Doyle on my adoption certificate."

"Jules, that's great! And what about a marriage certificate?"

"Nothing. They don't have any details of her getting married on the computer, but it doesn't matter. I sent the cheque for the birth certificate and it arrived yesterday. It has an address for her parents in Belfast and I looked them up in the phone directory on the internet, and guess what?"

She didn't give me any time to respond, but I knew what she was going to say and a sinking feeling competed with a sense of exhilaration in the pit of my stomach.

"The family's still living at that address, at least J and M Doyle are. I thought maybe it's her mother and father, coz you know she's Caitlin Mairhe, well she named me Gillian Mairhe and Jack was Francis John – and I thought, like, she might have given us her parents' names as second names. J and M – John and Mairhe. So I've got their phone number and I could just ring up and ask if it's them—"

"Wait, Jules. Slow down and listen." I tried to sound portentous enough to stop her in her tracks. "This next step is really, really important. If we don't get it right it could blow everything. It might be the difference between making contact and not, so please think carefully about this."

It worked. There was silence at her end and I launched into an explanation as to why a phone-call out of the blue was not the best way to greet a long-lost biological parent, and suggested, tentatively, that a letter from an intermediary, perhaps even me, would be a less threatening approach. Julia didn't sound thrilled by the brake this would put on her desire for instant relationship, but I went on talking and finally came up with the suggestion that she should write the letter I would sign, so it would only say what she wanted.

"But I wouldn't know what to write, Mo," she objected.

"OK, do you want me to have a go at drafting it, then, and you can change whatever you don't like?" I offered, cursing myself inwardly for getting yet more involved and giving myself more work when I needed all my Lily-free time to hunt down Robards. But Julia accepted, rapidly gaining enthusiasm for this new strategy.

"Could you, Mo? You know I can't write and I really wouldn't have a clue what to say to her. I'm glad we thought of a letter rather than a phone-call."

"Sure, OK. I'll try and get it done and bring it when we come down for your mum's – Betty's – birthday next week. Just don't pick up the phone, right? Think about how you'd feel if someone suddenly rang you and threatened to expose the biggest secret of your life."

"But what if she doesn't answer the letter?" Julia challenged.

"Let's think about that when it happens – and we've got to give her time. It might have to be sent on, she probably doesn't live with her parents at her age."

"Hmm, s'pose. OK, thanks, Mo. I'll see you Saturday. It's so weird," she added, "to think she could just be out there and I could get to meet her. But she's fifty-seven now. I keep thinking of her as eighteen, you know, this girl who got pregnant and went off to London and had these babies on her own. It's hard to think that she's lived a whole life since then. She might not have married, but perhaps she's had loads of lovers."

I wrote up some of the most shocking stats on teenage pregnancy, contraception and sexually transmitted diseases for Erica, which I lifted directly from the sex ed research:

In 2003, there were over 45,000 teen pregnancies in the UK, costing the taxpayer billions.

The UK has the highest rates of teen pregnancy in Europe; in countries with the lowest rates sex education and contraception is much more readily available.

As many as 25% of fourteen-year-old girls in the UK are having sex – mostly unprotected.

Sexually Transmitted Infection treatment costs the NHS over £1 billion a year.

The Family Planning Association has claimed that "for every £1 spent on family planning provision, £11 is saved from health and social welfare budgets".

I tacked on some slivers of non-information about the Robards for Erica, and listed all the so-called leads I was following up. Within minutes I had a sharp, emailed reply, thanking me for my hard work, but pointing out that I had uncovered nothing yet that wasn't already in the public domain and she looked forward to more useful information at my earliest convenience.

Pushing Lily back and forth on the swing with the winter sun in my eyes became quite hypnotic and I had allowed my mind to drift for several seconds before I realised she was shouting at me to stop. I lifted her out of the rubberised base of the baby swing she'd insisted on getting into. It caught her feet and pulled off one of her Wellington boots, which fell onto the ground. I tried to pick it up without letting her go, but she slithered through my arms and ran, single-booted, across the wet, sprung tarmac. As I turned to chase after her, I saw she was heading, not for her favourite roundabout, but towards the bench on the far side of the playground where a single, bundled-up figure sat watching her progress with a smile. To my surprise, Lily clambered up on the seat next to Old Peggy, who offered her a doughnut out of a grubby Morrison's bag.

"No, Lily, don't spoil your tea," I called, running up to them and peeling off her soggy sock before shoving her foot back into the pink, Barbie gumboot. "Thanks, Peggy, but you keep it. She's a devil for sweet things and I'm trying to stop her snacking too much between meals."

Peggy broke off a small piece of doughnut with her grimy fingers and popped it into Lily's expectant mouth.

"Little bit won't hurt, princess. Only one day past the sell-by date, they give it me this morning."

I looked round furtively to see if any of the young mums were watching this unhygienic transaction with horror, but no one seemed to be taking any notice. Lily finished munching and held out her hand for another piece, which Peggy gladly provided. I hoped that Lily's instincts were sharper than mine – usually she was the first to complain about anything smelly, and damp weather had not diminished the sour aroma of the man's overcoat Old Peggy habitually wore, secured around her waist with an old Etonian tie, and now steaming gently in the winter warmth.

"Did they give you a new trolley as well?" I asked, spying a more up-to-date model with double baby seat parked behind the bench. Peggy smiled at me over Lily's head and winked. I wondered if I could ask her how long she had lived round here and whether her current lifestyle was by choice, but before I could devise an inoffensive form of words, she had said something to Lily, who slid down from the bench and ran off to play on the roundabout. Peggy turned to me with an expectant look. "She seems to have taken a shine to you," I told her.

"She know a Gipsy Queen when she see one," she wheezed. "Last of the Norwood Gipsies is Peggy Finch, but little princess can sense I still got the gift of telling. Give me your hand, lovely," and once again she grabbed my wrist and turned my palm upward. "You made the choice, then, lovely, and a brave one. You saw the picture—" but before she had a chance to say any more, I pulled my arm away and leaped up as if I had seen Lily in difficulties.

"Time to go home, Li'l Girl," I told her, stopping the roundabout with my foot, to her annoyance, and lifting her off swiftly. "Let's go and see if Beth and Noah can come over for tea," I resorted to my most persuasive inducement.

"Bye bye, bye bye, cake lady!" Lily shouted and waved to Peggy as I walked her briskly towards the lake. For a child who still could be very shy with strangers and was fastidious about dirt and smells, her enthusiasm for a bag lady seemed odd. But Peggy's interpretation of their surprising relationship was far too fantastic to give any credence to.

Spring seemed to have come early on the day of Betty's birthday and we were able to sit on the patio of her and Colin's neatly manicured garden for drinks before lunch, albeit wearing fleeces and jackets. Jack seemed relaxed and divided his time between entertaining his daughter and being solicitous of his mother's every need. Sometimes the two were one and the same, as preventing Lily from causing chaos in Betty's perfectly tidy house was key to the harmony of all parties.

Colin and Betty loved entertaining, so as well as Jack, Lily and me, they had invited both their next door neighbours – retired, self-made couples like themselves – to celebrate her sixty-fifth. Julia and Danny arrived late, as usual, bearing a pile of colour-coordinated presents wrapped in Julia's usual professional style, with a birthday cake and card for Nanny, both supposedly home-made by Danny, but suspiciously neat for an eight-year-old. Betty was touched and delighted; she ruffled her grandson's auburn corkscrew curls, which Julia liked to keep as long as he would allow, and stiffened only slightly as he hugged creases into her flawless, cream silk blouse. I noticed that despite the gener-osity of Julia's presents, Betty seemed tentative as she offered her cheek to her daughter. Jules, though, behaved as if nothing had happened to upset their usual relationship and stood for a few seconds with an arm around the shoulders of her diminutive mother, exclaiming how well the sky blue cashmere cardigan she had bought set off Betty's beige-blonde bob.

As we sipped chilled bucks fizz in the chillier air, the conver-sation became mildly competitive, between the older couples, as to the relative achievements of their children and grandchil-dren. When Pete Next-door-on-the-right mentioned that his eldest grandson was studying to become a neurosurgeon, Colin quickly asked Jack about the next medical conference he was going to. Jack was non-committal.

"All that research on heart disease you're doing and a full surgery to look after, son, I don't know how you do it. Makes my old job in the bank look easy, and I used to get stressed managing all those people, didn't I, Betty?" he asked rhetorically. "These days you can get signed off work for stress any time you want, there's no stamina, no staying power today …" He shook his head disapprovingly. Jack and I exchanged micro-smiles and he narrowed his eyes at me to stop me jumping in – but Julia had no such qualms.

"You idiot, Dad," she scoffed from across the garden, where she was kicking a ball with Danny. "First you say Jack must be stressed out because he's a hard-working doctor and then you say no one's got any staying power and you as good as blame him for being soft on people with stress. Put your brain in gear before you open your mouth."

Colin started to bluster, but Betty smiled brightly. "Now then, dear, no disagreements on my birthday, please." She came and put her hands on Colin's shoulders and I was close enough to hear her say quietly to him, "Careful now, she's edgy. We don't want an incident today."

"An incident" had become Betty's euphemism for Julia's ability to black out at will whenever she was crossed or wanted attention. Not that her parents saw it that way. "Delicate" was how they described their daughter's behaviour, and during her teens had taken her to numerous specialists who had variously diagnosed her as having a nervous disposition, allergic reactions, mild asthma and even petit mal. Danny, though on the whole a sweet boy (and currently helping Lily to feed the Koi carp in their granddad's beloved fish-pond), seemed to be learning some of Julia's manipulative tendencies, including playing the "delicate" card when it suited him.

Seeing Colin looking at the quantity of fish pellets floating on top of his pond, Betty shepherded the children into the house to "help" her lay out the fork luncheon. Keen to move back into the warmth, the rest of us stood up from the wrought-iron garden seats and Julia came over to where I was clearing glasses and bottles onto a tray.

"Have you got the letter?" she asked in a conspiratorial stage whisper. Jack frowned at us and turned to go inside with his father.

"Yes. I'll show you after lunch, OK? Just don't make it obvious, please, Jules. It's your mum's day and I don't want to piss Jack off, either."

She nodded and took the bowls of nibbles and dips into the kitchen. Betty was allowing Lily and Danny to carry through unbreakables like serviettes and cutlery, while she arranged pretty bowls of salads and platters of cold meat, smoked salmon roulade and coronation chicken on the lacy cloth covering their reproduction antique dining table.

"Could you girls bring through the cruets and the mayonnaise and vinaigrette?" she asked. "Then I think we're ready to serve out." Betty tinkled the little silver bell that stood on a doily on the sideboard and everyone moved through to load their plates with the cold collation.

While agreeing with Margaret Next-door-on-the-left how quickly Lily was growing up and receiving a progress report on her three-year-old granddaughter, I could hear Jack charming his mother and Sandra Next-door-on-the-right with amusing but anodyne tales from the surgery. Julia was being quizzed by Margaret's husband, Les, about how she was managing as a single mother, whether her school-hours job in an up-market gift shop paid enough to live on and if Ian, Danny's father, was keeping up his maintenance payments.

"Now, someone like you, left on your own with a child through no fault of your own and working to pay your way, is no drain on the state," pontificated Les, as he forked up pink salmon topped by yellow chicken. "You face up to your responsibility and don't ask the taxpayer to help out. Not like these young single mothers who get themselves in the family way just to claim all these benefits."

"Dead right," agreed Colin. "I think that MP fellow, Robards, has got a good point about stopping teenagers getting contraceptives. That'd put an end to all these unwanted pregnancies if they had to wait till they got married."

"Dad," groaned Julia, "you're talking rubbish again." But the older generation was in full flow now and unconcerned by the illogicality of their viewpoint.

"And as for all these abortions being paid for on the National Health, no wonder decent people have to wait for an ordinary operation. It's not right," added Sandra, daintily removing a sliver of salami skin from her dentures and wiping it off her finger onto the edge of her plate. I couldn't help rising to the bait, even though I knew that Jack was willing me not to get involved.

"But it's much cheaper for the tax payer to fund an abortion than even to pay for a hospital birth, let alone all the social security benefits and tax credits to a single woman who has her baby." I bit furiously on a cherry tomato and sprayed seeds onto my new, white t-shirt.

"Mo's our resident socialist," Colin announced genially to the room at large. "We always enjoy a good ding-dong about politics, don't we, love?" But I wasn't to be put off.

"And cheaper still to give women the morning-after pill if they've had unprotected sex, especially if they can get it from a chemist, rather than having to front up to a doctor," I went on, opening Jack up to what I knew would be the next line of attack.

"You don't prescribe those things to young girls, do you, son?" asked Colin. Jack sighed, and I wasn't sure why I'd wanted to drop him in it with his parents.

"Of course I do, Dad," he replied. "Even if I disagreed with it—"

"Which you don't," I put in.

"Which I don't, it's a woman's right by law."

"Come and have some dessert, everyone, or there's a cheese platter and some fruit," said Betty, quickly standing up and starting to collect empty plates.

"Better education, that's what we really need," I flung in before catching Jack's steely expression. He picked up Sandra and Margaret's plates and said quietly, "Don't start on the sex education," as he stooped to add my plate and Lily's plastic bowl to the stack, accidentally treading hard on my toe as he turned towards the kitchen.

I saw my chance when everyone was sitting, replete with chocolate pavlova and whipped cream, and told Betty to open her presents from the other guests while Julia and I made the coffee. Pulling the kitchen door closed, I dug out the draft letter from my bag for her to read while I found the filters, spooned in coffee and poured water into the tank of the electric coffee maker. Julia sat at the breakfast bar, her long legs in faded denims twisted round the stool, her head bent over the paper until it was almost obscured by her mane of curly hair. I watched surreptitiously as she silently mouthed the words I knew almost by heart, whilst I quietly laid out the white and gold coffee cups, bowl of lump sugar and jugs of milk and cream on the tray. The coffee pot chugged and steamed as I waited for her to finish reading.

Dear Caitlin Doyle,

I am writing on behalf of Julia Patterson, whose name you may or may not be familiar with. She was born a twin on April the 15 1966 and was then named Gillian Mairhe Doyle. She realises that this letter will probably come as a shock to you and that you may need some time to think about how to respond to it. This is why she has asked me to act as an intermediary by making contact with you in the first instance.

Julia would like to get in touch with you if and when you are willing for her to do so, but she has no wish to cause any upset to your personal life. The documents in her adoption file say that you never told your family about her and her brother and this may well still be the situation.

In the meantime, she has asked me to let you know that she and her twin brother have had a very happy and comfortable life with her parents, Betty and Colin Patterson. She still lives very near them in Surrey and has an eight-year-old son, Danny, who looks enormously like her.

I have known Julia for several years and would like to tell you that she is a tall, slim and attractive woman with auburn hair and blue eyes. She is bright, funny, honest and determined; a devoted mother, loyal daughter and a good friend – definitely someone to be proud of. Due to some health problems she has had a variety of jobs and currently sells and wraps exclusive gifts while Danny is at school or being looked after by his grandparents in the holidays.

Please feel free to get in touch with me in whatever way you prefer – letter, phone, fax or email – at the above address and I will pass on your response and wishes to Julia. If and when it seems to be what you both want, then the two of you can get in touch personally.

I hope you will be pleased to hear from her, whatever your present circumstances, and that you will let me know what you would like to do next. If possible, could you try to reply in the next couple of weeks – it will also be a tense time for Julia, waiting for your response.

Looking forward to hearing from you.

With best wishes,

Mary Mozart

The atmosphere in the kitchen was growing dense with the aroma of fresh coffee and tension. Julia reached the end and looked up as the last drops of water bubbled through the filter into the jug. Silently she slid off the stool and added teaspoons and the coffee pot to the tray.

"Well?" I asked eventually. "See, I've signed it Mozart rather than Patterson, so she doesn't feel threatened by any family connection."

"Thanks, Mo. I don't know what to say." Julia's eyes were shiny and her lips trembled slightly. "That's really nice what you said about me and I think it's a great letter. Just, do we have to say I've had, like, a happy life and mention my parents?"

"Well, think about it, Jules. If you'd had Danny adopted, what would you most want to know about him? That he'd been miserable? I don't think so."

"No," she agreed. You're right. And I have had a happy and comfortable life, haven't I, compared to lots of people? I could have been a single teenage mother in a council flat, whatever the old gits say."

"There, but for the grace of God, go any of us," I agreed.

"I mean it's all very well Les saying it was no fault of mine, but it was at least half my fault that Ian left. And I'm getting Family Tax Credit, though I wouldn't dare tell Mum and Dad—"

I hastily motioned for her to put the letter away as Jack opened the kitchen door to let Lily in. She ran in wailing and hugged me round the legs.

"Your daughter's been crying for you and everyone else is waiting for their coffee, while you two sit here gossiping," Jack said, looking round suspiciously. Danny's come over all tired and he's having a lie down on Mum and Dad's bed. Is he OK?" he asked his sister.

"Of course he is, Dr Jack, don't be such a grump," laughed Julia, putting her arm round him affectionately. Standing in such close proximity they looked almost absurdly alike: the only differences were his extra three inches of height and short hair, fading slightly at the temples, whilst Julia's colour glowed through a henna rinse. "Come on, help me light the candles and we can take in Mum's birthday cake together," she smiled.

Later, when we'd said our goodbyes and Jack was strapping Lily into her car seat, Betty stood beside me on the doorstep.

"Thanks for giving Julia a little break in the kitchen, dear," she said, lifting her lightly blushered cheek for a kiss. "You know she's been on edge lately and she can't take too much stress, let alone noise levels, so it was good of you. I hope young Danny's not going to turn out as delicate as his mother." I felt somewhat guilty about her misinterpretation of my actions, but reassured her that I thought Danny was absolutely fine. He and Julia came out of the house at that moment and Jules walked with me to the car.

"Will you send the letter then, Mo?" she asked quietly.

"Sure?" I mouthed.

"Yeah, very sure," Jules replied. "Let me know as soon as you hear anything. Fingers crossed."

Lily fell asleep and Jack was silent in the car on the way home. Torn between wanting to avoid the issue and hoping to clear the air, I needled him into telling me what was wrong and then regretted it. Jack accused me of behaving like a child, starting an inappropriate political row at his mother's birthday lunch and then disappearing off into the kitchen for ages with Julia while everybody wondered what on earth we were up to. I'd upset Lily into the bargain, by shutting her out of the kitchen and making myself unavailable to her. I retorted that Betty had thanked me for taking Julia out of the line of fire and Jack shook his head.

"I wish more people had such a charitable disposition as my mother. She means a lot to me, Mo, and I won't have her hurt. It's one thing for Julia to behave badly, but you're old enough to know better."

"Oh, thanks very much," I shot back, spotting a diversion. "What's my age got to do with it? Julia's nearly forty, just like you, in case it had slipped your mind. Just because I'm a few years older it doesn't mean I have to behave like your parents' generation." I feigned hurt and Jack apologised, but I couldn't pretend that Caitlin Doyle wasn't driving a wedge between us. I closed my eyes for the rest of the journey down the A3, pretending to doze, but trying unsuccessfully to contact the Ultimate Source for directions on the right way forward.

Chapter Four

Jack was taking Lily for a wet walk to feed the ducks and swans in South Norwood Country Park when Mark rang to say he and Zoe were at Crystal Palace Station and was there any chance of a lift home, given the weather. I drove up to collect them, relieved to have avoided the front door welcome, which increasingly seemed to label Mark as a visitor to the house rather than a resident of it. They ran out of the station hand in hand when they saw the car pull up in the rain, and both clambered into the back seat. I surmised that, quite apart from not wanting to lose physical contact, had Mark sat in the front it might have indicated a closeness with me over Zoe, whilst offering her the front seat might have designated her as guest. They had stayed the previous night in Camden with Zoe's parents who, it seemed clearer than ever, were becoming Mark's second family on a permanent basis. At twenty-one and in their last year of university, he and Zoe were making exuberant plans to find jobs and a shared flat when the summer term ended – the only point of discussion was whether they would base themselves in North London near Zoe's home territory, or South London and Mark's stamping ground. I would have to be careful not to appear partisan in case that swung the decision against me as a potentially interfering proto-mother-in-law.

Having dumped their damp backpacks and coats in the hall, they came through to the kitchen, where I had the kettle already boiling, and sat next to each other at the table, never missing an opportunity to keep some part of their bodies entwined. By the time I put mugs of tea and slabs of carrot cake from the South Norwood bakery on the table, they were filling me in on the love-lives of their house-mates, moaning about the work still to do for their finals and outlining the jobs they were thinking of applying for.

"There's no way Mark's not going to get a first," grumbled Zoe with pride. "He's the hardest working person I've ever met – I sometimes wake up in the morning and he's already up, sitting writing an essay at the desk. And it's not as if I sleep in late myself."

"You'll get a first without doing the work, babe," beamed Mark, "so you must be cleverer than me – and I'm sure it's going to be easier for you to find the job you want. It's a woman's world these days – and quite right too. It's all good."

I snorted. "Wait till you get out there in the real world, and then wait till you have children and see whether you still think that," I interjected, unable to keep a sour tone out of my voice, which Mark picked up on immediately.

"So what's been going on with you, Ma?" he asked, turning his gaze fully on me while still holding Zoe's hand in both of his.

"Oh, I'm trying to dig some dirt on Maxwell Robards for Erica and not getting anywhere. It's all just a bit frustrating at the moment. No big deal."

"And Jack, and Lily?" he probed, as I'd known he would as soon as I revealed a hint of my state of mind. It was he, not Jess, who shared my mother's sensitivity to my moods. There was never any point in trying to hide anything from either of them, so I was thankful that the front door burst open and Lily, in a wet mac and sou'wester, ran down the hall and threw herself onto her big brother's lap.

"Li'l-woman! How's my little sis? Cool hat, baby." And he took the red and white polka-dotted hat off Lily and plonked it on Zoe's long, blonde hair, where it looked like a designer fashion accessory. Lifting Lily with ease onto his left hip as he stood up, Mark reached out to give Jack a warm handshake. "Jack, man. Good to see you, how's the doctoring?"

And the next hour was spent in a pleasant family confusion of chat, updates and questions with answers inevitably interrupted by Lily, and me dispensing rounds of tea until the consensus was to move on to alcohol. The Australian Shiraz might not have been the best choice for me, as it seemed to rush straight to my cheeks and envelope my head in an invisible sauna. I avoided looking in any mirrors, not wanting to see my face unattractively flushed and giving the impression, no doubt, of being over-emotional.

Mark and Zoe decided that Indian would be the takeaway of choice so I took orders and rang the Golden Curry, whilst Lily demanded to stay up and have popadoms with us. In the end she was mollified by Zoe offering to give her a bath, and when Jack also snuck off to his study for a few minutes peace I knew that Mark would take advantage of the time alone with me to find out what was up.

"I got this great long email from Jess," I said, leading the way towards the privacy of my office, "she sounds really happy – read it and see what you think." Mark scrolled quickly down the screen and turned away.

"I got the same one, Ma, already read it. She just said something on the end of mine about some Thai guy she fancies, but

I don't think there's anything going on with him."

I felt totally deflated; I had been copied-in on a general email to Mark and her friends, with mine sent separately, not because Jess had anything more personal to tell me, but rather to delete what probably mattered most to her.

"Was I a crap mother to you and Jess?" I demanded of Mark. "Was it the break-up, living without a father, or the tiny flat and the insecurity that interfered with me and her bonding properly? I thought things got better for you both after Jack came along, but did having to cope with a step-father make it worse? If I got it all wrong, I need to know. I don't want to blow it a second time."

"Easy, Ma, what's brought all this on?" Mark was obviously shaken by my outburst. "I'm sorry I told you Jess had sent me the same email – you know she doesn't get much chance to send them, she was probably in a rush. It doesn't mean she doesn't love you – almost as much as I do … joke," he said, seeing my face.

I started to tell him how Jack wanted me to work less and spend more time with Lily before she went to school; how he disapproved of what I was working on at the moment; and how torn I felt between wanting to be a good – even a better – mother this time round while needing to maintain my sense of self, through the work I was good at and enjoyed. At the same time as listening out for the click of Jack's study door and any sounds of distress from Lily, I rambled on about my frustration over people's disapproval of the sex education project, and my desire to show Robards, and the other doubters, its value and importance. But Mark seemed to understand what I was trying to say and have the response I needed to hear.

"OK, Ma, you're throwing a lot at me here, but there's a

couple of things you've got no worries about. For starters, you were, and are, a great mother to me and Jess. It wasn't your fault that Dad left – I love him but he's no way a family man and he wouldn't have been with anyone. Hasn't Jess ever told you how we think Lily's the luckiest little sproglet in the world to have you and Jack for parents? No? Well, perhaps she wouldn't have – but that doesn't mean she doesn't love you. Jess is difficult because she finds life difficult, but it's not your fault and she's getting there."

"Do you two talk about me, and Dad, and stuff, then?" I asked, surprised that Jess held such different attitudes to the ones she acted out with me.

"Yeah, sometimes. We wonder why the two of you ever got together, but that's another story. No, look, tell me another time if you want to, everyone'll be down in a minute."

I shut my mouth; it would take too long to explain my complex relationship with his father. Paul, a thrilling but unstable artist, had been the love of my life at university and for a couple of nomadic years of travelling after that. I wasn't sure that I would ever tell Mark his conception hadn't exactly been planned, but his birth had delighted both of us and we even had a quick, registry office wedding, to make it legal. Unfortunately the realities of parenting, including the need for stability and money, had affected our relationship badly and after Jess came along, Paul had become unable to cope with life in the tiny flat my parents had helped me to buy. His hold on reality had grown increasingly tenuous, his behaviour increasingly erratic; finally I had packed his belongings, asked him to leave and changed the locks on the door. The three of us didn't hear from Paul for another five years and now, prematurely aged and drinking too much, he sporadically contacted and saw the children. I was not surprised Mark and Jess wondered why we had ever been together, but that could wait until another time, as Mark clearly had useful things to tell me now.

"Go on, what about me being a working mother? Was it a problem for you?"

"No, of course not. I don't know, probably all kids want to spend more time with their parents, but we were proud of your work and we learned to look after ourselves more that way. You were a role model, and me and Jess both want to make you proud of us – you gotta believe me." Mark was talking with an urgency he rarely let show through the laid back persona he had adopted as a student. I tried to lighten the tone.

"But you think I'm a bit crazy too, with my yoga and meditation and believing in the Universal Spirit," I laughed off my deeply held convictions. "Jack certainly does – I don't know any more, maybe he's right."

Upstairs we heard Zoe and Lily emerge from the bathroom giggling and shrieking, and head towards Lily's bedroom. Any minute now they would be downstairs.

"Ma, you know I love Jack and he's the best step-dad we could have had – he's as together as Dad is off the planet. But he sees things in black and white, and that's sometimes a little … limiting. No criticism, but me, I'm more of a shades of grey man," Mark offered hesitantly.

"OK, I take your point," I replied. "But if he's black and white and you're shades of grey, but you're both balanced and sensible, what does that make me?"

"Well, this might sound stupid, and you know I can't hack your Zen spirit, energy stuff, but to me you're like colours of the rainbow. How you see things is probably much more exciting, more beautiful than our black and white and grey lives, but from the outside it's a bit 'now you see it, now you don't'. But where would we all be without it? And for what it's worth, I think you're the pot of gold as well – so go for what you believe in, because it will be right for you, and for Lily."

His strong hug was both gratifying and nostalgic. The latter for the little boy who used to want a hug from me to solve his problems, and the former because he had grown into a man who could offer me such intelligent support when I needed it, despite, or because of, his upbringing. "I hope Zoe knows how lucky she is – don't let her ever hurt my boy," I flashed involuntarily to the Source and, as if on cue, Zoe came through the door with Lily in her arms, clinging like a bush baby round her neck.

"Thanks so much, Zoe," I smiled and moved forward to disentangle my unwilling daughter as Mark reclaimed his beloved, and they slid back into each other's arms. The door bell rang and Jack came downstairs feeling for his wallet to pay the delivery man.

"Sort out the plates and stuff and I'll be down as soon as I can," I told Mark and Zoe, and bore Lily up to her room quickly before the aroma of balti and crackle of popadoms made her any less sleepy.

I lay next to her warm little body and read *Mog's Bad Thing* for the umpteenth time and Lily giggled, for the umpteenth time, at Mog the cat weeing on the chair. Putting the book down at the end of the story I automatically began to stroke the bridge of her nose with the back of my index finger to keep her eyes closed while sleep overtook her. It seemed impossible that it was fifteen and more years since I had been doing the same to Mark and Jess, watching for their fluttering eyelids to become still and listening for the rhythmic breath of sleep. I used to wonder how they could drift off so peacefully when I felt such a sense of turmoil surrounding my little family. Mark was right; Lily was growing up in far more secure surroundings than my first two had found themselves in at her age. How could I make sure that nothing went wrong this time, when confusion threatened to break through every way I turned?

I had just dropped Lily off at Mel's and was heading back past our house up to the station, when I heard the phone ringing. I dashed indoors and picked it up on its last ring.

"Hello, sorry, just made it—" I gasped into the receiver. There was a split second's silence in which I knew the caller had heard me, then the burr of the dial tone. Was it Ellie, checking to see whether I'd left the house and was going to be in on time? I dialled the number to find out the last caller.

"... the caller withheld their number," the digital voice told me dispassionately. I couldn't imagine Ellie would be that secretive about checking up on me, but rushed back out and trotted as fast as I could up the hill to the station. Inevitably, my train had been cancelled and I had to wait twenty minutes for the next one into Victoria, which was by then horribly overloaded. It was a relief to leave the foetid atmosphere of the carriage and head for the tube, which was a little less packed on the three-stop journey to Warren Street.

I added to my lateness by picking up a cappuccino and ciabatta before turning off Tottenham Court Road into media land. The basement offices of Generation Productions were far from luxurious, but the white-washed brick walls, ultra modern office furniture, array of awards and six designer clocks showing world-wide time-zones, lent it a suitably buzzy ambience. I silently greeted Ellie, who was sitting at her reception desk talking animatedly on the phone. She looked pointedly at her watch with kohl-lined eyes and held out my bundle of mail in one magenta-taloned hand, while continuing her clearly personal conversation. I grabbed it and made my way between the senior producers' outsize desks, past the two edit suites with their flickering screens and squealing soundtracks, into the more dilapidated back office where the sex education team was based.

Jane, our producer, a slim, glamorous woman in her early fifties, was sitting on her desk talking intensely to Peter Braithwaite. He was the young, photogenic sex therapist, ambitious to become a media star, on whose credentials the project was relying. Not wanting to interrupt, I smiled and sat down at the adjacent desk which was mine on a Wednesday, and Jane's dumping ground the rest of the week. I moved aside piles of accumulated scripts, videos and sex manuals, booted up the computer and started to open my mail. I had just skimmed through a press release on some heavy-looking adult sex programmes that another company were launching on a satellite channel, and was about to bin a list of new research posts sent through from an agency, when Jane leaned over and said in her low, ex-smoker's voice,

"You might want to hang onto that, Mo. We've got a teensy little problem."

I looked up questioningly. "What sort of problem, Jane? Was it the interviews? I know they got to you a day late, something went wrong with the email … or did I not get the information you wanted out of the couples …?" I trailed off. She and Peter Braithwaite were both looking intently at me with concerned expressions.

"You've heard about Maxwell Robards' campaign?" he asked quietly. I nodded guiltily, as if I was somehow implicated in it.

"Well his Family Fellowship researchers were on to us last week. They came round and asked us what was going into the programme, took reams of notes, and then lectured us about the kind of information they considered appropriate sex education for young people. A lot of moralistic stuff about abstinence, the dangers of abortion, pro-life propaganda – you know."

I nodded again.

"Well obviously we said thanks but no thanks," Jane told me, adjusting her exquisitely cut, leather jacket over the tight-fitting t-shirt. "I thought we were on safe ground and they were peddling extremist views that were never supposed to be part of our brief. The Department for Education had OK'd it all, given us the go-ahead and agreed to fund – well, you know that bit, you were here."

Peter moved in closer, so the rest of the production team, busy on their phones and PCs, didn't hear what he was going to say. I got a waft of Hugo Boss aftershave and peppermint mouthwash.

"In the House of Commons yesterday Robards asked the Education Secretary how much the Department was planning to spend on what he called pornography for school children. He totally exaggerated the explicit material that's going into the visuals and generally stirred things up. He's made the whole project look like some tacky blue movie and it's not doing my reputation any good, I can tell you. The only reason it's not in the papers this morning is because he did it late in the day, but I've already had a couple of tabloids onto me. I'm not sure I can continue on the project if it's going to undermine my integrity as a media therapist."

Jane looked exasperated now, as well as worried, and ran her fingers through her short, silver-blonde crop. "I know this could be bad publicity for you, Peter," she whispered, looking over her shoulder to check no one else was listening. "But if you felt you had to pull out we would be able to find another expert. The point is, the whole project is at risk now. And if this production goes down it could take the company with it – the Department funding was a life-saver. Generation Productions hasn't got much else on at the moment; without this we'd certainly have to make some of the staff redundant."

As concerned for my own welfare as Dr Braithwaite, my first thought was that as a part-timer, contracted exclusively for the sex education project, I would be the first to go. I hadn't even got round to invoicing Generation for the work I'd done so far, and if the company went into liquidation I'd be unlikely to see a penny of what I was owed.

"So what's the situation, Jane?" I queried. "Surely the Education Department can't withdraw funding now?"

"That's what we thought," she replied. "But they rang this morning to 'remind' us that they hadn't signed off the project as yet, their call last week was only 'an indication' that they 'might' be involved, and they would come back to us with more information later today. So, mum's the word," she glanced over her shoulder at the rest of the team, "until we know for sure one way or the other. I guess we'd just better get on with the work in hand, after all we may just get the all clear. Peter?" Jane looked challengingly at our vacillating expert. "Should Mo start looking for a replacement presenter?"

"I didn't say I was pulling out," said Dr Braithwaite defensively. "I'll just tell Ellie to screen my calls." And he walked briskly out towards reception. Jane shook her head and sat down behind her desk.

"About those interviews, Mo," she made a severe face, and

then laughed. "They were great! Can you work on Peter's script for Programme One. That's next in the shooting schedule – in the event that his delicate reputation allows him to continue working with us," she added sardonically, as she swivelled round in her chair, swung her long legs in their tight black jeans and spike-heeled boots over the arm and picked up the phone.

I answered emails, checked some facts on the internet and tried to write Dr Braithwaite's to-camera introduction. With Jane jumping at every phone call, and my mind involuntarily slithering off the job to Robards, Caitlin, Miranda and Old Peggy, I tried several times to capture the right tone. Reading back my first draft, I felt I'd made Peter sound as if he was trying too hard to be young and hip; the second contained some unintended double entendres which would appear sleazy; the third was simply pompous and my fourth attempt sounded like an old-fashioned text book. I was almost relieved when David, the Managing Director of Generation Productions, appeared at the office door and gestured to Jane and Peter to come with him. As he ushered them through, he turned back to me as an afterthought.

"Mo, you'd better come as well."

Hoping this inclusion might mean good news, I followed the others into the formally titled board room and closed the door behind me. 'The goldfish bowl', as we dubbed it, was partitioned off by glass panels but efficiently sound-proofed, so every move was visible but no sound emerged. A proficient lip-reader would have had a field day watching some of the meetings that took place here; the regular clash of egos fuelled by a constant adrenalin rush ignited sparks on a regular basis. This morning's mood, though, was sober as David outlined the call he'd had from the Department of Education.

"It could be worse, it's not an outright no," he informed us. "That bloody Robards man has just put the wind up them by stirring up a media feeding-frenzy. Basically, the funding is frozen, so they can truthfully say they're not committed to the project at this moment in time. But they're going through the content again with a fine toothcomb and if they do decide to go ahead, they're undoubtedly going to ask us to adjust the visuals and add in some material which 'takes into account other views' – i.e. at least some lip-service to the moral majority, Family Fellowship line."

"That's outrageous—" started Jane, at the same time as Peter Braithwaite began to bluster about his precious integrity. David held up his hand for silence.

"In the meantime," he continued, "with our financial situation being what it is, I have no choice but to put the whole production on hold, and no further debts can be accrued. Jane, as an employee you'll have to work on development until this is sorted. Peter and Mo, I'm sorry but your contracts are suspended until further notice and no more invoices can be accepted. As soon as the situation is clarified we'll get back to you. You might as well go home, Mo; Peter and Jane, we'd better discuss a united approach to any publicity."

I got up and left the other three to plan their tactics, my face burning with indignation and the close atmosphere of the goldfish bowl. As it was lunchtime, none of the others in the production office commented on my exit, complete with bag and papers, and it certainly wasn't my place to break the bad news to them.

Peace and calm, I am relaxed and in control, breathe in the calm … I tried to maintain the three-part breath throughout my journey home, but fury at Robards, imminent loss of face with Jack, and anxiety about the financial situation intruded on my communion with the Universal Spirit. When the train pulled into Crystal Palace Station, I had to rush to the door and half fell onto the platform, twisting my ankle in the process. Cursing my vanity for wearing high-heeled boots this morning so as not to look unnecessarily dowdy next to Jane and Ellie, I limped up the long flight of Victorian stone steps, along the enclosed walkway over the tracks, down the steps the other side and back up the modern iron staircase to the ground level ticket office. Breathing heavily and in considerable pain, I relinquished all thoughts of a healthy walk down Auckland Road, and took a waiting cab from the taxi office across the road.

I had paid the driver and was hobbling to the front door when I heard the phone start to ring and once more managed to get in and pick it up just in time. For a second time, the caller hung up on hearing my voice, and had again withheld their number. A notion of Miranda trying to get through to Jack in his lunch hour flashed into my mind, as my husband opened the front door and looked taken aback to see me in the hall. I pulled off my boot, showed him my swollen ankle and burst into tears.

"Well it sounds to me as though Jack reacted rather reasonably and hasn't given you a hard time about the money or not invoicing – excuse me a minute while I whiz this up."

Ros pressed the button on her smoothie-maker and, with a raucous noise that stopped the conversation dead, the fruit, cranberry juice and live yoghurt frothed up into a pretty pink liquid. She filled two tall glasses from the machine's tap and handed one to me. I had chosen Ros to take my troubles to, partly for her professional expertise, but also because she took a naturally impartial view of events and people and could be relied on for absolute discretion. I did not want my worries about Miranda circulating around my other friends; however, I hadn't confided them to Ros as yet, and I had a favour to ask as well.

"Yeah, he was pretty nice about it – bound my foot up and made me rest it as much as possible. I think he was a bit worried that I was so upset about being laid off after what he'd said about unsuitable projects." I took a gulp of Ros's fortifying cocktail. "Mmm, this is delicious, I must start making them at home. What are you taking with yours?"

Ros was tipping capsules and pills from a range of bottles into her hand and swallowing them with big swigs of the smoothie.

"Just my daily supplements," she answered, between gulps.

"I didn't know you were a health fanatic. I thought Miranda had cornered the market in that, but those look really serious, prescription even, some of them." Ros smiled, finished off her smoothie and rinsed out the glass in the butler's sink that she and Joe had bought in France, along with the other fittings for their perfectly tasteful kitchen and bathroom. Their flat was the top floor of a massive, early Victorian house at the bottom of Sylvan Road, with huge windows on one side, giving fabulous views over South Norwood Lakes Park and out to the Kent countryside beyond. Classic/minimalist was the closest I could get to describing their taste in décor, to which the two Dalmatians, one black and white and one liver-spotted, added the final touches.

"So, tell me what this morning's really all about," said Ros, to-the-point as ever. "I'm guessing that you didn't come round on a working morning just to tell me that Jack bandaged your ankle and made you lie down. What can I do for you, Mo?"

"Well, whichever way you look at it, I really need to get something on Robards." I returned the compliment of taking the bull by the horns. "Erica won't pay me if I don't come up with the goods, and if I can publicly undermine his campaign, it makes it much more likely the sex ed programme will go ahead – and I really believe in that, Ros, as well as needing the dosh."

"Your point being …?" Ros raised her dark, shapely eyebrows, and waited.

"You know his wife. If there's anything dodgy with him, she'll know about it and if I just had the chance to meet her I might get a lead, even a hint I could follow up. I just thought, if there was a charity event you knew she was going to be at, I might be able to come along with you, get an introduction, arrange an interview … Please, Ros?"

Ros walked over to her desk across their open-plan living space that encompassed the kitchen and her study as well as their expansive leather sofas and an original Shaker dining table and chairs. She flicked through the tidy, leather-bound volume on her roll-top desk and made a note with a silver pen.

"There is something in the offing, as it happens, but I'm not sure whether Kathleen's coming or not. It's at the Early Childhood Clinic in Bethnal Green, a fund-raising lunch to buy more specialised play equipment. I could ask you along as a researcher, especially if you could get Erica to write a piece about us." Ros gave me an arch smile, knowing I would appreciate the quid pro quo. I nodded excitedly, certain that Erica would agree to anything which facilitated a meeting with Kathleen Robards.

"But, Mo – nothing controversial at the event itself. Promise? And you're not to upset Kathleen if you do get an interview, just subtle probing, right?"

"Of course," I agreed. "Thanks, Ros, you're a star. But, you know I did come to talk to you about me and Jack as well. He is being really nice and everything, but I don't feel things are right while I'm doing this stuff about his birth mother behind his back – even though he's agreed to it. What is your secret, how do you and Joe manage to maintain the perfect relationship? Venetia only snipes because she's jealous, just like the rest of us."

Ros turned away. It seemed a long time before she answered, and I was left feeling I'd intruded beyond the boundaries of our friendship. When she turned back her face was quite composed, other than a tiny tic in one smoothly powdered cheek. I realised that she was the only member of the group whom I had never seen reduced to tears. She made a slightly rueful face.

"Venetia's not all wrong," she said at last. "It's not perfect at the moment, but that's just circumstances, it won't last." She seemed to be examining my face minutely, to see if it was safe to continue. Apparently I passed the test. "This doesn't go beyond these four walls, Mo?" I nodded. "When Joe's on tour or out of town, I don't own him – you understand? I don't like it, but some people need to … play with matches in order to keep the home fires burning."

I was flabbergasted. Ros let Joe sleep around, and that was the secret of their perfect relationship – surely not? All those jibes from Venetia were right on target, and I would bet she knew it, or had more than an inkling. Ros could clearly read what was going through my mind: "No, Venetia doesn't know anything; she's just having a go. Joe and I have strict rules and absolute discretion is one of them. And that I have his total, long- term commitment and when he's home he's completely mine."

The impact of what she was saying hit me in the solar plexus. "And presumably you have the same freedom … if you wanted to exercise it?" Ros's face gave nothing away. "Are you saying, Ros, that if Jack's telling me I can do something he doesn't like as long as he doesn't have to know about it, he might assume he can do the same? But with something different? I mean, do you think he might be having an affair and think it's OK just so long as I don't find out?"

Ros shook her head. "Why on earth would you jump to that conclusion, Mo? Joe and I are totally different from you and Jack, and I don't mean either better or worse. All I can say is, there are things between us that we don't share with anyone else, and I guess that's a big part of what makes our relationship special. It's the glue that holds us together and it's strong enough to allow us to give each other some space. Secrets within a relationship can be a bond; having secrets from your partner can pull you apart," she added gently, the closest she would come to offering direct advice.

"I suppose it's easier when kids don't come into the equation," I said without thinking, and wished I hadn't when I saw the twitch in Ros's cheek mutate into a grimace of pain. "Sorry, Ros, that was as tactless as Venetia," I responded quickly, but still something made me push on. "I've never asked you why you and Joe don't have kids, especially when you'd make such a fantastic mother, but tell me to mind my own business if . . ."

"Mind your own business, Mo," she returned curtly. "We knew early on that children weren't an option, and even that's more than anyone else knows. Perhaps it makes things easier in some ways, but not in others, believe me." And she stood up, making it clear that it was time for me to leave. I apologised again for my thoughtlessness, which she accepted with good grace and said she was sorry if she'd been sharp – it was a sensitive area and one she and Joe had agreed to keep to themselves.

"We're completely open with each other and we operate on very clear boundaries – he respects mine and I respect his. It may sound like a cliché, but it works for us." Ros smiled to release the tension I had created.

"Well, I still think your relationship looks more perfect than the rest of ours," I smiled back as I picked up my bag and coat. "I haven't blown my chance to meet Kathleen Robards, have I?"

"Of course not, you idiot. I'll check that she's coming to the lunch, you ask Erica about a story and we'll sort it out." Ros walked me to her front door and put her arm round my shoulders, making me feel small and dumpy next to her sinewy six foot.

"By the way," I said casually, as I walked out onto the landing, "do you think Miranda's the type to have affairs? What with Si so engrossed in his thesis, you could hardly blame her."

Ros shrugged. "People aren't 'types' and I don't make uninformed judgements – part of my professional training. I'll call you, Mo," she added lightly, as she closed the door and I started down the stairs.

I pondered our conversation as I walked round the corner, and down to Anerley Hill to pick up some vitamins at the chemist. If they were the secret of Ros's looks and physique, I was going to try some too. As I came out of the shop clutching a bag of bottles and boxes that had set me back more than I intended, or could afford, I almost bumped into Old Peggy. She was leaning on a couple of mismatched walking sticks rather than her trolley and I tried to slip past, rummaging through my purchases as if I hadn't seen her.

"There you are, lovely." She grinned at me, and took my arm in her pincer grip, forcing me to slow down and support her. Once again my gaze was drawn into her hooded black eyes; the deep bags beneath them, and the rest of her pointed, wizened face seemed to fade away. "She's coming soon, you'll see …" she intoned, and the busy street seemed to grow fainter, while that sunlit river bank I had visited once before materialised around me. In an instant I was aware of standing, naked, up to my waist in the ice-cold water, enjoying the pressure of the flowing current and the warmth of the sun on my torso. I started to call out to a figure standing on the bank to join me, but the bright sunlight from behind meant I couldn't make out their features as they started down the slope towards me. As I strained to see who it was, the scene faded and I was back on the pavement, with Peggy looking intently into my eyes and smiling her almost toothless smile. "You saw her," she nodded at me, with satisfaction.

I pulled away from her, nearly knocking her off her feet and ran across the road, causing brakes to squeal and horns to hoot as cars driving both ways tried to avoid me. I panted my way back onto Auckland Road. Safely home in my kitchen, I ignored the remains of breakfast still on the table and poured myself a glass of orange juice. Swallowing down a selection of vitamins and supplements, I assured myself that it must be the lack of some essential minerals that was causing my brain to have these episodes. Either that or my hormones were in uproar.

Chapter Five

It was as an almost throw-away remark, on the doorstep as he left for work, that Jack delivered his bombshell.

"Now you're not really earning anything, hon, it doesn't make much sense to go on paying Mel. This could be one of your 'meant to be' opportunities, a gift from above, to spend time with Lily till she goes to school in September." And he kissed me on the lips and our daughter on the head, adjusted his scarf and closed the front door behind him. At the same time as hoping Lily hadn't taken in what he had said and resisting the desire to open the door and shout furiously after him, I noted that not only had he smelled good, but he had a rash on the back of his neck where his hair had recently been cut. Only the expensive aftershave I had bought him for his last birthday gave him that particular allergic reaction, so he reserved it for special occasions. What was so special about today that was worth the itching?

I didn't say anything to Mel about cutting down, let alone stopping, her child-minding hours when I dropped Lily off an hour later. But I felt guilt like a snake-bite in my heart, spreading its poison round my system as I walked up the hill to meet my friends at the French café. Why did I not feel joy that the Universal Spirit was offering me the chance to spend all my time with my daughter in the few months before she became locked into school days and terms? Why could I not feel comfortable being supported by my very willing husband from his secure and socially responsible job?

I couldn't answer those questions, nor the greater one of how, in such a short space of time, my world had lurched from one in which I had a growing sense of being in the flow – what Jack called my sense of 'meant to be' – to the feeling that I was swimming against the current, and losing my grip on reality to boot. And why did I feel that it must all be my fault? Perhaps it was just because I'd woken up this morning with the start of a cold that filled my nose and prickled in the back of my throat.

I felt quite sick and over-heated when I arrived and ordered mineral water rather than my usual cappuccino. I kept my deepest discomforts to myself, but told Venetia, Suzy, Miranda and Ros that every aspect of my life seemed blocked. As well as my work problems, there had been no response from Caitlin Doyle and I feared that if there wasn't one soon, Julia would get impatient, take matters into her own hands and Jack would end up being forcibly dragged into the situation.

"They just can't help themselves, can they, even the decent ones?" asked Venetia impenetrably. We looked at her, waiting for an explanation. "Men!" she responded, as though her meaning had been blindingly obvious. "Jack always seemed like one of the good guys, reasonably on-message, if a bit too straight for my taste. I really thought you'd found the perfect partner there, Mo, but I guess there's no such thing!"

"What do you mean, Venetia?" I demanded, my heart in my mouth as I anticipated the worst.

"It must be genetic, this desire to control women – like chattels." I almost smiled with relief that this was all she was

accusing Jack of. "You've been earning your living all your life,"
Venetia continued, "brought up two perfectly nice human beings
more or less on your own, but now he thinks he knows best. *His*
daughter needs *his* wife to look after her full-time, so you can
both be dependent on him as provider. Then when you want to
do something, or go somewhere, or buy something for yourself,
who do you have to ask?" Venetia finished her rant and took a
gulp of her steaming double espresso. The rest of us looked at
each other, unsure whether to take her seriously and how best to
react. If we got it wrong, Venetia was quite capable of storming
off and freezing out any perceived miscreants for at least a week.
For a moment no one spoke, then Suzy, the least vulnerable
target for Venetia's wrath, risked a light-hearted approach:

"So, do we take it from this little outburst that Charlie's had
something to say about your future lifestyle? Duncan says he's
quite a traditional type beneath his racy exterior."

There was a tense silence as we awaited Venetia's reaction.
She looked up defensively and then crashed her cup back on its
saucer with a reluctant, wrong-footed smile.

"OK, God damn it, it is a sore point just now. Playing the sex
kitten had the desired effect on my team, but it's got back to
Charlie and he's come over all jealous and protective. He thinks
I should give up work when – if – we get married, and allow him
to pamper me, after the 'tough life' I've had. He wants me to
open fêtes in his constituency and do the social stuff around
Westminster."

Suzy gave her infectious, boisterous laugh and the rest of us
joined her, partly from relief and partly because the thought of
Venetia playing loyal wife and charming hostess was genuinely
hilarious. "Duncan bumped into him at the club last night and
they had a bit of a man-to-man chat, so I gathered there might

be a few clouds on the romantic horizon." She put her hand on Venetia's, who didn't withdraw hers; a clear sign that there was some genuine turmoil beneath the spiky exterior.

"There's a traditional side to most men, deep down," offered Ros. "It tends to manifest in situations where they feel vulnerable. It's the old, primal drives coming out when some fundamental aspect of their lives seems to be threatened, whether the menace is real or perceived."

"Oh thank you, doctor, for that profound insight," spat Venetia. "And what do you recommend as a cure for their poor little egos? Become a Stepford wife and give them all their own way?"

"You know that's not a solution I'd recommend," returned Ros equably, "unless it suited both parties. You're clever enough to find a way of neutralising the threat and achieving a workable *modus operandi*, Venetia. The question is, do you want to?"

That silenced Venetia briefly and I attempted to lighten the mood once more.

"I can't wait till you're going to Foreign Office dinners with visiting dignitaries. Where do you think she'll spark off the first diplomatic incident?" I asked around the table.

"Airing her views on corporate social responsibility to a group of our neo-con Republicans could have interesting results," suggested Miranda, with a grin.

"Or slagging off corrupt officialdom to a delegation of Eastern bloc politicians? That could put paid to Charlie's ministerial career and then you'd have to go back to work and support him," I teased, and fumbled for a tissue to blow my nose.

"Yes! That's it! Mo, you've done it again. You're a genius." A look of exhilaration lit up Venetia's previously downcast face and I could see that some wicked plan was forming in her mind.

"Agree to what he wants – that's neutralising the threat, hey, Ros? Then give him a taste of what it would really be like – a kind of trial-run Stepford wife, Venetia style. He might just end up begging for me to stay involved in my own career ..."

"I don't know why you have to make everything so difficult for yourselves, sometimes," Suzy interjected plaintively. "Duncan's supported me for eighteen years now, and I've never felt controlled or demeaned by that. And don't you dare say I haven't achieved anything during that time."

We all looked a bit uncomfortable. If any of the rest of us had had a disabled child like Olly, our choices might have been very different. It had been a huge blow to both Suzy, who was a perfectionist in everything she did, and Duncan with his formidable intellect, that their first-born son had been both physically and mentally handicapped. Together they had decided that Suzy would not return to the chambers in which she had been a young, high-flying barrister; she would give up her career, stay at home to look after their Down's Syndrome son and give him the highest quality of life they could. His younger brother Martin had been born two years later without complications or abnormality and Suzy had worked tirelessly to create a comfortable family life where all needs were met: Olly had an indefatigable carer; Martin's promising academic and musical talents were unstintingly fostered; and Duncan's personal and professional needs for a busy social life were always catered for.

Devoted as she was to her family, Suzy had also put her personal and professional experience to wider use. When Olly and Martin had started school, she had refocused some of her boundless energy on setting up and initially running a charity which campaigned, and provided practical support, for the families of disabled children. Now the boys were older and she

had handed over the day-to-day running of Big Hand to profes-
sionals, Suzy had found a creative outlet in the local arts community of Dulwich, where she and Duncan were long-standing
residents. No, not even Venetia would suggest that Suzy's
achievements were anything but substantial.

"I think you're right," agreed Miranda, surprisingly. "I don't
have the option to take a sabbatical from my career – the pharmaceutical industry waits for no man, or woman – and Simon's
salary wouldn't keep us in the manner to which the girls have
become accustomed. But Jack's offering you a gift, Mo. Nine
months, or whatever, to take time out, enjoy your daughter
before she starts to grow away from you. What's happened; I
always thought you two communicated so well about everything?"

I felt a flush of anger suffuse my face, particularly because
Miranda's choice of words echoed those that Jack had used this
morning. Had he discussed it with her, and if so where? Was it
for her almond eyes and Hispanic features that he had splashed
on the toxic aftershave? Luckily Venetia took up the cudgels on
my behalf before I could say something I might regret.

"What's this, a return to your Catholic roots? Come on,
Miranda, when was Si ever the head of your household – I can't
see you handing back the trousers and agreeing to sit at home
like a good little *señora*, even if he won the Lottery."

"Alright, girls, that's enough," trilled Suzy, seeing the situation could turn nasty. She fanned herself with a paper napkin.
"Oh dear, is the heating up high in here or is it just one of my
hot flushes coming on?" I took her cue and stood to leave one of
our less satisfactory mornings. Ros caught my eye.

"Kathleen has accepted for the lunch – she's even going to
make a short speech. Did you raise the idea of writing some-

thing with Erica?" she asked quietly, while Venetia and Miranda continued to bicker.

"She's happy for me to put a piece together and she'll do her best to sell it in, but she can't guarantee which paper will take it. Whichever one does will probably need to sort out a photo at a later date. Is that good enough to get me in?"

Ros smiled and gave me a discreet thumbs up. I said my goodbyes and left feeling at least something had been achieved that morning, even if no one had come up with a more concrete lead on Robards or offered any useful advice about how to deal with Jack or Julia.

And then there was Miranda.

The rational side of me said that she was my friend, that she had never shown any interest in Jack in the past and surely wouldn't have the audacity to have coffee with us and offer me advice if she was involved with my husband. My intuition retorted that something was going on between them, that I shouldn't ignore my instincts and the growing number of suspicious signs, let alone my worsening relationship with Jack.

I walked home, feeling a bit shivery, checked the post and my emails – still nothing from Caitlin Doyle and the only work-related message was a confirmation from Generation Productions of the cancellation of my contract – and found nothing that needed doing in my in-tray or diary. I was beginning to feel I would have to accept the inevitable. I got out my yoga blocks and did some alternate nostril breathing – *Anuloma Viloma*, as my yoga teacher called it, to equalise the flow of prana in my body. I held my right nostril closed and breathed in through the left; held my breath; breathed out through the right; in through the right, hold and out through the left. The teacher had told us this week that western science had finally caught up with the

Yogis and 'discovered' that the nasal cycle affected brain function. A blocked left nostril would make your right brain work less well and vice versa. With this cold my right nostril was the worse blocked, so perhaps this was suppressing my logical thoughts. I moved onto meditation, nervous though I was of finding myself back at the sunlit river, in someone else's body and unsure who I would find was with me in that idyllic spot. But I didn't even make it to my normal level of meditation – no peace or calm enveloped me, my nose filled up again, my throat throbbed and my brain buzzed with the events and issues I wanted to rise above.

By the time I knocked on Mel's door I had made enough of a decision to accept, for once, her offer of 'a bite of lunch', even though Lily's presence might mean it added an extra hour to my weekly child-minding bill. I sat down at the formica-topped kitchen table with Beth, Noah and Lily and watched Mel finish preparing the meal in her fluid, leisurely Caribbean style. No wonder I couldn't get Lily to eat much tea at home on her long days here, I thought, as Mel dished up massive portions of jerk chicken, rice and peas and a layered vegetable dish which I couldn't identify.

"What's this, Mel, it's delicious?" I asked, forking the melting, tangy mixture into my mouth and feeling it run soothingly down my sore throat.

"Sweet potato and callaloo pie," she smiled. "I'll give you the recipe – you can use spinach instead, or they got tinned callaloo up at Sergio's on the Triangle."

I resolved to be more adventurous with my cooking in the future – after all, I would have all the time in the world to shop for more exotic ingredients, and Lily probably already knew Sergio's Delicatessen's eclectic, multi-cultural stock better than I did. I didn't broach my subject until the children had finished their delectable mango fool and disappeared off to play, and Mel and I were drinking mugs of strong, Blue Mountain coffee that Andrew regularly had sent over by his family in Jamaica.

"Mel, I've got some bad news and I hope it's not going to cause you problems," I began, feeling hot already at the prospect of burning my bridges.

"No problem's too big that the Lord won't help us sort it," she smiled sunnily back at me. "What's happened, girl, you don't look yourself?"

I blew my nose and explained about the sex education project being on hold, possibly for good, about Jack wanting me to spend more time with Lily before she started school; and I stressed how happy I was with Mel's childminding and reluctant to change our current arrangements.

"I think Lily has a wonderful balance of care and a great sense of extended family with you," I assured Mel. "I don't want to reduce her time here at all, but it's hard to justify if I'm not earning much money myself at the moment." Mel didn't look at all perturbed by her own potential loss of income, but took a long draught of coffee and bit into one of the little cookies she called 'bullas'.

"I know you don't see things like me and Andrew, Mo," she started cautiously, "but the way I was brought up, Jack's the head of your household and in the long run you'll be happiest if you respect his wishes. Lily's a fine little girl and we love her company, but time is your gift to her; the more she gets the happier she'll be." She smiled beatifically at me and rested her hands on the worn table top.

There it was again, this talk of 'gifts': Jack's to me, mine to Lily. Why didn't this round of family benevolence give me the warm, glowing feeling I was clearly expected to have? I sighed.

"I don't know about that, Mel," I admitted. "No, I don't agree that Jack's word goes – when I get forms to fill in that ask who's the head of the household I cross it out and write 'none', or put both our names in. And it's not that I don't want to spend time with Lily, just not all my time, when I can use my 'gifts' on work I believe in." There, I'd got my own back on the gift thing. Surely no one in this day and age would suggest I shouldn't use the talents I had, whether they considered them God-given or part of my DNA.

"You know, girl, there are seasons in our lives, especially for us women," Mel responded calmly. "We have our monthly seasons and we have a season for child-bearing, then it's gone. We're not like men in that way; they make money and babies all through their lives, that's why we can rely on them. Maybe this is not your season to work, but to be a baby mother. Seasons come and seasons pass, girl, *Ecclesiastes:* three. It's not forever."

"But that's just it, Mel. I'm older, maybe too old to be a full-time mother again. I've done it all before, but even then I worked right through – had no choice first time around. If I give up work now, I may never get back in. I'll lose contacts, won't keep my skills and knowledge up to date. I'm scared of losing it forever if I dip out now. And I don't want to be totally dependent on Jack. My independence is important to me. Anyway, what about you and your income? This is your work, after all."

Mel looked sympathetically at me and explained that she and Andrew simply did what God wanted them to and that made life so much simpler than the complicated decisions I had to make on my own. He had provided Andrew with a job that paid enough for the family to live on, and when they had asked for guidance, led Mel in the direction of child-minding.

"But how did you know God wanted you to do that, Mel?" I asked, exasperated but envious of her self-assured connection to the Almighty. "Did he write it in stone or zap you like Paul on the road to Tarsus? Why doesn't he tell me what he wants me to do if he has these plans for us all?"

"He surely will if you listen, girl." Mel leaned forward earnestly. "Jake and I, we pray every night and then we listen and look for the signs He gives. Next day after we prayed about what I should be doing, I got a leaflet through the door from the council, about child-minding. Then it was on the news about the government wanting more childcare for working mothers, and a couple of days later you told me you were pregnant. They come in threes, mostly, the signs."

"So when I meditate and use the Source to get into the energy flow," I suggested, "I'm doing exactly the same as you? Same process, different words. Except I do it on my own and Jack wouldn't have anything to do with it even if I wanted him to."

Mel shook her head. "If you don't accept Jesus Christ as your saviour, girl, you're playing with fire. You're opening yourself up to the tempter to lead you astray. If it's not in scripture, it's not from God. Our pastor, he had a reading for me after I'd had my signs. 'Mark: ten: fourteen,' he told me that very Sunday. 'That's what I've been given for you, Mel.'"

"Sorry, I don't know my Bible that well," I admitted. "What did it say?"

"Why, 'Suffer the little children to come unto me, and forbid them not: for of such is the kingdom of God,'" recited Mel with awe. "That was confirmation and it worked out just fine, didn't it? Now I don't know what God has in store for the future, but

I'm surely going to pray for you tonight, girl."

"Thanks, Mel," I said, unsure how to respond, but relieved that she hadn't offered to do so there and then. "I'll let you know what Jack and I decide – and thanks."

I gathered up a reluctant Lily from her dolly game with Beth in the toy-strewn lounge – Noah had fallen asleep on the floor as I'd distracted Mel from putting him down for his nap – and dragged her off to get dressed for her weekly ballet class in Norbury. The little blue leotard and skirt, along with the hand-ful of Smarties the teacher gave out at the end, were the best bits as far as Lily was concerned and I wasn't sure how much longer I could persuade her to keep going.

I sat, sweaty and snuffling, in the stuffy little changing-room at the back, where the parents waited out the lessons. I had even-tually persuaded Lily to join in the pointy-toe steps with which Miss Denise, the teenage teacher, was leading the class around the front "studio". I wondered how the family lived in the upper storey of the small terraced house with their ground floor ded-icated to the dancing school. A burst of loud discussion above our heads suggested not in total harmony, and a spike-haired adolescent boy came crashing down the stairs and slammed out of the front door.

"Everyone alright, today? We've got a lovely range of tights and ballet shoes just in, if anybody needs new ones." Miss Joan, mother of Miss Denise and presumably the hacked-off teenager, and owner of The Norbury Dance Academy, popped her head round the door. The disjunction between her youthful dancer's body in leotard and leg-warmers and her haggard face with its stage-heavy makeup and ballerina-black hair scraped back in a chiffon scarf, made it hard to estimate her age, but I guessed it was not far off mine.

I recognised the high stress-levels in her taut smile and remembered back to when Mark, Jess and I had lived in such cramped conditions that Mark had to put his makeshift bed away each morning to make space to dress in the tiny room he shared with his sister; and my "desk" was a stool at a cleared work-surface in our minute kitchen. Now I had a house with more than enough space for my three children, an entirely comfortable, if not affluent, lifestyle and choices which did not involve having to turn my home into a business to make enough money to live on.

I tuned in to the sporadic conversation going on around me: one mum was cooing at the baby she was rocking in a buggy; another sat, hand on her heavily pregnant belly, smiling as she felt her unborn baby kick, and discussing birth plans with her friend whose toddler twins were busy turning out the contents of their mother's handbag. Only the lone father was out of the loop, trying to read the paper and ignore the female disorder around him. Was my only real choice, I ruminated, to either join the community of totally-involved mothers, or else remain on the fringes of my daughter's little life – part-time mum, part-time worker, maybe part-time wife in Jack's eyes?

We rushed into the house and straight up to the bathroom, Lily desperate for a wee after refusing to use the windowless loo at dancing and drinking a full carton of apple juice on the way home in the car. Struggling to peel off her leotard and tights in time, I couldn't even attempt to reach the phone when it started to ring, but went next door to Jack's study when she was safely ensconced on the loo. No message on voicemail and once again the caller had withheld their number. When I went back into the bathroom, I found Lily happily unwrapping tampons from a dusty box I kept by the toilet.

"What are these, Mummy?" she asked, testing one in her mouth.

"Oh yuck, not for eating, darling." I took the box from her and started to pick up the curls of cellophane festooning the floor.

"Are they your toy mouses?" Lily enquired, swinging one by the tail. "Eee, eee, eee."

"No, they're not mice, they're for … keeping Mummy's knickers clean," I told her truthfully but uninformatively. "Wash your hands, Lily," as she half pulled up her tights and tottered out of the bathroom with her leotard round her ankles.

"I will in a minute," she called back. "I just going to change my knickers, they're a bit wet. You can clean them with a mouse."

An unwelcome thought wiped the smile off my face as I put the box away out of Lily's reach. The box was dusty because I hadn't had occasion to use it for some time. Was it six weeks, two months, or more since I'd had a period? I tried to think back, but failed to identify the date of the last time I'd had to bother with tampons. It occurred to me that Suzy's talk of hot flushes and Mel mentioning the limits of the child-bearing season had set off little shockwaves of recognition in my head that until now I had chosen to ignore. Forty-five was young – but not too young for the menopause to start, as I knew from Suzy's experience. I ran after Lily and found her in her room, surrounded by clothes and the open drawers from which she had pulled them in the hunt for her Barbie knickers-and-bra set, which I remembered were in the wash.

"Wear these knickers and your vest with the pink bow," I urged her. "It's much warmer than the Barbie bra anyway."

"I don't want to be warm, I want to be a lady," she huffed at me, standing hands on hips, pouting and tossing her curls. Four-going-on-fourteen, I thought regretfully and reached out to hug her.

"Don't be a lady too soon, it's nice to be a little girl," I told her, but she pulled away and started emptying her dressing-up box to find some suitably ladylike attire.

I recalled my anger at Jack when he called Lily an "achievement". Of course he hadn't been implying she was some project we were working on. No, he had been referring to the two years it took to conceive her and my resulting age on becoming a mother again. I knew that he would have liked another child, though we never spoke of it any more, he for reasons of tact and I for fear of making explicit my failure in this area. Six years was not a huge age difference and, had he been the elder, it would have been entirely unremarkable, but I knew he had taken a risk in marrying a woman nearing the end of her fertility. For a man with few genetic connections in his life, it seemed especially unreasonable that my body had now decided to end his chances of producing a vital addition to his biological family.

I told Jack that I had talked to Mel about reducing her hours, but said I wanted to leave the final decision for a couple of weeks in case the Department of Education funding came through for the sex education project after all. In case I could find something to put a spanner in the works of Maxwell Robards' retrogressive campaign against us, I thought, though didn't say aloud. Jack nodded and seemed pleased that I'd come round to his opinion, though not as delighted as I felt my con-cession warranted. After we had eaten dinner in front of the TV, he said he had some research to do and went upstairs to his study. I thought I heard him talking on the phone, but he had Dave Brubeck playing on his perfectly balanced sound system and I couldn't bring myself to listen at the door.

I went into my own, almost redundant, office and did an internet search for menopausal symptoms. "Hot flushes, night sweats, palpitations, insomnia, headaches, dizziness …" Yes, I had been feeling unseasonably warm and prone to flushing recently, had not been sleeping well and dizziness was the least of the problems with my head. "Mood swings, irritability, anxiety, difficulty concentrating, difficulty coping," continued the web page, and worse, "vaginal dryness, loss of libido and passing urine more often by day and/or by night". It was true, I had been getting up in the night recently, and our sex life hadn't been great or frequent in the last few months. I couldn't remember when I had last instigated love-making; without my realising it, our physical relationship had been down to Jack for some time now. I stopped reading when I got to "later menopausal symptoms: the skin may become dryer, thinner, less elastic, more prone to bruising; hair thinning, dryness and the growth of unwanted hair …"

I checked my email, and found a brusque message from Erica confirming that she was sure she could sell the Early Childhood Clinic story to one of the left-leaning broadsheets, but if this line of enquiry into Robards didn't produce anything useful she would have to terminate the story and there wouldn't be a fee. I clicked hopefully on an email from Jess, but it was just a round-robin collection of anti-men jokes she had sent to all her girl friends with a note saying she was still having a great time and making new friends. Was this the Thai boy she had failed to tell me about last time, I wondered as I scrolled down through the mildly amusing, but predictable humour? The last one gave me pause for thought, however:

> A woman marries a man expecting he will change, but he doesn't.
>
> A man marries a woman expecting that she won't change, and she does.

Had I changed since marrying Jack? Was I no longer the person he had fallen in love with? And had I expected Jack to change and been disappointed by his consistency?

I was debating this in my head when I absent-mindedly clicked on a message from an address that didn't ring any bells: n.oconnor@nics.org.uk. My heart lurched – this was about, if not from, Julia and Jack's birth mother.

> Dear Ms Mozart,
>
> I am writing to you following your letter to Caitlin Doyle about her daughter, Julia Patterson.
>
> Miss Doyle has received your letter and has asked me to reply on her behalf.
>
> I am a social worker and work part-time in the Post-Adoption Service at the Northern Ireland Children's Society.
>
> As you rightly guessed, Miss Doyle was extremely shocked to receive a letter in relation to her children at her parents' home whilst she was visiting them recently. Indeed, the distress caused by your letter to Miss Doyle made her quite ill and to date she has been unable to respond at all. Not knowing what to do, she came to the NICS Post-Adoption Service for advice.
>
> Although Miss Doyle was pleased to hear that her daughter has had a happy life with her adopted family, this contact from her

causes Miss Doyle serious personal problems. As you pointed out in your letter, Miss Doyle never told anyone in her family, or indeed anyone else, about the birth of her twins and their subsequent adoption. To do so now would cause considerable upset to Miss Doyle's elderly parents and to other people close to her.

Because of this, Miss Doyle hopes that Julia will understand that she cannot enter into a relationship with her or meet her at this time. She will, though, write her a letter telling her something of her own background and that of her father and why she felt it was in the twins' best interest to be adopted.

In the mean time, Miss Doyle begs you to respect her privacy, and that neither you nor Julia try to get in touch with her at her parents' address, where she is not resident, or in any other way. As soon as she is well enough, she will write to Julia c/o your address.

Please do not hesitate to contact me if I can be of any further assistance.

Yours sincerely,

Niamh O'Connor
Post-Adoption Services Counsellor
Northern Ireland Children's Society

After reading it through a couple of times, ensuring that Jack's study door was still closed and *Blue Rondo a la Turk* was playing loudly enough to cover my voice, I picked up the phone and dialled Julia's number. When she answered, I tried to lower her expectations as far as possible before reading Niamh O'Connor's email through to her, but inevitably she found it a massive disappointment.

"Oh my God, I can't believe it," she cried histrionically into my ear, "my own mother doesn't want to know me! What kind of woman is she? She must be a cold-hearted bitch – no wonder she had us adopted out," and Julia dissolved into tears. I decided against a sympathetic response, figuring that would send her further down the spiral of self-pity, and I couldn't afford to be on the phone too long sorting her out.

"Stop it, Julia!" I snapped, trying to deliver a verbal slap to her hysteria. "Calm down and listen. I told you to prepare yourself for the worst, and this is far from the worst."

"Why is it?" she wailed pathetically. "She doesn't want to see me or have a relationship with me. Ever."

"That's not what she said, at least the 'ever' bit. Just look at it from her point of view for a minute. This middle-aged woman with a life we know nothing about – she must have friends, could be married, could have children, possibly has a job, maybe does stuff in the community—"

"We know she's not married," Julia interrupted. "She's still Miss Doyle."

"Jules, do you think she's going to give you her married name if she doesn't want you to find her? I'd say all those references to 'Miss Doyle' are probably a smoke screen. Anyway, shut up and listen for a minute," I cut in hurriedly before she could interrupt again. "Whatever her circumstances, she goes to visit her elderly parents who assume she's always been a good girl and an upright woman. She's just standing chatting to them, say, opening some junk mail that still gets sent to the wrong address, when bang, there's this letter from someone who she last saw as a tiny baby thirty-nine years ago, and never thought she would ever hear from again. No one anywhere, possibly even your birth father, knows anything about this part of her life, and she's so freaked by it, she gets physically sick. Think what would have happened if you'd actually rung her up, she might have had a heart-attack on the spot."

"Yeah, I suppose," agreed Julia reluctantly. "But she still doesn't want to know."

"Look," I continued, trying to get my point across as quickly as possible, "what she's done is very sensible. She's gone for professional help, replied to you as quickly as she could, and she's said she's writing a letter. That's contact, so don't knock it. We've found the right person and she's going to give you information. It's been really quick and it's just a first step. You've got to give her time to think things through and she may well change her mind, agree to meet you later on. This is a good response, don't be so negative."

Julia exhaled loudly. "Yeah, sorry Mo. It was just such a shock. I don't know if I ever really thought she'd get back to me at all. I'll wait for her to write."

"That's better, Jules. OK, I'm going to forward you this email now. Read it through a couple of times and see if you can't see how this social worker is trying to get a dialogue going. That's what social workers do – they always want to get parents and children together. She says Caitlin came to her for advice, and clearly she's advised her to write to you, not back off completely. She's also advising you – us – not to mess around with Caitlin's feelings and try to get in touch, but to give her time to come round. I need to let her know whether you're going to do that."

"Oh, yeah. You're right, Mo, wow! Email back and tell her I'll wait for Caitlin to write. It's all going to be OK. Of course she'll want to get to know me when she thinks about it. And there's Danny, she'll realise she's a granny. Maybe she doesn't have any other children or grandchildren." Julia's mercurial temperament flew up the positive gauge to the point where I had now to bring her down to earth.

"Jules, remember one more thing. You cannot tell Jack anything about this email, and I wouldn't say anything to your parents, either. I know it's hard, but if you need to talk about it, it has to be to me and no one else, OK?"

I heard Jack's footsteps on the stairs and swiftly clicked off my email programme so he didn't see Niamh O'Connor's email.

"OK, Jane," I said loudly into the phone. "Thanks for the update, let me know if there's any change in the situation." I put the phone down, hoping that Julia would have the nous to realise Jack had come in, and wouldn't try to call me back.

"You're not putting the menopause into the sex education package – that's a bit beyond the needs of teenagers, isn't it?" asked Jack, reading over my shoulder.

"What? Oh, I must have clicked on the wrong link, I was looking up contraceptive pills, not HRT," I lied quickly. I closed down my web browser, stood up and put my arms round Jack's neck. "You smell nice," I nuzzled his cheek. "Been anywhere special today?" I moved my hands down his body. "Is it bedtime, would you say?" I whispered in his ear seductively. Jack took my hands off him and gave me a peck on the cheek.

"Not tonight, Josephine. We had a partners' meeting and I've got some admin to do as a result. Don't wait up, it might take some time." And Jack went back into his study and closed the door.

Chapter Six

I wasn't aware of Jack coming to bed, having fallen into a deep sleep as soon as I turned out my light, and woke early in the morning after what seemed like an endless and complicated anxiety dream. I was trying to buy a ticket on Victoria Station to go on an important journey, but didn't have any money. My dead father, in the velvet-collared overcoat he wore when I was young, was selling his paintings on the street outside and offered me the coppers from his hat. I wanted to ask him a vital question but couldn't remember what it was I needed to know. He didn't speak, but smiled at me and pointed; I looked and saw he was showing me Jack and Miranda, arms around each other, getting on a bus. When I tried to run after them it felt like I was wading through water, and then I was in that unknown river again, but this time alone and frightened, the water swirling round me, threatening to knock me off my feet and pull me under.

I woke up in a sweat, kicked back the duvet and pushed my damp hair off my face. Still half in the reality of the dream, I turned to check that Jack was in bed with me – of course he was, sleeping undisturbed by my movements, but when I put a hand on his arm for reassurance, he turned over and faced the other way. Wide awake, now, and with a little time before Lily was likely to surface, I tiptoed downstairs, avoiding the creaky boards, to sort some things out in my mind. As I sat at the kitchen table, warming my hands round a steaming mug and, when the green tea had cooled sufficiently, swallowing another selection of vitamins, I reflected on my options.

The last thing I wanted to admit to Jack was that I might be menopausal; it could only affect our relationship for the worse and, if he was even tempted to look elsewhere, would inevitably add lustre to the charms of a younger woman. Despite supposed patient confidentiality, I couldn't bring myself to be checked out by my own GP, the woman partner in his surgery. If Jack himself didn't see me in the waiting room, the receptionist would and probably mention it to him in her chatty way. Then I couldn't lie; we would have to discuss whether I should take HRT or live with my symptoms and he would scoff at the alternative treatments it would be my first inclination to try. No, I would keep this to myself, or at least not share it with Jack, for the moment, and pay a visit to the health shop on Westow Hill, this morning.

If I wanted to keep Lily going to Mel, I would have to find more work for it to make economic sense in which case I would also have to convince Jack of the value of my sticking to some kind of career path. There had been nothing in my line of expertise on the list of jobs from the Research Agency I had looked through in the office, so I would have to put out some feelers among my contacts and see if any other projects were coming up. Erica was often a good source of such information, being too grand to work at that level herself, but I didn't want to speak to her until I had something more concrete on Robards to offer.

That was as far as I had got in sorting out my life when Lily came pattering down the stairs, having found my side of the bed empty. She climbed onto my knee and put her arms round my neck.

"I love you Mummy. Can I have some of your cuppa tea?" she asked, eyeing up a golden omega oil capsule and a red St John's Wort pill which I had yet to consume. "Can I have one of your sweeties?"

"No, these are Mummy's pills," I replied, swigging them down, and poured some cooling milk into the last third of my tea, which I relinquished to my daughter's greedy slurps. "What shall we do this afternoon when I finish work?"

"Go to the swings and see the cake lady," she replied without hesitation. "I like her, she might give me more doughnut. And can I have a baby sister soon? Or a brother, like Noah, so I got someone to play with at home?"

"You don't really want to share your toys and your books and your dressing-up clothes with a baby, do you?" I asked, wishing small children didn't have such an impressive ability to raise the subjects you least wanted them to. And when she nodded, without taking her lips off the mug of tea, I resorted to the adult standby of, "Well, we'll see."

The very knowledgeable Indian man in the health shop was full of information about alternative treatments for menopausal symptoms.

"There are many plants which contain phytoestrogens. These are naturally occurring oestrogens, which mimic the action of the female oestrogen hormone," he told me. "Now the one that is considered most helpful with hot flushes is black cohosh, which grows in North America. The American Indians call it squaw root – they use it for menstrual problems and pain in childbirth, so it has a long history as one of nature's medicines for women. Then there is red clover and alfalfa – but that can stimulate the appetite and therefore make you gain weight."

I mentally crossed that one off the list.

"What about evening primrose oil," I asked. "Isn't that supposed to help with the menopause as well as PMT?"

"Oh, indeed," he went on, scarcely drawing breath, "evening primrose oil contains fatty acids which help your body synthesise prostaglandins – you've heard of those I'm sure," he smiled and nodded at me. "These help to regulate the action of oestrogen, progesterone and prolactin."

"Well, maybe I'll just take some of the black cohosh," I ventured, blinded by alternative science, "and see how that goes."

He picked out a pack from the shelf and took it to the till.

"Now tell me, miss, do you have a history of breast cancer or other oestrogen-related cancers in your family, because it is a strong substance and those are contra-indications. And are you sure you are menopausal and not suffering from any other condition? One must be careful before starting on a course of treatment."

"Well, no," I replied tentatively, "but I've got most of the symptoms. I'm a bit young, but in the right age range."

The door opened with a rush of cold wind and in walked Miranda, of all people, wearing an expensive, red suit over a black lacy top that accentuated her Spanish looks. Her eyes fell on the counter and immediately took in my packet of black cohosh pills lying there. She turned to me and without even a greeting asked, almost accusingly:

"Mo, are these for you?"

"Well, yes," I started sheepishly. "They're for …"

"I know exactly what they're for, Mo, and let's talk before you buy them." Miranda picked up the packet authoritatively, replaced it on the shelf and swiftly picked out a couple of others.

"Gingko biloba and ginseng for Simon," she explained. "His concentration is very poor and he's becoming somewhat stressed about completing his thesis before the spring. I find the combination of these two is quite helpful in keeping him alert and relaxed." And she paid for them with the exact change, slipped them into the neat leather bag which matched her suit, took my arm and walked me out of the shop.

"Now, I'm sorry to interfere," started Miranda, "but as your friend, may I offer you some advice?"

"I'm sure you're going to, whether I like it or not," I answered, too unsure of my ground to protest very vehemently.

"First, have you had a proper check-up with your doctor?" I shook my head. "If you're only pre-menopausal, taking Black Cohosh or other oestrogen supplements could reduce your internal supply, which is not what you want. Our HRT team have carried out research into all the natural products so I know what I'm talking about. If you really are menopausal and the symptoms are unpleasant, I can recommend some of our new generation HRT – tablets or patches, see which suits you best. I'm all for alternative and herbal – you know me – but you can't beat pharmaceutical treatment for more acute problems. I presume Jack has a view on this?"

"I haven't said anything to him," I admitted, "nor to anyone else either, Miranda, so please let me tell people in my own time."

"I understand, Mo. But if you're not sure that you are menopausal, at least get yourself an FSH test from the pharmacy."

"What's an FHS test?" I asked. Miranda looked at her watch then started to speak fast.

"Alright, you know the ovaries produce oestrogen – obviously – but they're stimulated to do so by follicle stimulating hormone – FSH. As you go into menopause and blood levels of

oestrogen fall, your body secretes an increasing amount of FSH
into the bloodstream to try and increase oestrogen production.
The FSH is excreted into the urine and that's what the test
detects. It's simple, and almost 100% accurate, so go buy one."
Miranda finished her instruction to the simple-minded, and
glanced towards the bus stop, where a queue was growing.

"Thanks, Miranda, I might do that. And you won't mention
this?" We both heard the noisy grumble of the bus's engine
behind us. Miranda started to walk, talking to me over her
shoulder.

"You should talk it through with Jack, Mo. It affects both of
you and he's a very sensitive, caring man. Excuse me, I have to
go, I have a key meeting with my manager this morning. Catch
you later." And she was gone, clacking briskly down the street on
her elegant stilettos towards the bus stop, where she arrived in
perfect time to step in, season ticket in hand.

I was half inclined to go back into the shop and buy the
Black Cohosh, Red Clover, Evening Primrose Oil and Alfalfa just
to assert myself, but had to admit Miranda's advice was sensible.
Once again, though, she seemed to know more about Jack than
I was comfortable with.

"Thanks for coming over, Mo," cooed Suzy, opening the double
front doors of her handsome, Georgian mansion before I had
even reached the scrubbed stone steps flanked by lions
couchant, and was still crunching over the immaculate gravel
drive.

"Come in, come in. I've got a proposition I want to put to
you."

I left my coat on the oak pew and snuck a glance in the gilt-framed antique mirror which reflected the Ruskin vase holding one of Suzy's au-naturel flower-arrangements. My face was a bit flushed, my hair ruffled and my jeans and sweatshirt looked a little rough compared to my friend's gracefully flowing wool dress. But her and Duncan's kitchen, with its navy blue Aga, massive old pine table and Windsor chairs, was a second home to everyone in the group and all our children too. As Suzy steamed the milk for our cappuccinos, I could hear Olly singing along to one of his beloved musicals – *West Side Story*, I thought – in the adjacent playroom, and Martin practising a Chopin nocturne on the violin from somewhere upstairs.

"Half-term," smiled Suzy. "You'll be working round those again soon. My boys don't exactly share their tastes in music, but at least we've got the space for them to develop their predilections without getting in each other's hair."

She put two frothing cappuccinos in generous, bowl-shaped cups on the table, brought over home-made ginger biscuits on a matching plate and sat down opposite me.

"An idea came to me in the night which would get me out of a tight spot and might help you a little, too," she said happily. "Don't say no before I've spelled it out properly." And Suzy explained that she and Duncan were hosting their annual evening for the Dulwich Association in a month's time, that it was quite a high-profile affair with up to a hundred people likely to attend, a speaker to book, musicians and professional caterers to be engaged, invitations to be organised … and she was terribly behind with her art course, had Big Hand's AGM to organise and simply hadn't got the time to make it happen.

"So what I was hoping, Mo, was that I could persuade you to take on the whole admin of the event for the next month, as you've got a bit of a break in your otherwise busy schedule."

I winced inwardly at the thought of the work involved and wondered how Suzy could have me down as someone who could afford to do voluntary work on the scale she operated on, backed by Duncan's munificent income.

"Of course, Duncan and I have a budget for this event," Suzy went on quickly, as if reading my thoughts. "It's very good for his client-base and for Big Hand's profile and fund-raising. So I'd like you to tell me your hourly rate and how much of your time you think this would take up, Mo. It's a serious proposition, because it really gets me out of a tight spot, and if it helps you manage Lily's childcare until your proper work comes back on stream, then that's a bonus for you."

I was deeply touched by Suzy's offer, and the terms in which she'd couched it so as not to make me feel like the beneficiary of her charity. Although it wasn't exactly on my career path, it would certainly buy me some time, and perhaps Jack would see it as more suitable in both content and location. I named my usual daily rate, and also my caveats:

"If I got a lead on Robards, I would have to run with it, Suzy, and what if by some miraculous chance the sex education project got the go-ahead? Wouldn't that leave you in a worse position than if I'd never taken this on?"

Suzy reflected briefly. "No, I don't think so, Mo. This isn't going to take your full-time attention and so long as you keep a reasonable paper-trail I could take up where you left off, or get someone else onto it, if I had to. I'm quite prepared to pay what you've asked and I know you'll do a good job."

So we spent another hour running through the tasks to be undertaken, their timescale and the best way of tackling them. One of the first things Suzy wanted me to do was attend a lunchtime talk at the Dulwich Picture Gallery up the road from her, on the background to the Crystal Palace Exhibition including the history of the surrounding area. The speaker, a young historian named Dennis Reid, was getting quite a reputation locally. I was to check him out for substance and entertainment value, and if he came up to scratch, book him to talk on another subject for the Dulwich Association evening. I wrote the date in my diary, made some more notes and put Suzy's files into my bag, ready to return home and get started.

"I do have one other piece of information for you," Suzy said as I stood to leave, "but I don't think it's of much value. Duncan did a search through the files and Maxwell Robards did once take out an injunction against one of the tabloids for invasion of privacy when his wife was in hospital. Duncan thought he remembered that she was having a hysterectomy – though why that would make any kind of story, I don't know. It's just rather sad, really. It certainly explains why he doesn't have any children."

"Yes," I agreed, it was sad – but not so sad I couldn't pass it on to Erica as a useful snippet. Perhaps I could work on the theory that Robards was bitter and twisted towards fertile, young adolescents who could have unwanted babies at the drop of a hat; a perennial injustice to those who had difficulty conceiving.

Olly must have heard the movement of our wooden chairs on the red pamment tile floor as we stood up, and came loping in from the playroom to say goodbye.

"Hello, goodbye Auntie Mo, I love you," he declared, giving me a bear hug and a sloppy kiss on my cheek. "Did you hear me singing?" He broke into *I Feel Pretty* and did some dance steps around the kitchen. Suzy watched her son with deserved pride. Thanks to her dedication, Olly was coherent, sociable, could read and write at about the level of an eight-year-old and had wide-ranging interests. It looked as though, when he finished college in another three years, he would be able to lead a relatively independent life. At the other end of the scale, Martin was likely to get a scholarship to music college or a top university, and take his pick of careers in the arts world.

"To think I would have had an abortion if I'd had the amniocentesis and found out Olly was Down's while I was pregnant," Suzy said quietly as we walked down the passage from the kitchen into the hall. "My life would have been so much the poorer."

"But you do think you should have had the choice?" I queried, my mind still constantly flitting back to the sex ed package and Robards' pro-life views.

"Yes, of course I do," replied Suzy, checking to see that Olly was not listening. "But not knowing what Olly would be like and that caring for him would be more of a gift than a burden, it wouldn't have been a genuine choice, would it?"

"So you have some sympathy for Robards and his anti-abortion stance, then?" I asked, somewhat surprised.

"Well, not for the way he chooses to make his point," she said carefully. "You know I don't think promoting abstinence is helpful, or restricting access to contraception. But once a baby exists, *in utero*, it is much harder, and 'informed choice' – there's no such thing, is there, before you become a parent? No one can tell you how much you're going to love the little scrap of humanity you produce from your own body, however imperfect or damaged it is."

She stood with her back to me, adjusting her flower arrangement, but over her shoulder I could see her pensive smile in the mirror.

"So what do you think we should tell teenagers about abortion in the programme? That it's not OK, that they'll love their children more than they can imagine and that'll make it all worthwhile? Remember, Suze, you live in a very different world to a single teenage mother living on a housing estate, even if she has a perfectly normal baby."

Suzy snorted. "Don't patronise me, Mo. I know I live in the lap of luxury compared with most, but don't forget I've worked with people in all walks of life with disabled children. Money only goes a certain way. And just think of this: if Julia and Jack's birth mother had chosen to have a termination, four wonderful human beings would never have been born."

"Four? Oh, you mean Lily and Danny. Yes, I take your point, but Caitlin Doyle's hardly a good advert for adoption either: she's lived her whole life with a dreadful secret, it would seem, and now the thought of getting in touch with her daughter has made her ill with worry. God, it's a fraught area, isn't it? Well, it doesn't look as if I'll be having to make any decisions on the best message for teenagers now, so thanks a million for offering me your event to manage. I'll get onto it right away and I'll do my best to make it a really good evening for you, Suzy."

Olly came to the door, gave me another hug and asked me to marry him, while Martin, at Suzy's behest, called down a brief, "Bye, Mo," from the top of the wide, circular staircase before returning to his violin. I could hear his sweeping cadences through a top window as I drove my old Golf out of the drive, into College Road and round Dulwich College, where the Victorian neo-baroque library, red-brick halls and rolled green playing fields were silent and empty over the half-term break.

If people like Duncan and Suzy didn't pay to send their children to such privileged and sequestered educational establishments, I reasoned, but joined the bright and the dull from all walks of life in the state education system, it would raise standards for everyone and minimise those crucial differences between the haves and have-nots in our society. The support that parents like Suzy and Duncan gave to their children's schools was in itself a resource that would go half-way to solving state education problems. But the strongest influence on a child's success, I had learned when researching a previous project, was not the quality of teaching children received, nor even parental input, but the attributes of their peer group at school. If all the Dulwich College boys were spread around the local state schools, the resulting peer community would raise standards effortlessly and negate the them-and-us culture that was regularly acted out in fights between College boys and pupils from Kingsdale Comprehensive up the road.

And as for their female counterparts at James Allen Girls School, where Miranda's salary paid for Naomi and Lola to go; how many JAGS girls would end up as teenage mothers, I ruminated as I drove up Gipsy Hill? Probably none, unless they actively chose to. Girls in Social Class Five – the bottom of the pile – were ten times more likely to end up in that situation than those at the top. And girls with below-average educational achievement were also at far greater risk of becoming teenage mothers. We would never reduce our rates of juvenile pregnancies to those of other European countries until we could join them in offering an excellent state education which few parents saw the need to opt out of. The problems of teenage sex and unwanted pregnancies were not just about sex education, but about a just education system for all children.

Having worked myself into a righteous fury, I beeped the horn somewhat unnecessarily at a slow driver in front of me and decided that the traffic around the Triangle's one-way system was too heavy to stop off at the chemist and buy one of the tests Miranda had suggested.

Once home, I grabbed a hunk of cheddar and a Granny Smith, made a cup of raspberry tea – no more caffeine, Suzy's cappuccino had contained enough to raise my body heat and anxiety levels – and took it all through to my office where I intended to start work on the Dulwich Association evening forthwith. I was sorting through the address list for invitations, and planning a database which Suzy and Duncan could use for years to come, when the phone rang. I picked it up, half expecting silence then a click at the other end, but it was Venetia, in merry mood.

"Is that Mary Mozart, researcher extraordinaire?" she asked in a fake posh accent, and laughed raucously.

"Is that you, Venetia?" I answered, chomping on a mouthful of cheese and apple.

"Of course it's me, silly. Only joking." Her words were a little indistinct and she giggled in a way that reminded me of our drunken student evenings.

"Are you at work? You sound pissed?" I asked, amused.

"Well, I might be ever so slightly inebriated, and I think I'm at work. No, seriously, Mo, I've just had a very jolly lunch with my friend Perry, the disgraced newspaper-editor. A delayed part of my campaign, you know. Couldn't put him off, even though Charlie's in a strop. Oh well, anyway, what was I going to say …? She appeared to drift off into a reverie for a couple of seconds. I could only imagine what effect seeing Venetia like this was having on her team – I hoped it wouldn't negate the success she had achieved so far in asserting her senior managerial status.

"I don't know, Venetia, what have you rung me for? I'm just in the middle of doing a bit of work for Suzy."

"Ah, that's it," she slurred back, "you can stop whatever you're doing, whoever it's for. I've got the information you wanted."

And she stopped portentously, waiting for my response.

"And what information would that be?" I went back to sorting through names and addresses, unconvinced that Venetia had rung me for any particular reason other than to boast about her social contacts.

"Maxwell Robards," she hissed in a stage whisper. "I've got the low-down on his guilty past. Perry told me, so it's bound to be true."

I sat up instantly, pen in hand, pulling my notepad towards me from under Suzy's files.

"Go on, Venetia. What did he say?"

"Well. When Robards had just won his first election and was starting his career as an MP, he employed a rather attractive young secretary to manage his diary. About six months later he made her redundant, on the grounds that Mrs R was giving up her teaching job and was going to take over as his diary secretary. The bimbo PA was not best pleased about this, and went to the paper where Perry was then an up-and-coming political reporter, and he was assigned to get a juicy story on the new MP out of all this. So he interviewed the woman, who said that she had had an affair with Robards, he had got her pregnant, paid for her to have an abortion and then sacked her. At that point, the fragrant Kathleen got ill and was rushed into hospital, which enabled Robards to take out an injunction against the paper for invasion of privacy and basically sending his wife over the edge."

"She didn't go over the edge, she had a hysterectomy," I broke in. "Duncan's firm was acting for Robards."

"Ah, well, whatever. Anyway, the paper dropped the story and Perry moved on to higher things. But that would show Robards up for the charlatan he is, if you could prove he'd paid his ex-mistress to have an abortion to save his marriage, career and the rest!" Venetia ended triumphantly.

"That's completely brilliant, Venetia!" I exclaimed, pen at the ready. "So I need to find this secretary. What was her name and what contact details does Perry have for her?"

"That's the down side, Mo," admitted Venetia. "You are going to have to use all your investigative skills to find her, because the file's long gone. All he could remember was her name – which was at least an unusual one. She was called Ruby Wadilove, and she came from some village outside Oxford – she went back to her parents there when all this blew up. That's it, all the info I've got. But it's what you wanted, isn't it? The proof that Maxwell Robards is a total hypocrite who preaches one rule for the masses and lives by another himself."

"If I can find Ruby Wadilove, it's perfect," I responded gratefully. "Of course she's probably moved and married since then, so she'll have changed her name, but I'll track her down even if she's emigrated to Australia. Thanks, Vee, and thanks to Perry when you next see him."

"Well it won't be for another lunch like this in the near future," giggled Venetia. "I'm going to have to drink some strong coffee to get through this afternoon's meeting-schedule with any semblance of sanity. Must run, bye Mo."

By the time Lily needed picking up from Mel, I had rung Erica and told her the news.

"Excellent work, Mary, I knew you'd come up with the goods in the end." She sounded like a headmistress who had just read a decent piece of work from a pupil whose report always said "could do better". "Let's hope she's articulate and photogenic. If she's got a family we can get some pics of, that would help to get a major spread. Call me the minute you've seen her."

I had also searched Directory Enquiries, online and by

phone, for Wadiloves in Oxfordshire and found three, none of them with the initial R; I had sent off, online for a search for Ruby Wadilove on the electoral roll, which would take twenty-four hours; and looked for her in all the schools in the Oxfordshire area on Friends Reunited, with no success. I reckoned, though, that with a rare name like that, at least one of the Wadiloves living around Oxford must be related to Ruby, if not her parents themselves, so I rang all of them. One was an elderly man who had never heard of Ruby and was annoyed at being interrupted in the middle of his favourite television programme. The next number was no longer in operation and the third didn't reply, but a stilted recording on the answerphone asked me to leave a message.

I put the phone down and thought about what kind of message I should leave. If this was Ruby's parents' number, they might not welcome anyone digging into their daughter's past, so I decided on a bland approach which was truthful in letter, if not in spirit. I dialled again, and waited for the beep:

"Hello, this is Mary, with a message for Ruby, Ruby Wadilove. I wanted to get in touch – after that time we were both working in London, oh years ago now. I've got lots of news and I'd love to hear what you've been up to. If Ruby's not living here any more, could you let me know where she is, I'm on …"

And I left my contact details and signed off with a cheery, "Bye then, talk to you soon!"

I was determined to have a good evening with Jack, to clear the air between us and put our relationship back on its normal, easy footing. To this end, I cooked a roast lamb dinner for two with all the trimmings, laid the kitchen table with the good plates, the silver plate cutlery Betty and Colin had given us as a wedding present, napkins and candles, and uncorked a nice cabernet sauvignon. It made a satisfactory glugging sound as I poured it into two of our thick, green wine glasses when Jack came down from reading Lily her bedtime story. A few slurps of red, some potato wedges with my home-made guacamole as a starter, and the aroma of lamb cooking with garlic and rosemary would put him in a relaxed mood.

I asked him about his day, to which I got a fairly non-committal answer, then told him about Suzy's proposition, pointing out that it would at least cover child-minding costs until I knew for certain whether the sex ed project was dead or not.

"You might be able to carry that on, on a voluntary basis, if you do take a break," Jack suggested amicably. "There's a lot of arty people in Dulwich Village who share your interests, why not get to know some of them, get more involved locally?"

"Yes, I suppose I could," I agreed, trying to sound more enthusiastic than I felt. "How's the lamb, pink enough for you?"

Jack mumbled something that sounded like approval though a mouthful of lamb, and after telling him about the talk I was going to, my planned database and the catering arrangements I had to make, I thought it might be safe to mention Ruby Wadilove. I chose a casual approach, as if I didn't think it would really lead anywhere, but just mentioned that her parents used to live in Oxfordshire. This turned out to be a bad move, for reasons I couldn't have guessed.

"Well, I'm afraid you won't be able to go off looking for her if it takes you too long to get to, because you'll have to be here for Lily," Jack frowned. "I was going to tell you, when you'd finished about Suzy and her evening, that I've managed to get a last minute place at the Cardiovascular Research Conference at the

University of Utah. I'm taking part in a seminar, so the University will pay for my accommodation and the practice has agreed to pay my fare. I'm flying out next week and I'll be gone for six days in total, so I won't be here for babysitting if your work takes off again."

I was shocked that Jack hadn't mentioned even the possibility of this conference before. Usually we shared all our plans at an early stage.

"How long have you known about this?" I asked. "Why didn't you tell me – well, anything, before now?"

"It's all been very sudden," he answered wearily, and pushed away his half-eaten plate of lamb. "I hadn't even thought of going until a few days ago, when I was approached about ... taking part in a seminar. I didn't think I could make it, and then it all just came together today. It's something I have to do."

I looked at my husband more carefully than I had for some time. He looked pale beneath his freckles, and there were dark circles under his eyes.

"Are you OK? You look – is it me, Jack, or us?" I suddenly felt a pang of real worry. "Is something really wrong?"

He stood up and picked up his plate. "Sorry, hon, this was really nice – I'm just not very hungry. Got a lot of things to do for next week." He scraped the remains of his meal into the bin and put his plate by the sink. "It's not you or your work, it's me. There's some stuff I need to sort out. I'll be able to tell you about it when I get back, so just give me some space till then, OK?"

Jack put a hand briefly on my shoulder and walked out of the kitchen.

I would have run after him and demanded an explanation if the phone hadn't started to ring at that moment. I picked it up in the kitchen and was amazed to hear the tentative response to my somewhat abrupt greeting.

"Hello, is that Mary? It's Ruby here, I got your message on the machine. I just wasn't sure who … which Mary it was ringing after all this time."

Chapter Seven

"So then I explained that although it was true that we had both been working in London at the same time, she actually didn't know me. I hadn't wanted to leave a more explicit message in case it wasn't her phone number," I recounted to the group. "In fact, it was her aunt's number that I rang."

We were meeting in Venetia's compact terrace house on Camden Hill, one of the small roads leading off the top of Gipsy Hill, because she was waiting for a plumber to call and repair her central heating. In the meantime we were all sitting in the comfortable, mismatched armchairs in her front room, whose warm terracotta-painted walls belied the current chill in the air.

"And she didn't put the phone down on you?" asked Ros, pulling her classic camel overcoat round her shoulders.

"No, though I think she was a bit freaked when I started talking about Maxwell Robards and what had happened between them. To begin with she just kept saying that it was all a long time ago and she didn't want to cause any problems for anyone. So I asked if she knew about his current campaign, which she did, and whether she didn't think it was rather hypocritical given his history with her."

"She surely had to agree with that," stated Miranda. "How could she not?"

Miranda was warmer than the rest of us, having come straight from a session at the gym. She looked younger and more relaxed than usual, too; her petite frame softened by matching, pastel-coloured tracksuit and trainers, her hair pulled off her face by a wide, elasticated band.

"Well she went very quiet at that point, so I kept talking to keep her on the phone," I told them. "I told her about the sex education project and how valuable it was and how many teenage girls we could prevent getting pregnant or save from having to have abortions like she did. I explained that if she spoke out about how Robards had behaved to her, it would undermine his campaign and increase the chances of the project happening."

"And did that have the desired effect?" asked Suzy, her bright purple pashmina making Venetia's rust-coloured, velvet chaise longue look even more faded than usual.

"Well, then I had a brainwave and said that I doubted she was the only woman Robards had abused. If she didn't want to talk I'd keep looking till I found someone who did. She suddenly said that yes, it was time to set the record straight and she would meet me and tell me the whole story. The trouble is she now lives in Stratford – she works as a legal secretary. I'm going to have to drive up and see her in her lunch-hour next week, she can't do it sooner. Erica's all for sending a photographer with me, but I don't want to frighten Ruby off."

"Finally! Here he is." Venetia left her position at the window, with its autumnal William Morris curtains, from where she had been peering anxiously out. She went to the front door and we heard her showing the plumber down the narrow passage to her little kitchen. I glanced around the room at the framed examples of Aurora's art hanging on the walls, ranging from primary-school juvenilia to some of her more recent, exquisite still life studies in oils and gouache. A new, double portrait of her and Venetia was standing, waiting to be hung, in the empty Edwardian grate. She had captured the likeness between her and her mother, and also their differences; where Venetia's colouring was Scandinavian blonde and blue-eyed, Aurora's similar features were framed by dark chestnut hair and she stared out of the painting with lifelike green eyes.

"Normal service will be resumed shortly," smiled a relieved Venetia, coming back in and plonking down a refilled cafetiere and Morrisons chocolate cake, still in its box, on the stripped-pine linen-chest she used as a coffee table. "Apparently it's just the thermostat, which he's replacing as we speak. Did you finish your story, Mo?"

I nodded, and picked up the coffee pot to refill everyone's mugs, as Venetia was clearly not intending to take her hostess role any further and seemed keen to give us some news of her own.

"Well, not only have I discovered the existence of Ms Wadilove for Mo this week," she began, "I've also been formally invited to accompany Charlie to an exhibition of new Latin American art at the British Council, where I shall implement phase one of Mission Stepford. For a start I've bought this amazing new dress," and she plucked a shimmering garment out of an exclusive boutique's carrier bag placed conveniently on the floor, and held it up against herself. "With the wrap, it's oh-so demure," she demonstrated. "Without the wrap ..." And Venetia revealed a dress that was breathtaking in its minimal-ism, and which only someone as skinny as she could even con-sider getting away with.

"Charlie's going to love that!" chuckled Suzy.

"He would in the privacy of his own flat," grinned Venetia, "but I'm dying to see the look on his face when he gets an eyeful among all the diplomatic guests he's been invited to schmooze."

"And I bet you've got something else up your sleeve," I guessed. Venetia tapped the side of her nose and looked secretive.

"All in good time. I'll keep you posted." And she returned the wicked designer dress to its tissue paper nest in the bag.

"Well, you can give it another outing at my Dulwich Association evening – which will be extra specially good this year as I've persuaded Mo to take on the admin," said Suzy, subtly reminding me that I had more than Ruby Wadilove to occupy my time. "Formal invitations will be forthcoming – when Mo's had them printed and you've all been input into the hi-tech database she's creating – but in the meantime, you are all invited, with whomsoever you choose to bring, and don't anyone dare not to come!"

There was much shuffling through elegant diary (Ros), scruffy filofax (Venetia) and slick personal organiser (Miranda), checking the date and agreeing that everyone was free, or would instantly become so. Ros said she thought Joe would be back and would, of course, want to come; Venetia asked if it was OK to bring Charlie and Aurora; Miranda told us her family would all be there on pain of death, including Lola.

"Is Jack pleased with your new job as Event Manager?" she asked, with a bright smile. "I presume you've talked about that?"

"Of course, he's my right-hand man," I replied, hoping I sounded equally bright, rather than as brittle as I felt. I didn't appreciate her dig about our lack of communication.

"Mo's got some great ideas," Suzy cut in. "She's going to get us a brilliant speaker, the caterers she's found have a buffet menu to die for, we're going to have a jazz quartet, and she's already enlisted the kids to help. I'm just so relieved she's taken it on," she told the rest of the group. "What with half-term, getting Olly sorted out and keeping Martin on track for his A levels and violin exams, I was beginning to think I might have to cancel."

"Well, after the half term from hell I just had, I took a decision for myself." Miranda hugged her knees and looked pleased with herself. "My best friend from grade school called to say she was getting married again – a whimsical choice as she and Gerry have been co-habiting for years – and was there any chance I could make it. And I thought, yes, I could so use a break right now. So I booked a week's annual leave with my manager and just told Simon and the girls I was going home for the wedding and they would have to get along without me. They looked shocked, but I didn't give them any option for protest."

"Good for you, Miranda, you deserve it!" That was Ros, ever supportive of strong personal decision-making.

"And haven't you and Joe got a romantic break planned for when his season ends?" Venetia goaded Ros in return.

"We haven't booked anything yet, but we're thinking a city break in Prague might be relaxing," returned Ros, coolly. I wondered whether there was any truth in this or whether she had been driven to defend her relationship by Venetia's constant niggling.

At that point the plumber put his head round the door to tell Venetia the heating was on again, and she dived out to pay his doubtless exorbitant bill. To fill the silence that followed her exit, I told the group that we had still heard nothing directly from Caitlin Doyle and, once more, I wondered how long Julia's patience would hold out. Suzy and Ros sympathised; Miranda looked uncomfortable, I thought.

"Such a waste of time and energy!" Venetia's disparaging opinion was directed at me as she re-entered, checking a radiator for returning warmth as she walked back to her seat. "If Julia's got problems she needs to look to herself, not some spurious relationship with a mother who's never been near her in forty years. Aurora's always been happy with my decision about her father. She doesn't need to know who he is and I don't want him involved with us. He's got other children, who he's not much use to anyway, and it would get too complicated. As far as I'm concerned, I'm the person who brought her up and that's all that matters."

It seemed to be only me who noticed a sharp intake of breath from Miranda at this declaration. Could it conceivably be that Si was Aurora's father, and that he and Venetia had agreed on his non-involvement? Was that a source of friction between Miranda and Si, and perhaps another reason for her to look for comfort elsewhere?

"Miranda, when are you actually going to be away?" I asked. "I just want to make sure you get your invitation before you go – gives me a deadline to work to." I noted down the dates she gave me in my all-purpose notebook.

After we had consumed yet more caffeine, demolished the cake and talked further about Suzy's evening, Miranda's holiday and the challenges of our various children, we carried dirty mugs and plates to the kitchen and said our goodbyes. I was the last to leave, still rinsing out, through force of habit, Venetia's miscellaneous collection of handmade pottery, when she came back into the kitchen.

"I'm glad you're still here, Mo – thanks for the washing up," she said, making no effort to contribute to the task. "I wanted to ask a favour. Aurora's looking for some paid work – she's selling a few paintings and getting the odd commission, but it's not enough to live on. At her age she needs to be independent of me; I'm sure she'd like to get her own place."

"Why would she want to move out of here?" I asked, surprised. Venetia and Aurora had always maintained a very equal and adult relationship, and had plenty of room to lead autonomous lives within the house they had occupied since Aurora's birth. She had a bedroom, studio/sitting room and shower room to herself on the top floor and Venetia rarely used the kitchen. I didn't know how they arranged finances between them, but I guessed Venetia didn't charge her daughter rent or board. Aurora would be mad to take on that expense when she had such a comfortable lifestyle at home.

"Well, things may change, Mo. If I do settle down with Charlie, he wants to get rid of his bachelor pad and buy a new place for us close to Westminster – Kennington or Stockwell, probably. I can't ask him to take on my adult daughter and I don't suppose she'd want to be with us anyway. I mean, she and Charlie get on fine, but I don't think it would work with all three of us being in the same house. So I need her to be solvent." Venetia looked rueful. She had championed Aurora's artistic career in an admirably hands-off way through art college, and her decision to live only from her painting since graduating. But I could see her dilemma: if she wanted to make a life for herself with a new partner, Venetia was going to have to make compromises.

"How can I help?" I asked, not seeing the obvious connection.

"Would you give Aurora an introduction to your brother? The Mozart Gallery has to be one of the most successful in Cork Street and working with other artists is one of the few things she'd consider. Anthony might need an assistant, or know of another place that does. I don't want to force Aurora into something she hates, but I have to think ahead."

"Of course I will. She's so clever and gorgeous, she'd be an asset to any gallery. I'll give him a ring this afternoon. Does Aurora know what's happening?" I asked, not wanting to commit any faux pas.

"We have talked about it," Venetia said reluctantly. "But it would be easier if he could contact her direct – if there was anything he felt he could do. I don't want her to think I'm railroading her into this."

I made an addition to my 'to do' list and put my notebook away. "I'll ring him this afternoon, I'm sure he'll help if he can. Maybe take her out to lunch and talk through some options – he's nice like that."

I saw Old Peggy coming out of Morrisons as I walked home from Venetia's and, buoyed up by my forthcoming encounter with Ruby Wadilove, decided to say hello to make up for my last, abrupt leave-taking. Peggy pushed her new trolley past the car-park lifts then stopped to chat with a couple of the young guys who regularly played guitar, or simply asked, for money outside the adjacent Blockbusters store.

"Hi, Peggy. Did you get some more doughnuts today?" I asked her. She turned creakily and gave me a wide smile.

"Hello, lovely. No doughnuts, it's white mice today. Nice thick icing they got, hardly stale at all. Want one for little princess?" She showed me her bag full of the long, white-iced buns. I refused one on Lily's behalf, but did tell Peggy that my daughter called her 'Cake Lady' and had asked to see her again.

The old woman smiled knowingly. The scarf she had wound

around her head today gave her a certain exotic look and instead of her usual fag-end, she took up a broken clay pipe from the baby seat of her trolley and puffed on it. I resisted the inclination to tell her how bad it was for her lungs and instead apologised for running off last time I saw her. She looked me in the eye and I started to worry that she was going to take me to that other place again, but Old Peggy just nodded, and took my woolly glove in her grimy hand.

"The pictures are a gifting, not for fear," she said enigmatically. "You'll understand in time. You've found her, but now it's catch as catch can. She's got a battle with love and fear just like you, lovely."

I smiled calmly, trying to hide my bewilderment that Peggy could once again home in on events in my life with considerably more accuracy than random horoscope clichés. She couldn't possibly know about Ruby Wadilove and her internal struggle with revealing the truth about her erstwhile lover, but the so-called 'pictures' that had come into my head bore no relation to any of this. Peace, calm and reason, I inhaled, adding a Jack element to my mantra, and turned to go. Peggy squeezed my hand and patted her makeshift turban.

"Keeps my old head warm," she said, "and shows you Peggy's the queen. Ta ta, lovely."

I laughed inwardly and thanked the Universal Spirit for the rationality I had requested. No, there was nothing mystical about Peggy, she was just a deluded old woman who thought she could foretell the future and, better still, that she was the queen. I walked down Fox Hill in good spirits, hoping that I could get Anthony to find a job for Aurora. She had been like a big sister to Mark and Jess when they were small and, though she denied it, Jess still looked up to Aurora.

* * *

It always took a little courage for me to ring my brother, especially at his gallery. Though younger than me, his careless success and flawless family made me feel wrong-footed, immature and disappointing. But these were my own insecurities and never implied by Anthony, who, when I did pick up the phone, was in a frantic rush. His current exhibition of a protégé artist had all but sold out, and the provocative suite of paintings had garnered excellent reviews from the critics as well.

I quickly reminded him who Aurora was, emphasising her physical attractions as well as her degree in fine art from St Martins, and asked whether there were any jobs going at the Mozart Gallery. It seemed he had a new project in mind, and someone who combined creative flair with some business acumen and the ability to nurture budding talent, could be just what he was looking for. I talked up Aurora in all these areas and he agreed that he would see her, if she got in touch with him – he hadn't time to chase her up himself.

Before he rushed off to more important matters than chatting to his elder sister, I asked him whether he had seen our mother lately. He had to wrack his memory to recall the last time he had actually made the trek from the leafy avenues of Hampton Hill to the dusty streets of Pimlico, but eventually concluded it was just after they had returned from the New Year skiing trip.

"So, did Mum tell you that she's leaving the family portraits to you?" I asked.

"She did, indeed. Sally's not best pleased about it, I can tell you," Anthony laughed unconcernedly. "She's designed every inch of wall space in both our houses to hold the appropriately colour-coordinated painting, photo or relief, and now she's got half a dozen grim-faced Mozarts in ancient frames to find a home for! If she has her way they'll end up under blankets in the spare garage."

"Well, I'd be happy to take Mary Wilhelmina off your hands," I responded lightly.

"The gipsy girl? You always thought you looked like her," Anthony recalled. "She may be better looking than the others, but the quality of her portraiture lowers the tone. I'll have a word with Sal – though I don't think Mum's planning to pop her clogs or sell the house just yet. Must rush, talk soon, Sis."

My confidence in having paddled myself back into at least the slipstream of the energy flow was short-lived. I checked Miranda's dates in my desk diary and confirmed what I had dreaded the minute she mentioned her holiday: they coincided almost exactly with Jack's conference in Utah. And Miranda's home town of Montpelier, Idaho – if that was indeed where she was going – was a short journey, in American terms, from the conference location in Salt Lake City.

I parked on College Road and walked up the drive to what was in fact the back and least attractive façade of the Dulwich Picture Gallery. Even this side of Sir John Soanes's early nine-teenth-century design, though, was perfectly proportioned. Rick Mather's modern extension held The Café, a place where Suzy sometimes treated me to coffee and cake, or lunch and glass of wine. We would sit outside, if it was warm, or behind the glass wall in winter, watching tourists, school children and local residents wandering through the landscaped gardens. Though rarely crowded, a steady trickle of visitors came to

South London's answer to the National Gallery, to view its permanent collection of Poussins, Rubenses, Rembrandts, Van Dykes, Gainsboroughs and the rest, or one of the increasingly prestigious exhibitions the Gallery regularly hosted.

How incongruous, I considered, that Dulwich College, originally founded by a Shakespearian actor of dubious repute, to educate poor boys, should have come to own the last King of Poland's art collection, a unique Georgian building and a costly piece of real estate in this prime location. The thespian Edward Alleyn had wanted his paupers' school to be styled 'Of God's Gift', but were the current recipients of these munificent presents those for whom he had intended it?

I entered the hall, which doubled as the shop, and paid my entrance fee. I debated buying Lily a Dulwich Picture Gallery teddy bear, but on seeing the price decided she had quite enough cuddly toys. I filled in the fifteen minutes before today's Lunchtime Lecture by gazing at my favourite Rembrandt portrait of the red-haired young man – perhaps he reminded me a little of Jack.

Turning back to the central galleries, I observed, with sudden clarity, that Rubens's massive painting of *Venus, Mars and Cupid* was not the vulgar, mythological family portrait I had written it off as, but rather a celebration of the mother and child relationship. Soft, pale, tender Venus, playfully squirting breast milk at her happy son Cupid, were well-lit, complex figures, while father Mars, dark and shadowy at the back, was being literally disarmed by another cherub. Rubens seemed to see women as the central power in the family, taming the aggressive male and nourishing the children.

In the smaller Italian rooms at the end, I passed some other sensual representations of Venus and Cupid, which made the

Virgin and Child portraits hanging close by seem cold and love-less. I got so involved with comparing the warm, pagan moth-ers with their uptight, Christian counterparts that I ended up running through the Education Wing to the Linbury Room and creeping into a seat at the back whilst Dennis Reid was making his introduction.

I didn't think I would learn much this lunchtime, having read up about the Crystal Palace story over the years, but I was looking forward to hearing more about the earlier history of the Norwood area – as well as establishing whether Mr Reid would be a strong enough speaker for Suzy's – and mine, as I now thought of it – evening.

He was a youngish, academic type – in his early thirties, I estimated – dressed in trendy, casual clothes and not at all unat-tractive. He won points from me almost immediately, by deal-ing coolly and humorously with the recalcitrant laptop containing his PowerPoint presentation. He kept up his flow while re-programming the computer until it finally complied and filled the screen with an impressively diverse range of visu-als. Admittedly, these were a little thin on the ground to begin with; the Domesday Book in 1086 recorded our area as being controlled by the Archbishop of Canterbury for "pleasure-hunt-ing, fuel and pannage for two hundred swine" but didn't run to pictures of this intriguing description.

I opened my notebook to indicate serious interest and scrib-bled down that the name Norwood first appeared in the Assize Rolls of 1272 and came from the Great North Wood of Surrey, which stretched from Camberwell to Croydon and survived until well into the eighteenth century. A map dated 1611 flashed onto the screen and Dennis pointed out the present-day Norwood areas – Upper, South and West – shown as hills and woods encircled by some familiar place-names – Croydon, Mycham, Stretham, Dulwich, and Lewesham. I was glad to hear that my home ground had achieved its place in history by providing wood for the Navy's fighting ships in Tudor times, and that two of Francis Drake's vessels, the Golden Hinde and the Revenge, were constructed from Norwood oak.

I took a break from my notes to peer at the backs of the twenty-odd heads seated in front of me, and wondered what had drawn them to this genteel discourse today. The majority were older people, perhaps locals who used the Gallery as their art education centre; a handful were obvious tourists who had possibly wandered in by accident and stayed to rest their aching feet. A couple of art students stood out for their youth and unconventional dress and I thought I recognised one familiar profile at the front. When I refocused on the lecture, it was to discover that Norwood also held its place in literary annals: the diarist John Evelyn recounted passing through the area in 1652, when he was dragged from his horse, tied to a tree and robbed; references to Norwood as an area of woodland were to be found in the writings of John Aubrey and in Daniel Defoe's *Journal of the Plague Year*; and Samuel Pepys mentioned in his diary of 1668 that his wife and her companions visited the Norwood gipsies to have their fortunes told. Later, thanks to the establishment of Beulah Spa in 1831 and the Crystal Palace itself in 1854, writers such as Charles Dickens and Emile Zola were regular visitors and Arthur Conan Doyle lived for a time in Tennison Road and set a Sherlock Holmes story – *The Mystery of the Norwood Builder* – in the locale. Paintings and photos of these famous authors came and went, but a strange little aside from the main theme of Dennis Reid's talk sent shock waves through me.

Backtracking to the eighteenth-century inhabitants, he told

his attentive audience that crime had flourished in these dense and hilly areas. Dick Turpin was supposed to have lived in a cottage in Thornton Heath and hidden-out in another on Spa Hill – and smugglers bought tea, silk, brandy and lace this way from the south coast into the capital. A map of 1746 by John Roque showed us that by this time the forest was thinning out and much of the locality was common land. Then during the Napoleonic Wars, several Enclosure Acts dispossessed many people by parceling the woods and commons into owned properties. Most famously, the police were sent in under the Vagrancy Act in 1797, to break up the encampments of gipsies on the hill which had been their habitat for around two hundred years, and which, as Gipsy Hill, is still named for them today.

And then as he clicked the mouse once more, an electrifying picture appeared on the screen: a simple engraving of the woman who had been the most renowned fortune-teller, and known as the Queen of the Gipsies, one Margaret Finch. Squatting in what had apparently been her habitual position, her chin resting on her knees, the Gipsy Queen's long bony face with its small, dark eyes and deep bags, large hooked nose and tight mouth, was the spitting image of Old Peggy's. What was more disturbing, the old fortune-teller held a long, smoking pipe in her mouth and wore a turban in exactly the style of Peggy's headgear when I had last seen her outside Morrison's.

"Margaret Finch was probably the most famous of the gipsy fortune-tellers on account of her great age," enthused Dennis Reid. "She died aged a hundred-and-eight, -nine or -ten, depending on which source you believe, in 1740. She had lived in Norwood for years and local tavern owners got together and paid for her funeral, in gratitude for the many visitors she had attracted to the area. She was buried at Beckenham Church, in a

large square box because she had been sitting in this position—"
he indicated the engraving, "for so long that she couldn't be
straightened-out to lie in a normal coffin! As I said, another sixty
years after her death, the gipsy community was dispersed, though
many remained in the area and intermarried with local people."

I spent the rest of the lecture in a daze, not sure what significance the picture I had seen and the information I had heard held
for me. Some new and fascinating facts about the Crystal Palace's
transfer from Hyde Park to Sydenham went in one ear and out
the other. Even the slides of paintings by Tenniel, Pugin and
Holman Hunt, and the amazing array of contemporary photos of
every aspect, interior and exterior, of Joseph Paxton's remarkable
edifice, couldn't erase the earlier picture from my thoughts. Only
at the end, when the audience gave the lecturer's charismatic performance an enthusiastic round of applause, did I recall that I
had to go and speak to him and hopefully book him for Suzy.

I waited at the back of the small queue of people eager to talk
to Dennis Reid and have him sign copies of his recent book about
the history of this corner of South East London.

"Hello, how can I help?" He looked up at me, as the last elderly lady pocketed her autographed hardback and shuffled off,
with a charming smile. Inwardly I reminded myself that he was
probably nearer my son's age than my own and tried not to
respond flirtatiously.

"Well, there are two things I wanted to ask you, if you have a
minute," I began. Dennis took off his glasses, deleting another five
years from his age and pulled up a chair for me. I secured his
agreement to talk at the Dulwich Association evening with ease;
he would come up with a talk that would be suitably entertaining
and of interest to the guests who would be, by definition, well-
informed about their area.

"Perhaps more of an after-dinner speech than a history lecture," he suggested and I instantly concurred. "I might give them some anecdotes about my research methods and some of the people I've encountered on my travels round here."

"Well, perhaps we can discuss it when you've had time to think about an outline," I proposed, wondering simultaneously why I had done so. But he nodded enthusiastically and started to write something on the back of his lecture notes. "I, er, wondered if you'd come across any descendants of the Norwood Gipsies," I continued tentatively, "in your research. That picture of Margaret Finch—"

"Oh, it's priceless, isn't it?" agreed Dennis. "It's an engraving that was published in the *Gentleman Magazine* in 1740, which shows how famous the old Gipsy Queen was. But to answer your question, no, I didn't come across any of her descendants, though many of them stayed in Norwood and intermarried with *gadjes*, as they call the rest of us. Anecdotal evidence suggests that a few full-blood and many of the mixed-blood gipsies worked on the reconstruction of the Crystal Palace, and were then employed as staff. Why do you ask?"

"Well, there's an old bag-lady who hangs around the Park and the Crystal Palace Triangle; she claims she's a gipsy queen and does some fortune-telling. The strange thing is, she looks exactly like that portrait of Margaret Finch," I told him, expecting a dismissive response. But Dennis Reid was intensely interested and said he would very much like to speak to her. Next time I saw her, he asked, would I inquire whether she would agree to be interviewed by him? He gave me a couple of his cards and took down my details so he could send me an outline of his proposed talk for Suzy's evening. As I got up to leave, he stood and held out his hand.

"What a great pleasure it's been to meet you … Mary," he said, looking at my details on his lecture notes. "I really look forward to working with you and getting together soon."

"Call me Mo," I said, "all my friends do. Email the talk outline and I'll give you a ring."

Did I imagine he gave my hand an extra squeeze before letting go? As I walked out of the room I could still feel the warm, dry imprint of his palm in mine and the warmth of his smile lingered in my mind. Peace and calm, you're just menopausal, I told myself, and attributed my raised pulse-rate to low blood-sugar levels, requiring an instant food-injection at the café next-door.

I walked into the light and airy room, hoping to find an empty table, but they were all taken. Not wanting to share with a chatty old lady or bag-laden tourist, I was about to leave when a familiar voice called out:

"Mozart! Over here!" I looked around and caught sight of Si in the far corner sitting, somewhat surprisingly, with Aurora. I made my way through the tables and sat down on the spare moulded wooden chair. A sudden thought struck me.

"I'm not interrupting anything, am I?" I asked them both. "I was about to go and have a sandwich at home …"

"Of course not, Mozart," replied Si. "I've just escaped from my thesis for an hour – thought immersing myself in some serious art might get the muse flowing, and then I decided a spot of lunch might help her along. I found young Aurora had just bagged the last table, so I said I'd buy her lunch if she'd let me share it with her."

Aurora, who was a little bigger than her mother in every direction, looked ice-cool in black from head to toe, her thick, chestnut hair held off her face with trendy sunglasses and only mascara emphasizing the green eyes in her alabaster-smooth complexion.

"Hello, Mo," she greeted me. "Was that you coming in late to the lecture on Norwood? I thought I recognised you. He was well good, Dennis Reid, wasn't he?"

"Yes, it was really interesting," I agreed, "and I've booked him to speak on something else for Suzy's Dulwich Association evening."

"Cool," said Aurora, "I'll be there."

"Oh, Lord, a lecture as well as all those Dulwich snobs to talk to," said Simon. "I'm trying to get out of it this year, but Miranda's given me a three line whip. She's off home for a week, friend's wedding or something, did she tell you? I didn't get an invite to that event, though, did I?" He took a slurp of his Beck's beer and stared into space.

The waitress came up to take our orders and I quickly grabbed a menu while the other two gave her their requests. Aurora had chosen cold poached salmon with yogurt dressing and green leaves; Si had plumped for a serious meal of chicken breast stuffed with herb butter and roasted sweet potato mash, and selected a bottle of their most expensive white, Deakin Estate Chardonnay, with three glasses. I stuck a mental pin in the menu and got Thai fish cakes with cucumber-coriander salad and chilli dip, then added a bottle of sparkling water to the order. I couldn't afford to lose focus this afternoon and it was hardly surprising that Si wasn't achieving his deadlines if he habitually escaped like this. Though it wasn't like him to drink at lunchtime, I suspected he would have ordered a whole bottle even if he'd been alone at the table.

"This is such a good coincidence," I said to Aurora. "My brother Anthony's looking for someone to work on an interesting new project at his gallery and he asked me if I knew anyone suitable. I thought of you straight away – I'll give you his number in case you're interested." And I wrote Anthony's details on the back of a card I pulled out of my bag. "Do give him a ring, he could be a good connection for you anyway," I added, handing it to her. Aurora looked impassively at Anthony's name.

"Did Mum ask you to do this?" she asked, directly.

"Umm, she sort of mentioned you might be looking for something, but then I had to talk to Anthony about some family stuff and he mentioned this project, so ..." I tailed off lamely, not sure whether I had dropped Venetia in it with her daughter. Aurora's face gave nothing away.

"So, Venetia's got a new boyfriend, has she?" asked Si, coming out of his reverie at just the wrong moment. "I wonder if she'll stick with this one. Well, you're on husband number two, Mozart – I guess it's just the way with our generation, can't keep relationships going. What do women want from men these days – enlighten me, you two?" he demanded almost aggressively.

Aurora and I exchanged a quick glance and she laid a comforting hand on Si's wrist. I noticed that they looked at each other with similarly black-lashed green eyes. As luck would have it, the waitress returned with our drinks at that point and diverted our attention. I tried to steer the conversation to less controversial matters, but every subject seemed to feed in to a depth of despondency that I hadn't encountered in the twenty-five years I had known the usually easy-going Simon: his work, Miranda's work, Naomi and Lola, updates on our friends and their children. He grew quieter as we ate and drank, until Aurora and I were holding a conversation on our own. When the bill came, Simon paid for Aurora as he had promised and we all rose to leave the now almost empty café.

"Thanks for Anthony's number, I will give him a ring. It's cool about Mum – I know you know what's going down," smiled Aurora as she kissed me goodbye, declining a lift to West Dulwich station.

"Sorry to be so down, Mozart," mumbled Si, who had drunk most of the Chardonnay. "Things aren't great with Miranda or the girls at the moment. Seems I'm not enough of a man to hold my own in our house. Not surprised she's looking for the real thing …" and he turned and walked dejectedly away, leaving me to hope he wasn't implying what I suspected.

Chapter Eight

It came at pretty much the time I had anticipated: Julia's phone-call saying she wasn't prepared to wait any longer for Caitlin to get in touch, she was going to ring "my grandparents" and get "my mother's" phone number off them and ring her direct.

"Alright, then, Jules," I responded coolly, after she had vented her anger at Caitlin for a few minutes, "it's your decision. What exactly have you decided to say to your grandparents about who you are, or are you going to use a pseudonym?" Even this simple question gave her pause, as I hoped it would, because she had thought nothing through beyond the assumption that I would try to stop her acting. At first she tried bluster:

"I'll tell them exactly who I am and that their precious daughter's been hiding their first two grandchildren for nearly forty years and now she hasn't written to me when she said she would, so will they please give me her phone number."

"That could work, I suppose," I replied, sounding reflective. "I'm just wondering whether they would actually believe you – it might sound as if you're some kind of nutter, from their point of view. Then again, they might believe you, but would they give you Caitlin's number without talking to her first? She'd probably be furious that you'd broken your word, deny everything and cover her tracks completely."

"Right, right, OK, I'll pretend I'm, like, an old school-friend who's lost touch and wants her phone number." Julia knew she was losing the fight, but we had to wrestle it out to the conclusion.

"Do you know which schools Caitlin went to, Jules? And how good is your Irish accent? You'll need to have believable answers to any questions they might ask you." I felt a bit mean not playing the game by Julia's rules; what she had wanted was a reaction as emotional as hers, a tussle and then for me to find a solution for her. But I had too many problems needing solutions to involve myself in this one any further.

"OK, Mo, you've made your point!" Julia half sobbed at me. "So what do I do to make her write to me? I'm getting desperate here, with no one to talk to, thanks to you—"

I ignored another provocation and went for the knock-out blow.

"You wait, Jules. You stay patient and give the poor woman time to get herself together. She said she'd write, and she will. You said you'd wait, and you will. That's the deal. If nothing comes in another … week, let's say, I'll email the social worker again. Alright?"

Julia recognised that she had been beaten and agreed to my terms. All the same, I couldn't risk her getting worked up again at a time when I wasn't on tap to calm her down, so after she had hung up I instantly reneged on our deal and began a new email. I typed into the Name box: n.oconnor@nics.org.uk Subject: Patterson/Doyle search. After some deliberation, I wrote:

Dear Niamh,

Following my last email in which I told you that Julia was content to wait for Caitlin Doyle to contact her when she was ready, I feel I should now inform you both that Julia is finding the delay very difficult to deal with. She can be very emotional and I am afraid that if she does not receive some communication from Miss Doyle personally in the next few days, she might try to make contact herself. This is in no way a threat; I just feel that, acting as an intermediary in this matter, it would be sensible to let you know how Julia is feeling. I leave it in your hands as to the best way to explain the situation to Miss Doyle.

Yours sincerely,

Mary

I hoped it wouldn't come to that, but felt that if Julia did decide to do anything silly, I had at least given them notice, and kept my own integrity intact.

I drove out of London through Croydon, which for once was not as traffic-jammed as I had expected. Mel had taken Lily early for me and Jack, on the day before he left for Utah, was coming home in time to collect her so that my meeting with Ruby Wadilove could take as long as it needed. Rush hour on the M25 was dying down by the time I got to that motorway from hell, and I reached the M40 intersection without too many hold-ups.

Between High Wycombe and Oxford the road climbed gradually into the Chiltern Hills and the engine in my little old car strained to maintain even seventy miles-an-hour. At the summit the roadside foliage dropped away, the vista opened wide on the sunlit, chalky downs and the Golf seemed to heave a sigh of relief that it had made it and was now on a downward run. I glimpsed the distant villages as they came and went on either side of the road; church spires and farm houses, animals in fields and people walking dogs. Could there be a better environment for

Lily to grow up in than South London, with its intensity of people, traffic, noise and dirt?

A born and bred Londoner, I had always viewed our capital as the centre of the universe and to live outside it a kind of cop-out. Dr Johnson didn't know the twenty-first-century city when he pontificated that to be tired of London was to be tired of life, but was I tired – not of life, but emotionally, physically? Was my changing body trying to tell me that it was time to make other changes?

As the Golf achieved its top speed – a rattling seventy-eight miles an hour – I turned down the Madness tape that was play-ing and listened for any untoward engine noises: breaking down was not an option today. I couldn't detect anything to worry about so turned the volume back up to blot out my chattering thoughts.

> *"My girl's mad at me.*
> *Been on the telephone for an hour*
> *We hardly said a word*
> *I tried and tried but I could not be heard,"* I sang along with

Suggs.

> *"Why can't I explain*
> *Why do I feel this pain?*
> *Cause everything I say*
> *She doesn't understand,*
> *She doesn't realise*
> *She takes it all the wrong way."*

Are men and women really from two different planets, I won-dered pointlessly, and do we inevitably ascribe different mean-ings and values to the same words, making true communication impossible?

I passed the Cherwell Valley Welcome Break and decided not to stop off for a quick coffee. Ruby was taking an early lunch-break and I wanted to be settled and sorted before she arrived in our agreed meeting place. I made good time on the remaining third of the journey and reached the edge of the small, historic town by half past eleven. I turned into Waterside, with its magnificent theatres, and then right into Sheep Street. I manoeuvred slowly up the little road, checking out exactly where my destination stood before driving into the car-park on Ely Street. Sitting in the Golf, I tested the little tape-recorder, made sure I had spare batteries and at least two working pens, then pulled down the rear-view mirror, dusted the shine off my face, refreshed my lip gloss and ran a comb through my hair. I was ready to go and meet Ruby.

I walked back down Sheep Street, admiring its beautifully maintained Tudor façades. Number twelve was one of the oldest buildings in the whole town, pre-dating its most famous playwright inhabitant, and must once have been the centrepiece of a single house. Lewis Carroll's nieces had opened it as a tea shop in 1913, but it currently served tasty modern food at reasonable prices, catering to astute tourists and trendy locals. It also offered comfortable and judiciously arranged tables through its various asymmetrical rooms, and for all these reasons Ruby and I had settled on Lamb's Restaurant as our meeting place. I had agreed to buy her lunch and Erica had consented to foot the bill.

Although it was only quarter-to-twelve, Lambs was already half full, with a combination of morning coffee-drinkers and early lunchers booked in for matinee performances at the Royal Shakespeare Company venues round the corner. The very accommodating maitre d' had placed us just as I had requested. His choice of a table for two, in the little beamed alcove which gave it a feeling of seclusion, even had a large mirror hanging behind it so I could spot anyone approaching the table without looking too obvious. I put my tape recorder under a scarf on the table and casually perused the menu.

At twelve o'clock on the dot, I glimpsed the reflection of a plump woman with blonde, bouffant hair, frosted pink lipstick and a severe, black suit whose jacket was buttoned over a crisp white blouse, approaching the table. I turned towards her, trying not to look surprised at her appearance.

"Mary?" she asked in the little girl's voice I recognised from our phone conversation. It sounded incongruous coming from the robust-looking lady before me.

"Ruby, do sit down," I smiled up at her. "It's nice to meet you, thanks for coming."

She seemed nervous, pulling her chair awkwardly up to the table and taking the menu I offered her with small, tremulous hands. I suggested we order first and waited to see what she would choose. I watched discreetly as she carefully read through both the *a la carte* and fixed price menus, and came to the conclusion that the voice was a more accurate reflection of her character than the armour-plated exterior. When she indicated she was ready I smiled and beckoned the waiter. Ruby selected roast lamb steak and sticky toffee pudding from the fixed price menu and asked for a glass of Coca Cola. That was promising, I thought, she didn't intend to pick at a salad and rush off at the earliest opportunity. I hastily picked salmon and cod fishcakes followed by poached pear in red wine, with an elderflower pressé to wash it down.

"Have you come far?" I asked disingenuously, as an opening gambit, but Ruby was ahead of me.

"I work a few streets away, but I'd rather not say where, if that's alright with you," she replied primly, and sat, hands in her lap, waiting for me to make the next move.

There seemed no point in beating about the bush, so I established that she was happy for me to turn on the tape recorder and started the interview. Her age – thirty-nine – and the dates she had worked for Maxwell Robards presented no problems, but she seemed hesitant when I asked about her background and what had led up to her applying for the job with him.

"Would you rather just tell me everything in your own words, and I'll ask the odd question if I need to?" I enquired. Ruby seemed more comfortable with this modus operandi, so I pushed the tape recorder under its scarf to her side of the table. She took a breath, closed her eyes for an instant, then looked at me directly.

"I was quite a country girl, before I went to London," she started in her breathy, high-pitched tone. "I had ambitions though, thought that I could be somebody if I just made the right connections. I had a perfectly good job as a secretary in Bicester, but I'd worked for – an accountancy firm, since I'd left school and I wanted to 'better' myself, as I thought of it. So I kept looking in the paper for jobs in London; my parents really didn't want me to leave home, but I was determined. Then a friend of mine who had already made the move and was working for another MP, told me Maxwell – Mr Robards, I mean, was a new member and looking for a diary secretary. I was on the train the next day, had an interview with him and accepted the position when he offered it to me a week later." Ruby took a sip of her Coke, which the waiter had just placed on the table. Beneath the heavy foundation, her cheeks were slightly flushed and I could see a hint of the appealing young woman she must have been.

"Well," she continued, smiling at the memory, "I thought I'd won the pools, this was it, a job in the big smoke and for a really important man. I moved into my friend's flat in Balham and we'd get the tube to Westminster together every morning – well, we'd get out at Embankment and walk, to save changing lines, unless it was pouring down." She paused for a moment, and I tried to refocus her on her work with Maxwell Robards.

"So you worked in his office at the House of Commons?" I asked.

"Oh yes, not that it was much bigger than a broom cup-board, and it had to fit both our desks, but I was in seventh heaven, I really was."

"So you worked very close to him, in every sense, right from the start?" I probed further, homing in on angles and phrases that would fit the tabloid style. Ruby bridled.

"It was cosy, but nothing else," she said tartly, sitting up straight so the waiter could place her lamb steak and minted spring vegetables in front of her.

"To begin with," I prompted, pleased with the arrangement of watercress sauce and spinach on my healthy-looking fish-cakes. Ruby looked put out.

"You said I could tell you in my own way," she frowned at me. I apologised hastily and turned my attention to my food. Ruby ate doggedly, but with evident pleasure, as she continued her story.

"Maxwell, which was what he asked me to call him straight away, was a joy to work for. He was courteous and thoughtful and, once I'd got the hang of it, I enjoyed the work – and I was good at it. I'm very efficient and I organised a system that suited him perfectly. No, if there was a problem it was her. Mrs Robards. She was always polite but I never got the feeling she liked me, never treated me as part of the family like he did. But then that was the trouble. They didn't have a family and that was what he really wanted."

Ruby stopped to mop up some gravy on her plate with the crusty bread roll she had kept on her side plate for the purpose. Now we were getting to the heart of the matter, I thought excitedly. "Robards Got Secretary Pregnant Because of Infertile Wife"; "MP's Wife Demanded Secretary's Abortion". I tried out headlines in my mind while the waiter took our plates.

"Pity everywhere's gone non-smoking, I could really do with a fag," Ruby announced as she took out an old-fashioned, enamelled powder-compact and dabbed at her now ruddy cheeks. "Never mind, I want to get this over with." I waited with anticipation while she applied a slick of lipstick and approved her appearance before returning the compact to her bag.

"After a couple of months working for Maxwell, and seeing how Mrs Robards was with him when she came into the office, which she did occasionally, I realised that it wasn't just me that was getting the cold shoulder. She could be very frosty with him, which he didn't deserve at all, poor soul. And then just after we'd had a break for Christmas and the New Year, I came back after lunch and found them having this awful row. She had her back to me when I came in so she didn't see me and went on shouting at him; horrible things she was saying. 'You can't make me do this, it's not you that has to go through all the needles and chemicals they put into you. You don't care about me; it's all about your career!' Well she was quite wrong. He did care about her and he really thought she was unhappy because they couldn't have children. That's why he wanted them to try fertility treatment, but she wasn't having any of it."

The waiter brought our desserts. Ruby looked delighted at

her choice and I almost envied her vanilla bean ice-cream on the side as opposed to my slim line mascarpone garnish. It turned out to be, though, the perfect complement to my melt-in-the-mouth pear, which I ate slowly while waiting for Ruby to reach the climax of her narrative.

"I know all this," she said indistinctly through a mouthful of sticky toffee pudding, "because after that Maxwell started to confide in me about how worried he was about Kathleen, he thought she was making herself ill. And then whenever she had a go at me after that – she'd ring up and complain that I'd booked him for something when she wanted him at home or to go somewhere with her, or come into the office and tell me I'd filled in his diary all wrong – he'd buy me a box of chocolates or a bunch of flowers to make up. We did get very close, you know, and I …well, I was very young, remember. I did, I fell in love with him." She stopped talking and ate silently for a bit. This kept her lips from trembling, but her eyes looked moist. I changed the tape over to give her some time, then encouraged her to spell out the facts that would give me what I wanted.

Since Ruby had finished her account shortly after she had scraped up the last of her sweet, and I had recognised that she had said everything there was to say about her relationship with Robards, I was standing in the queue for returned tickets for the 1.30pm matinee at the Swan Theatre. Ruby's time-management was obviously still exemplary as she had left promptly at 12.55 so as not to be late for her colleague's lunch break. I had paid our bill and, free unexpectedly earlier than I had planned, decided to give my brain a break from sifting through Ruby's information by engaging it with my favourite Shakespeare com-

edy, *As You Like It*, which just happened to be playing. Jack and
Lily could have their planned time together – I needed some to
myself. At 1.29, with several people in front of me and thinking
the Life Force must have other plans for my afternoon, a
harassed-looking man came in and announced his wife had
been held up and he had one ticket to spare.

"I'll take it!" I called out and rummaged in my bag for the
cash to pay him. He handed me the ticket and told me it was
mine for free. His wife had paid for them and if she was so dis-
organised as to double-book herself with an aromatherapy
facial, she didn't deserve to have her money refunded. I wasn't
going to look a gift horse in the mouth, so followed my benefac-
tor up the long flight of stairs to our excellent seats at the front
of Gallery One. It felt peculiar to be going to the theatre with a
strange man but, I reminded myself, I was always in the right
place at the right time with the right people. Perhaps the precision timing of Ruby's departure and the offer of this seat meant
there was a message for me in the play this afternoon.

The huge thrust stage in the galleried auditorium gave actors
and directors scope to use the space as they believed Shakespeare's
troupe would have in the sixteenth century. It could equally
accommodate the most modern of interpretations, and this production, I read hurriedly in my programme as the lights went
down, combined elements of the two. I skimmed down the cast
list before the seating area became too dark to read, and saw to my
pleasure that I had caught a part of the repertory season in which
Joe was acting.

The stage lights came up on Scene One and the audience
drew an excited breath. The token set, suggesting an urban environment as much avant-garde twenty-first-century as classic
sixteenth, was lit in garishly modern colours, and the young

actors playing Orlando and his compatriots were dressed in a creative and sexy fusion of Elizabethan and modern street clothes. It was not, though, until the next scene, when the leading female characters appeared, that I realised the director had chosen to highlight the homoeroticism of the play by using a device both classic and ultra-modern. He, or she, I hadn't caught the name, was exploiting an all male cast – as, of course, it would have been in Shakespeare's day – to explore complex levels of relationship between members of the same sex. No chance this afternoon, then, to observe whether there was any sexual tension between Joe and the gorgeous young actresses that Venetia had taunted Ros with.

The plot unfolded all its contrivances and complexities with less light comedy and more bitter-sweetness than the play usually conveyed. I felt it was to the credit of the director and cast that no crude representations of bi- or homosexuality came to mind with regard to any of the actors or the characters they were playing. Celia, performed by a slight, blonde young man who projected femininity without make-up or camp gesture, declared her affection for her friend with all the intensity of a lover. Rosalind, a darkly androgynous actor, instantly established a radiant presence which was credibly attractive to both men and women.

Indeed, the production seemed designed to celebrate, rather than mock, the range of intimacy and sexual possibilities that the confused identities and disguises of the story line unleashed. I looked around the audience of mainly elderly day-trippers and American tourists to see whether they were shocked or taking offence, but the nuances of the performance were so delicate that the deeper meanings of Shakespeare's words seemed to resonate through any stylistic provocation.

Joe was playing Jacques, the melancholy but acerbic commentator on the convoluted liaisons of the assorted lovers. Under the softer lighting of the pastoral scenes, I was pleased and relieved that he delivered the famous Act Two speech on the phases of human life – man passing from infancy to boyhood; becoming a lover, a soldier and a wise civic leader; then growing increasingly foolish until he is returned to his "second childishness and mere oblivion" – in a way which avoided cliché and made it instead an eloquent commentary on how quickly and thoroughly human beings can and do change. I would be able to tell Ros with absolute honesty how strong I'd thought his performance of a character that could come across as a cynical bore.

In the interval I treated myself to the vanilla ice-cream I had missed out on at lunch and made polite conversation to my neighbour whose wife's seat I was benefiting from. He had seen almost every RSC production in the last twenty years and agreed with me, and apparently the rest of the audience, on the quality of this one.

"Brilliant, really, for a first time director," he mused. "You never know if an actor's got it in him to make that transition."

I looked swiftly down at the programme credits and saw, to my surprise, that Joe, as well as acting in it, had directed the play.

"Oh, I know him!" I boasted to my new friend, before I could stop myself. "Joe's a good mate of mine." He was thrilled, but I had cause to wish I hadn't opened my mouth.

"This was meant to be!" he enthused. "I've always wanted to go backstage and meet a real director and actors, congratulate them on the show. I'm just a fan, don't know any theatre people personally. And now thanks to you … Would you take me with you when you go and see him – in exchange for the ticket?"

I could hardly refuse, even though I had planned to nip off

smartly just as the final applause started and make the car park before it got clogged up. My unintended delay, though, didn't prevent me from enjoying the second half, in which the web of sexual confusion grew more tangled and then unravelled with aplomb.

I watched delightedly as the lovelorn hero practiced his courting skills on Ganymede, the young boy who was really Rosalind in disguise – and who in this production was a man acting a woman now disguised as a boy. The dazzling actor in question made the double cross-dressing seem natural and believable, whilst drawing anyone in the audience with an iota of awareness to the inference that even the most heterosexual amongst them had it in them to be attracted by someone of the same sex, given the right circumstances. The actor playing Orlando presented, without any effeminacy, a credible enjoyment of rehearsing his romantic moves with the beautiful, young Ganymede – almost as if a boy who looked like the woman he loved was even more appealing than the woman herself.

The audience loved it and applauded loud and long at the end. I led my companion away as soon as I could, and we found our way backstage. Passing the two actors who had played the rustic couple, Phoebe and Silvius, chatting urbanely in the passage, I asked them where we could find Joe. They pointed out a door and walked on, arm in arm. As we approached, I could hear loud music and laughter from inside the dressing room. I knocked a couple of times, and called Joe's name, but no one seemed to hear so I turned the handle and pushed open the door. As soon as I stepped into the small, sweaty room, I wished I had waited.

"Mo!" Joe jumped to his feet, pulled his towelling robe around him and came towards me, a warm smile quickly replacing the shock on his still made-up face. "You should have let me know you were coming; how did you like the show?" But I knew that he knew I had seen the alluring dark man who had played Rosalind, kneeling on the floor between his legs, while Joe stroked his thick hair. I was relieved to be able to usher in my admiring friend who, standing behind me in the passage, had seen nothing of the tableau, nor the look of ecstasy on Joe's face.

Joe, to his credit, was entirely charming and entered into a technical discussion about the staging of his and other directors' productions of *As You Like It* with alacrity. The other actor smiled enigmatically, and turned down the music, but didn't seem disposed to leave Joe alone to talk to his visitors. After five minutes of effusive congratulations, I escaped on the excuse that I had to get home to Lily, leaving Joe to deal with the theatre nerd who had already enthusiastically accepted the offer of a drink in the Dirty Duck.

Well he damn well deserved it, and more, I thought furiously, embarrassment and distress vying for centre stage in my feelings, as I half-walked, half-ran back along Sheep Street to the car-park. Getting out took as long as I had feared, with what seemed like half the audience queuing for the exit, and my stress levels were high as I drove back towards the motorway.

Poor Ros, she already felt she had to let Joe sleep with other women to keep her place in his heart, and now he was abusing her trust by getting involved with men as well. We'd all – well, Venetia and I, among others – had experimented with same-sex relationships, but it had been a phase which belonged to student life, singledom and the seventies. It wasn't likely to be something a long-term, mature relationship could survive. So, I worried as I drove back down the M40, should I tell Ros and risk being responsible for the destruction of her and Joe's relationship, not to mention her friendship with me; or keep it from her in the belief that I was protecting her. Although I was very fond of Joe, my first allegiance was unquestionably to Ros. How should I act in her best interests?

Mental close-ups of Joe's and the androgynous actor's bodies, hands, and eyes replayed involuntarily in my head. A hold-up outside Oxford gave me the opportunity to attempt a quick meditation to clear my thoughts and seek guidance, but the Universal Spirit wasn't minded to communicate in that particular traffic jam. However much peace and calm I tried to breathe in, they made no contact with the synapses in my brain.

None of the miscellany of tapes, which had lingered for years in the Golf, seemed soothing or even life-affirming: *Madness Greatest Hits* simply jangled; *Take That and Party* trilled camply; *Abba Gold* sang of tragic lives. I fished on the floor for my bag and managed to extract the tape of Ruby's interview and insert it in the car stereo without taking my eyes from the road. I rewound and listened to the all-important side two.

Through the speakers I heard the clatter of her spoon and fork as she scraped up her sticky toffee pudding, against the background chatter of the other patrons. There was a loud sniff and I recalled Ruby dabbing a paper napkin to her eyes and nose. Then her little girl voice sounded out close to the microphone.

"It was completely one-sided, of course. I think Maxwell realised I was infatuated, but he never used it against me or took advantage. No – " she had put up a hand to stop me interrupting. "I know what I said to that journalist, but it was all a lie. I'm sorry, but that's the record I wanted to set straight. What happened was Mrs Robards, Kathleen, got worse. Now I look back, I think she was having a bit of a breakdown, mentally I mean.

She started to get paranoid, accuse me of trying to break up her marriage and crazy things like that. Now I was young, but I wasn't … that kind of girl. I loved him alright, but he didn't try anything on and I certainly didn't. I just used to go back to the flat and dream a little …"

There was some rustling, and I envisaged Ruby rummaging in her bag, bringing out the worn photo in a cardboard frame, and passing it over to me. It had showed her, young and slim, standing on the steps of the House of Commons with a darker haired and smoother-faced Maxwell Robards. I had looked at it, smiled and handed it back, the sick feeling in my stomach detracting from the taste of my delectable pear and mascarpone. So there was no story for Erica, no dirt on Robards, no hope for the sex education project. Still I had had to listen to the end. Ruby had taken the photo back, stroked it as if to remove my contaminating fingerprints and replaced it in her handbag.

"I would have given anything to be his wife, and I hated her for not appreciating what she had. I knew that I could have looked after him, given him the children he wanted and been a good mother and MP's wife. But I never did anything to try and make that happen. Then one Monday Maxwell came in and he looked really terrible. As if he'd not slept and been crying too. He told me that Kathleen had got really bad over the weekend, ill with terrible stomach pain and bleeding, as well as the mental thing, and then last night she'd been taken to hospital in an ambulance. He said he was terribly sorry, but he was going to have to give me my notice, to take effect immediately, with three months pay in lieu.

"I was devastated and asked him what I'd done wrong. He said I'd done nothing. It was Kathleen, she didn't want me working with him anymore and she was going to give up teaching and be his secretary when she was better. He'd promised her as she went into the operating theatre that he would tell me today." By now Ruby's eyes were sparkling with recollected anger. She reached involuntarily into her bag for a pack of cigarettes, remembered she couldn't smoke here and put them back.

"So what did you do?" I heard my own voice ask, even then hopeful that some sliver of scandal could be salvaged from the shattered story.

"Well, I went back to the flat and cried my eyes out, then I told my friend when she came home. She was furious, said I should get my own back and go to the papers. I said there was nothing to say, but she wouldn't have it. Said both of them deserved to suffer, and I was feeling so weak that I let her make up this story of me being pregnant with Maxwell's baby – that was to spite Kathleen. And then she came up with the idea that he'd made me have an abortion – she said that was to ruin his career and stop him hurting anyone else like he'd hurt me. And she phoned a paper and I had to meet this journalist, Perry something. I told him the story my friend had made up, but I knew I couldn't go through with it.

"Perry must have contacted Maxwell and told him, because he kept phoning the flat, but my friend wouldn't let him speak to me. Anyway, I don't know why but the paper dropped it in the end and I went back home to my parents. I was ill myself for a while after that. It was about six months before I could work again. I went back to my old job and I stayed there till my parents were killed in a car crash. Then when I'd cleared out the house and sorted their affairs, I decided it was time for a fresh start, and I took a job here in Stratford." Ruby's voice stopped abruptly. Even though she, or her conniving friend, had cost me time and effort, I had wanted to know how her life had turned out.

"So did you marry, have children, Ruby?" I had asked her, gently.

"No. You'll probably think I'm silly, but I never met anyone who came near Maxwell and I'm sure I never will. I have a nice flat, a good job, two cats who are like children to me, and a few close friends. I visit my aunt and uncle in Bicester every weekend, and that's my life. I've a nest egg from my parents' house and I'm happy enough. If it hadn't been for Kathleen Robards I might have got over my feelings for Maxwell and moved on in my own good time. As it is …" she paused. "And now I'd like to go. Thank you for lunch. I'm sorry I can't help you with your sex programme. For what it's worth I'm sure Maxwell's quite right in what he says. I just couldn't let you go chasing round for other women that Maxwell had abused, like you said, and upsetting his life again. There won't be any." And I heard the scraping of her chair as she had risen to leave. I ejected the tape.

I not only had to decide what I should say to Ros about Joe, but also how I was going to tell Erica about Ruby. Would she refund the money I had spent on the meal and petrol, or was I yet again out of pocket on the sex education project? And what, above all, was I going to say to Jack about everything that had happened today, when I had left him and our daughter alone on his last day at home?

Jack had spent all yesterday evening packing his efficiently slim case and printing off documents in his study, for the conference I assumed. There was nothing I could do to help, he had assured me, he had everything under control; shirts ironed, suit cleaned, shoes polished. He had given me his flight details but said there was no useful contact number for the University of Utah's

School of Medicine, he'd have his mobile with him – turned off, of course, when the Conference was in session.

He and Lily seemed to have had a good time in my absence. She had been fed and bathed by the time I got home, and was bubbling with excitement about the presents she claimed Jack was going to bring her back from America. I wondered if I too figured on the present list. After I had created some semblance of order in her room and put Lily to bed, I had at least been allowed to cook dinner. When we had eventually sat down to a hastily-assembled stir-fry, and glass of white wine for me – Jack had refused alcohol on the grounds of his early flight in the morning – he had listened inscrutably to my account of lunch with Ruby.

"I'm sorry it didn't turn out as you hoped," he'd remarked. "We'll have to sort out your work plans and Lily's childcare when I get back and things are clearer."

His words had sent a chill through me, but I didn't dare press him on their significance. Nor did I feel able to share my problem about Joe and Ros. Talk of infidelity and strained relationships felt too close to home. I didn't want to crack our relationship wide open and be left with an emotional rift valley yawning between us with no way of bridging it, while he was physically so far away.

There had been no bodily farewell in bed. As was happening more and more lately, I had fallen asleep over a book and hadn't noticed when Jack had come in and carefully marked my place, put the book on my bedside table and turned out my light.

Now he had sprung out of bed, simultaneously silencing the five a.m. wake-up-call he had booked. I pulled on my dressing gown and slipped downstairs to make him a coffee before he left, but the taxi gave a quiet hoot from the street just as Jack emerged, washed, dressed and smelling of mouthwash and aftershave, from the bathroom.

"You drink it," he said, as I offered him the steaming mug, and picked up his waiting case and briefcase. "I'll just put these in the cab and come back for my mobile and the charger." While he took his bags down the path to the taxi, and freezing misty air scented with exhaust fumes filled the hall, I ran up to his study to save him time. As I pulled the phone off its charger lead, its dark display lit up. I read:

> 2 missed calls
> MIRANDA

I thrust the charger into his hand on the doorstep, my heart pounding and a sick feeling in my stomach.

"Jack?" I whispered hoarsely, holding up the phone to show him the tell-tale screen. He looked at it, put it in his pocket and kissed me lightly on the forehead.

"Thanks," he said, coolly. "I'll ring when I've arrived. Look after Lily." And he strode to the pavement and climbed into the back seat of the cab, which pulled away swiftly.

I hardly had time to close the front door before I had to run to the downstairs loo, where I retched and threw up violently into the toilet bowl.

Chapter Nine

"That's extremely disappointing news, Mary. I really thought you'd got us a front page story."

Erica was not pleased. I'd chickened out of ringing and sent her an email about Ruby and Robards. But typically she'd picked up the phone to me the minute it pinged into her Inbox, and caught me on the hop.

"It's particularly unfortunate that you wasted all that time going up to Stratford and taking her out to lunch. I don't quite understand why you couldn't have established that she didn't have any kind of affair with Robards over the phone."

"I know, I'm sorry, Erica. She sounded as if she was going to spill the beans on him, or I wouldn't have bothered going." She was making me feel like a naughty schoolgirl being told off by the Head.

"Well I can't pay your expenses on a non-story. Have we any other leads? The whole thing's going to go cold if we can't come up with something soon."

I remembered that I was going to meet Kathleen Robards at Ros's fundraising event this week and Erica seemed somewhat mollified by this.

"If that leads to a decent story, then I may be able to include your expenses with Ruby in the total bill," she conceded.

I tried to sound grateful, but I didn't hold out much hope that, after Ruby's description of Robards, Kathleen would lead me to any great revelations, even if I could persuade her to give me an interview. I didn't voice these thoughts to Erica, but rang off assuring her I would use all my journalistic skills to uncover whatever skeletons were lurking in the Robards' cupboards.

I thought about Jack, who would be in the air by now. His flight touched-down at Dallas before he arrived in Salt Lake City in the evening, so I couldn't expect to hear from him until after Lily was in bed tonight at the earliest. The sick feeling returned to my stomach as I allowed myself to wonder whether he had returned Miranda's calls, had plans to get together with her during his time away, or was even sitting next to her at this moment.

I diverted my thoughts, did twenty cleansing *Kapalabhati* breaths, snorting negative thoughts out of my nose at speed, and checked my email again to see if anything had arrived that would give me something else to think about. As I looked, an email arrived from Dennis Reid, lifting my spirits a little.

Hello Mo,

It was so good to meet you at the Gallery the other day – you were a welcome surprise at the end of the queue of old dears, charming though they were.

I was flattered that you asked me to speak at the Dulwich Association evening, and I'm very much looking forward to the event. The fee you mentioned was more than adequate, the guests will be an ideal audience for my work, and it gives me a chance to meet up with you again. Perhaps we could do that sooner, if you would like to give me your feedback in person on the proposed outline of my talk, which I attach.

I was so interested in what you said about the possible descendant of Margaret Finch; you are obviously a skilled researcher with sharp powers of observation. The old lady might feel more comfortable if we had a chat with her together.

Do let me know when you're free and maybe I could buy you a drink. Look forward to hearing from you.

Take care,
Dennis

Was I imagining it, or had I pulled, as Jess would have put it? As he was at least ten years younger than me, he was probably just being nice to someone who could increase his contacts base, but what the hell? I could do with a bit of male attention to boost my wilting ego, and the way things were going I might soon be free to make the most of it. I opened his talk outline and skimmed through what he planned to say to the Dulwich Association. It looked like the perfect balance of new information to feed to the voracious amateur local historians, laced with entertaining anecdotes giving insight into his research methodology. Still, I could work up a few suggestions for improvement to justify a meeting.

Hi Dennis,

Good to hear from you and thanks for the outline. It seems well thought-out and very suitable for this audience, but maybe we could discuss a couple of other ideas too.

I'll probably see Peggy Finch in the next day or so and will ask her if she'd like to talk to you about her life and background.

It would make sense to catch up on both things at the same time, so shall we meet for a drink tomorrow evening? Drop in at my place around 8.30, if that suits, and we can sort it all out over a bottle of wine.

If I don't hear, I'll expect you then.

Cheers,
Mo

Did I sound very forward, I wondered, asking him to my house instead of meeting somewhere neutral like a pub? My reason was simply babysitting. I didn't want to ask Mel and have her disapprove of me abandoning Lily in Jack's absence, nor did I want to ask Aurora or Naomi, my alternative evening sitters, and start rumours flying around their parents. And now, here I was already mentally flicking through my wardrobe and wavering between my best jeans and a trendily revealing top, or tailored trousers and my favourite cashmere cardigan.

I needed to ring Ros and confirm arrangements about the Early Childhood Clinic lunch and meeting Kathleen Robards, but I had come to no decision about telling her what I had seen in Joe's dressing room. If I was going to grass on Joe, it would have to be sooner rather than later. To phone now and say nothing would make it much harder to do so at another time.

The sound of the post flapping onto the doormat came as a welcome distraction and I brought it back to my desk to sort through. The usual junk mail, a couple of bills, which I put on one side for Jack, a letter for him from Utah, USA – something that he should have received before leaving? – and a thick envelope postmarked Belfast and addressed to Miss Julia Patterson, c/o Mary Mozart.

So, Caitlin had finally written.

I knew Julia would be at work in the shop, but would have her mobile in her pocket.

> Letter arrived. Let me know what you
> want me to do   open or send to you.
>
> MO X

She would pick up my text at her next break and doubtless phone me instantly. I stuffed my mobile and the letter in my bag, pulled on my coat and scarf and picked up the car keys. I drove up Fox Hill, into the one-way flow of the Triangle and peered left towards Morrisons as I passed. There was no sign of Peggy around the green outside or with the other beggars. She wasn't pushing her trolley up Westow Street nor along Westow Hill. Not finding her on Anerley Hill either, I pulled into Crystal Palace Park and drove down to the car-park. The quickest way to the swings was past the outsize, Victorian stone bust of Joseph Paxton and across the high walkway over the sports ground, but I didn't have to go so far. Peggy was in the anomalous seating area, with its hideous, concrete sub-Stonehenge décor, dozing in a patch of thin sunlight. Her skin looked so waxen and pale as I approached, that I thought she might have passed out, but she opened her eyes when she heard my footsteps and smiled.

"Found Peggy, did you, lovely?" she wheezed. "Now what is it you want to know?"

I sat down beside her and related the information I had garnered about the Norwood Gipsies, Margaret Finch, and our shared local history. She listened for a bit, alternately sucking on her fag-end and giving rasping coughs which shook her whole body. When I ran out of steam, Old Peggy fumbled in her overcoat pocket and brought out a handful of grubby objects which she placed between us on the bench. There was a hunk of mouldering bread, the broken clay pipe, a tattered piece of red cloth and some folded newsprint.

"You got there in the end, lovely," she cackled with amusement. "Needed some help, though, didn't you? Lucky my great, great, great, great – I've forgotten how many greats she were – grandma got her picture drawed, and that I favoured her so much in looks. Never get nobody to understand without her."

"So you are related to Margaret Finch?" I asked the old lady.
"How do you know, Peggy?"

She handed me the stumpy pipe.

"You see her in the picture, smoking her baccy? This was hers.
Old Gipsy Queen's smoking pipe. Broken off now, but you got
gadje doctors who can tell how old things are. They'd know this
was old as Margaret Finch. Been passed down through mother
and daughter, from *drabardi* to *drabardi* – them's the tellers," she
explained as I looked puzzled. "In secret, from the men, though.
The Roma don't keep what belongs to the dead, but the women
said the old Queen's pipe had special powers. Keeps the *mulo* –
bad spirits – and sickness away. She smoke it till she were hun-
dred-and-ten year-old and didn't get no cancers nor nothing."

I refrained from pointing out that Peggy herself didn't seem
to be in the rudest of health from smoking 'baccy', but asked her
instead whether she would like to talk about her life to the historian who had shown me her ancestor's portrait. I would be
there, I reassured her, and would make sure she felt comfortable
answering anything he asked her. She puffed and coughed a
couple of times before replying, and then asked, "He *gadje*, this
doctor of yours?"

"He's not … Roma, as far as I know," I answered hesitantly. I
had no reason to suppose Dennis had gipsy blood. "And he's not
actually a doctor. He's written a book about this area and he's a
nice man. He'd be really interested to meet you and hear about
your life and your family history."

"Then you bring him and you stay with Peggy. Time's not
long for me and the Roma need family around them when the
end's near. No, you're not Finch," she added quickly, seeing the
concern on my face, "but you Romni from another *compania*.
Peggy is Romni through the mothers back to the Queen and

before her. That's why she has the powers of telling – but Peggy Finch is the last of the Norwood gipsies. You have the blood through father's line, I can tell, but there are powers come through from the mothers before. You see the past, the pictures, if you don't let your *gadje* ideas get in the way. You'll thank Old Peggy for opening your gift when you understand."

She looked into my eyes again, but I was ready for her and resisted her ability to transport my mind elsewhere. She laughed, setting off another series of wracking coughs, and when she could speak again, put her hand on my arm. "Ah, lovely," she croaked, "you got control, now. You can come and go as you please. Learn to use the gift, it's all Peggy can be leaving you – and little princess, she has it too."

She started to replace the contents of her pocket, while I was left to absorb, once more, the content of her ramblings. The sight of her putting the mouldy bread back into the overcoat stirred me into speech.

"Oh, Peggy, you can't eat that. I'll go and buy you some fresh rolls from the bakers," and I made to take it from her hand. She pulled away and shoved the greening crust in her pocket.

"Now, lovely, being Romni don't mean you know the ways. This *bogacha* ain't for eating, it's for keeping away the *mulo*, like the Queen's pipe. And this," she picked up the red rag, "this *diklo*'s for luck, for life, colour of blood."

"And what about those press clippings?" I enquired, as the yellow wad followed the other objects into Peggy's pocket.

"These papers are for *gadje* doctor to see, when you bring him. Peggy'll be here when you want her."

I put my hand on her arm, and although she seemed to be fading into a doze, Old Peggy turned it over and ran her thumb back and forth across my palm.

"The woman will come soon, who you're looking for. She brings you work – what you want, eh, lovely? And she brings love. Careful with the man – your man. There's new love in his life, but don't you fear. Keep him in your heart and he brings love back to you. Go home, lovely. Let Peggy sleep. The owl's been hooting ..." and with that unfathomable statement, she appeared to drift off into sleep or some other place that was not with me.

My mobile rang as I was unlocking the car. I knew without looking that it would be Julia.

"Mo, open it now and read it to me." She was practically hyperventilating. I pulled out the envelope from my bag and was about to tear it open. "No, no don't touch it. I need to read it myself. It's to me, my mother. Mo, you couldn't—"

"I'll drive down this afternoon, Jules, OK?" I guessed her question and answered. It was fair enough that she wanted to read the letter immediately, and without me as mediator, but I wanted to be there when she did, to brace her if there was bad news, or check her enthusiasm if there was progress to be made.

"I'll collect Lily, give her a quick lunch and with a bit of luck she'll doze in the car. Then she can see Danny for a bit when he gets back from school."

"Danny's here – he's off school today with a headache, so he'll look after Lily while I read the letter then we can talk about what to do next," enthused Julia. I hoped there was a 'next' option, rather than a closed door, and tried to concentrate my mind on possible responses to best- and worst-case scenarios.

As Danny was at home and Julia was desperate, I decided to set off for Surrey as soon as I had picked Lily up from next door. While I was making some sandwiches for Lily and me to eat in the car, I turned over Peggy's words in my mind. The parts about her being a descendant of Margaret Finch were quite believable, and Dennis might indeed be able to date the clay pipe back to the eighteenth century. But how did she know I had gipsy blood on my father's side and in what way was the mind-game she played with me any kind of gift?

Why did everyone seem to be offering me gifts that I didn't want, while what I desired most – Jack's love, stability for Lily, meaningful work for me – seemed increasingly elusive? Although I could make no sense of Peggy's reference to a woman who was going to bring me work and love – it certainly hadn't been Ruby – her words about Jack both frightened and gave me hope. How could I keep him in my heart and ensure he brought his love back to me?

I rang next door's bell, intending to make a speedy departure with Lily, but the children were painting in the kitchen and Mel said she had something to show me. While she went upstairs, I admired all three works of art, hurried Lily out of her plastic apron and washed her multicoloured hands in the sink. She stopped protesting when I told her we were off to see Danny and Auntie Julia.

"And Nanny and Granddad too?" she asked, excitedly. Not this time, I told her, they were busy and we'd see them another day. Mel returned with a brightly-covered hardback book under her arm and a piece of paper in her hand.

"Now I don't know how you feel about this, girl, but when Andrew and I prayed for you the other night, we were given some verses. We both felt the Lord telling us this was for you, so I'm going to pass it on. We weren't given clarity on the meaning, but maybe it will just speak to you direct. It's Matthew: seven, verses seven to eight."

"Oh, right, thanks Mel." I was a bit taken aback at this. "What does it say – The Bible's not really my thing."

Mel opened what turned out to be the book in question, flicked through the wafer-thin pages and pointed to the middle of a column. I leaned over to follow her finger, and read:

"Ask, and it will be given to you; seek, and you will find; knock and the door will be opened to you. For every one who asks receives; he who seeks finds; and to him who knocks the door will be opened."

I thanked Mel without giving her the satisfaction of a reaction and swept Lily into the car. Whether it was a direct missive to me from Mel's God, or a well-timed piece of intuition didn't matter too much. It cleared a space in my mind and there was something I needed to do. Once we were through the worst of the Thornton Heath traffic, I pulled out my mobile, put it in hands-free mode and dialled Jack's number.

"Let's leave Daddy a message for when he gets off the plane," I told Lily. When his voicemail message had finished I spoke.

"Hello darling, it's me and Lily hoping you've had a good flight and that you get a good night's sleep. We miss you already and we love you to bits and want you back home with us where you belong. But have a good conference. Tell Daddy you love him," I told Lily, and through a mouthful of sandwich she obliged. "I love you too, Jack. Call me tonight, any time. Bye for now." That was my knock at Jack's door and I hoped it would open a little wider when he rang in tonight. At least he could be in no doubt that his wife and daughter needed him, and if Miranda was with him when he listened to his messages, perhaps it would give her pause.

* * *

We had only been in her small but artfully-decorated house long enough to take our coats off and for Danny to lead an adoring Lily up to his room before Julia had grabbed my bag to search for Caitlin's letter. I found it for her and offered to make coffee while she sat alone to read it. Finding she only had instant in her minute kitchen, I unearthed a teabag and made myself a cup of tea. Then I washed up the remains of hers and Danny's lunch and waited what I thought was a reasonable time before making her coffee with hot milk, as she liked it, and taking her mug through.

Julia had her knees under her in an armchair, a thick blue sheaf of writing paper in one hand, the other twisting her curls into ringlets as she frowned with concentration. She ignored the coffee I placed on the table beside her. I turned to go out again.

"No, stay, Mo. I need you to read this, I'm not sure ..." and she put the top page to the back and carried on reading.

I sat and waited while she scanned down to the end then handed the bundle to me, picked up a photo from the arm of the chair and stared at it intently. I took the letter and started to read the elegant script written in black fountain pen.

My Dear Julia,

Please forgive me for not writing to you sooner. As you will have heard from Niamh, your letter, or rather that of your friend Mary Mozart, came as a great shock to me and I have had to make some extremely difficult decisions as a result.

First, let me tell you that when you and your brother were born, you were quite the most beautiful babies I had ever seen. As you will know from your own son's birth, nothing can prepare you for the emotions a mother feels for her own children and despite the circumstances, I was no exception. You and John, as I called him, were perfect and I loved you completely – which was why I wanted the very best for your little lives and better parents than I could be to give you that. But I am jumping ahead. Let me go back to the beginning.

I was brought up in Belfast in the fifties, a time of strict morals and especially in our household. My parents were Catholic and frequent church-goers, my father was our church's organist and my mother involved in all the women's church groups. He was a teacher and believed that to spare the rod was to spoil the child. For all that, they were loving parents and my sister and I grew up in a stable, caring home. We attended a private church school, for which our parents just managed to pay the fees by leading a frugal life. Our academic success was everything to them, so we worked hard, but of course we were surrounded by other girls who came from more affluent and less authoritarian homes.

My best friend was one of these and when I was sixteen, I was allowed to stay weekends with her, go to approved parties and events and even on holiday with her family. She had older twin brothers, who were both wonderful boys, but the elder, Patrick, and I fell deeply in love and we planned to marry. Because we came from such different backgrounds, only his twin brother and my friend, his sister, knew of our relationship, and they were sworn to secrecy. If my parents had found out I would have been banned from their household – I couldn't even risk telling my sister, who I was very close to but who sometimes found it useful to get me into trouble with my parents. His parents would not have minded so much, but would probably have thought their son could have made a better match.

Patrick was three years older than me, and was studying law at Queen's University while I was in my last year at school. He was going to graduate and turn 21 the same summer that I took my A-levels. I would be celebrating my 18th birthday that September and when that happened we were planning to announce our engagement and get married as soon as possible. During the summer holidays I was allowed to go on holiday with Patrick's family to their holiday house on the coast. My friend and her other brother allowed me and your father as much time alone as they dared: we would set out for the day with all four of us, they would leave us alone for a few hours then we would all return to the house together.

During that time, Patrick and I became more intimate than we had previously been – we were so close to getting engaged and married, as we thought, and I'm sure I don't need to spell out to you what happened. But on the day before I was due to go home to my parents, the most terrible thing happened. Patrick and I were on our own by a river, the day was scorching hot and I suggested we swim. He was unsure, not because he wasn't a strong swimmer, but because he had occasional blackouts. I was determined, though, took all my clothes off and plunged into the icy water. I called him to join me –

I stopped reading and shut my eyes, hoping Julia was still intent on her photo. I found I could come and go with ease, as Peggy had said, and took myself back to the river where I had experienced feelings of such intense happiness. I let the scene play out from where I had called my companion to join me, and now I saw he was a handsome, blonde-haired young man, smiling at me in a familiarly loving way. I watched, laughing, as he took a running jump into the river, then felt fear grip me in the gut as he failed to reappear.

I swam over to where he had jumped, and found myself calling "Patrick! Patrick!" I reached down into the water, found his limp arm and pulled him to the surface; his eyes were closed and his mouth blue. I struggled to drag him to the water's edge and more so to heave him out onto the grassy bank. I tried to re-suscitate him, but felt his lips lifeless beneath my own as I desperately blew hot breath into his lungs. The sense of desolation and loss that flooded over me by that secluded river bank was more than I could take and I used my consciousness to bring myself back to Julia's sitting room. Her eyes flicked up at me from the photo.

"You alright, Mo? You looked a bit funny then."

"Yeah, fine," I muttered. "It's just a bit … let me finish reading."

I read through the paragraphs where Caitlin described what I had just experienced and wondered whether I could have let my eyes wander ahead without realising it. But that didn't account for the times that Peggy had taken me there, long before this letter had been written. Caitlin carried on her story:

> Eventually my friend and Patrick's twin returned, but it was too late. Patrick was dead. I had dressed and put some clothes back on him, but other than that I told them what had happened. His twin brother blamed me for luring Patrick into the water and over-exciting him, and the whole family was naturally devastated. His parents were never told about my relationship with Patrick, mine never knew and it would have been bad enough to live with the fact that I was responsible for the death of the love of my life, if I hadn't realised, a month later, that I was pregnant. You will find it hard to believe that young people in that day and age had little understanding of, and no access to, contraception, but we had thought the 'precautions' we took made us safe.
>
> I had no one to turn to – Patrick's family were still grieving, my friend had gone away to college and though I did tell her brother, Frank, about my condition, he made me promise never to tell his parents and to stay away. My own

parents would have been horrified, so I endured my 18th birthday then booked myself on the ferry to England where, I told everyone, I was going to enrol in college. In fact I did not do this for another year, but found a bed-sit and worked as a waitress through most of my pregnancy. I contacted an adoption agency and in the last weeks went to live in a house in Hammersmith along with several other girls in my position.

I now knew that I was having twins, which, as I hope you will understand, Julia, made it even more impossible for me to consider keeping you both. After you were born, I spent two more weeks at the agency home, living with and looking after you and John. I loved you more than I have ever loved any person again in my life, but knowing you would be fatherless and without support from extended family, I thought it kindest to my darling babies to give them loving parents and a better life than I could. After the fortnight with you, I was told to pack my things and prepare to say goodbye. I dressed you in your best clothes and, when a social worker came to the house, handed the two most precious things I would ever have over to her, never to see them again.

At least that was what I believed, and that was the law until it changed ten years later. It was months before I could put you out of my mind for even a few minutes at a time, but I told no one, slowly learned to live with my loss and made a new life for myself. Then, Julia, your letter came out of the blue, nearly forty years later, and I have been beside myself with worry. Of course I want to see my daughter and find out who she is and meet my grandson. But telling my parents, who are now old and frail, might literally kill them, and it could have truly serious consequences for the other people in my life.

I enclose a photo of your father, Patrick, who was a wonderful young man and would have adored you if he had lived and we had been able to bring you up together. I don't have any of me as I don't like being photographed, but will send you one at some point (don't worry, it's not because I am a monster!). I believe Patrick's parents are now dead and his brother and sister both emigrated many years ago – I have no contact details for them. I must ask you, Julia, not to ask me for more at the moment. It is simply not possible for me to communicate with or meet you, let alone introduce you to other members of my family. I am very sorry it has to be this way, but please keep Niamh in touch with your whereabouts, and if my situation changes I will contact you.

With very much love to you and your brother,
Caitlin Doyle

As I finished reading, Julia passed me the worn photograph of Patrick. He smiled out of a face that reminded me in features and character of Jack, especially, but topped by light blond hair rather than auburn. I gave her back the photo and letter, and she hugged them to her possessively.

"Are you OK, Jules?" I asked, surprised not to have seen tears or anger yet.

"It's such a lot to take in," she replied. "I know she says she can't see me, but she's told me so much I almost feel like I know her already."

Not half as much as I do, I thought. I've actually lived some of her life thanks to a mad gipsy fortune-teller. I think I've just watched my own daughter's grandfather die.

"If you wanted to," I said, "you could write your own letter, tell her about yourself and send her a photo of you and Danny, via Niamh. She might not answer but at least you'd know she had it."

"I wish I knew what would happen that was so bad if she told anyone about me. Maybe not her parents, but she's a bit mysterious about the other people in her life. Oh my God—" she broke off, looking out of her front window. "Here's Mum." And she ran down the hall and opened the front door to Betty.

Before I had time to stop her, Julia had thrust her birth mother's letter into her adoptive mother's hand and suddenly burst into tears.

"Oh, Mum," she wept, following a confused-looking Betty into the living room, "I've found my birth mother and now she doesn't want to see me. Jack didn't want to know so Mo's helped me find her. I should have talked to you about it before, but Mo said I couldn't, and now it's all so horrible." She dissolved in tears on the sofa; Betty sat beside her and stroked her hair, making shushing noises. When Julia had calmed down a little, Betty sent her upstairs to wash her face and without speaking a word to me, read through Caitlin's letter and looked briefly at the photo of the twins' father. Eventually she looked up at me, and in a voice that was so cold I shivered, said, "Mary, this is a terrible thing you've done. I expected better of you."

Jack finally phoned the following night. Yes, he had picked up mine and Lily's message; no he hadn't been able to phone before now, the schedule was very busy; no, there was no one there that he knew. I told him all was well this end, and snatched the phone out of Lily's hand when she started to tell him that Nanny had got cross when we were at Auntie Julia's house.

"Just a minor spat between Danny and Lily," I lied. "We went down because Dan was off school with a bad headache and I had nothing much to do." Jack seemed more interested in his nephew's illness than anything else, while all I wanted to do was tell him the tragic story of his biological parents and how Betty had blamed me for turning Julia against her and feeding her false hopes about her birth mother. I was asking, but receiving nothing of the love and support I craved from Jack; knocking, but he was shutting the door in my face. I tried to keep him talking, but knew I was losing him.

"Look, Mo," he finally cut in, "this is a bad time. The conference is really hectic and – there are things happening that I can't go into now. You'll have to wait till I get back, then we'll go through everything and sort things out. I'll call again when I can. Bye for now."

I was sure this was his way of flagging up the end of our relationship. If Miranda wasn't with him at the conference, it seemed clear they were going to decide on a plan of action for when they came back. Si had perhaps been more aware than me of the looming demise of his family. Strange that Miranda and Jack, the two responsible, grounded parties, were the ones behaving in a way that would be considered reckless and crazy if it were me and Simon. Perhaps they had both had enough of being married to idealistic dreamers and had fallen for a mirror image of their own attitudes and values.

It might have been these thoughts that swayed me in favour of the tight denims, but when I tried them on I found I had put on a few pounds too many and had to revert to the more generously-tailored trousers. The menopause wasn't going to stop me wearing the low-necked top, though, and I was quite pleased with the fuller cleavage it showed off.

Dennis arrived on time, in black jeans, a soft wool shirt and leather jacket, and proffered a cold bottle of Prosecco Frizzante – a clever choice, I noted; bubbly but not champagne.

"What are we celebrating?" I asked, showing him into the sitting room which always looked its best lit only by the low table-lamps.

"The best Dulwich Association event ever," he answered, grinning his boyish grin, "and the start of a working partnership?" He popped the cork out of his bottle with precision and poured the frothy Italian wine into glasses that were glinting beside bowls of shiny olives on the coffee table. "Here's to you, Mo," Dennis said easily. We clinked glasses and sat down at right-angles to each other on adjacent ends of the two sofas.

We chatted effortlessly and after we had made some perfunctory additions to his talk and agreed that we would meet in the park tomorrow morning to interview Old Peggy, I discovered that he was currently unattached after the break up of a long-term relationship and sympathetic about the unsatisfactory nature of communications between the sexes.

"I was the one who loved to talk, do everyday things together and make romantic gestures in our relationship," he confessed. "I thought that was what women liked, but it didn't do me any good with Rachel."

"She must have been mad," I smiled. "Most women I know would give their right arm for a partner who did those things without prompting or complaining. I know I would."

Somehow our legs made contact as we leaned to pick up our glasses together, and neither of us moved away.

"I can't imagine why anyone would think of giving up on someone like you," Dennis said gently. "You're attractive, intelligent, creative … I can't imagine a dull moment with you around, and yet you're obviously such a carer, a home-maker." He gestured at the room, and brought his hand down, perhaps accidentally, perhaps not, on the sofa arm between us, touching mine. An electric current seemed to run between us. His hand moved up to caress my cheek and I leaned towards him. We kissed softly on the lips. I was about to slide my arm around his neck when there was a piercing scream from upstairs.

"Sorry, my daughter," I mumbled, jumping up, cursing Lily's timing. I ran upstairs and found her sitting bolt-upright in bed, her eyes wide open but seeing nothing but her nightmare.

"The fire, it's burning me," she cried. "Dada, Dada, come out! It's melting, all falling down!" she shrieked, and shielded her face with her arms from some imaginary furnace. Wherever her dream had taken her, it was horribly real and inescapable.

"Shhh, darling, Daddy's not here, it's Mummy, you're alright, there's no fire, shhhh …" I rocked her and tried to bring her back from the nightmare, but it took me some time to calm the terrified little girl, get her to lie down and go back to a quiet sleep. As I stroked the bridge of her nose, I thought I heard movement downstairs and wondered whether the mood had been irretrievably broken, and if so whether that was not perhaps for the best. What was I doing, snogging a man I'd only just met when my daughter was lying innocently upstairs? Whatever her father was doing thousands of miles away, I was hardly maintaining my position on the moral high ground.

I would have to tell Dennis I'd made a mistake and apologise.

When I got down, I found no one to apologise to. Dennis had let himself out, leaving a note, scribbled in green pencil on the back of a drawing of Lily's, under his empty glass.

Mo,

I apologise for my behaviour tonight. You are a lovely woman, but I didn't realise you had a small child. Whatever your problems, you and your husband will work them out

and I don't want to be responsible for causing you more trouble. Thank you for a very enjoyable evening and please let's meet Peggy Finch together tomorrow.
No regrets, no embarrassment, I hope.

Love
Dennis

I smiled at the evidence of his sensitivity. Some younger woman – someone attractive, intelligent, creative, a carer and home-maker – was going to be very happy with Dennis Reid as a part-ner. I tried not to envy her.

Chapter Ten

I woke with the same sick, anxious feeling that had greeted me every morning since Jack had left, and was still feeling queasy when I met Dennis at the Cintra Gate. We greeted each other crisply in the cold morning air, and then relaxed. There were no regrets nor embarrassment on either side, we established wordlessly, chatting about the exact location of the burned down Crystal Palace and the view we would now be sharing if we had lived a hundred years earlier, as we walked down, through the South Terrace Gates to where Peggy was sitting, in the concrete Stonehenge.

Had she been there since I left her, I wondered, seeing that her trolley was in exactly the same position? Once more she appeared to be dozing, her breathing sounding even more laboured as we approached. Dennis and I exchanged glances as we took the plastic seats on either side of hers; I put my hand on her arm and shook her gently.

"Peggy? Are you OK? I've brought Dennis to talk to you, the *gadje* doctor."

Old Peggy's eyelids flickered but didn't open.

"Perhaps I should call an ambulance," said Dennis, pulling his mobile out of his pocket. "She doesn't look at all well to me."

As if stung, Peggy opened her eyes and struggled to sit up straight.

"No ambulance for Peggy," she rasped, coughing. I poured her some hot tea from the Thermos I'd made before leaving – to maintain my caring-homemaker status in Dennis's eyes. She drank it greedily and held out the plastic cup for more.

"That's better," she wheezed, "just a bit chill last night. Fine now, is Peggy." But she didn't look fine: her skin was greasy and colourless, her breath short and the bony hands around the warm tea were shaking. I decided not to offer Dennis a cup, but to keep it all for Peggy.

Once more I couldn't fault his handling of the situation, as he considerately asked 'Miss Finch' whether she was happy for him to record the conversation and told her to stop him when she was tired. Peggy sat impassively while he took some photos of her with his neat camera. When he put it away and turned on the tape recorder, she ran through the information she had given me about her Romany ancestry through the female line and rummaged in her pocket to find Margaret Finch's clay pipe, which she handed over to Dennis. He took a plastic specimen bag from his briefcase and placed the pipe carefully inside, promising to return it as soon as he had run tests on it.

"Peggy won't be needing it no more," she replied to this. "Give it to lovely, here, if she want it."

In answer to further questions about her own life, Peggy told us that she had been born in 1927, to Maggs Finch who, like all the Finch women, had not been married to any of the fathers of her children. Peggy had had three older half-brothers, whose two fathers had moved on, but her own Dada had been one Edward Smith, a Romany from Epping Forest who had met her mother on his travels. He had moved into Maggs's family *vardo*, a stationary caravan, in the Dulwich Woods, at some point before Peggy's birth. The area had still been heavily forested in the twenties and thirties and, as Peggy described it, the gipsy families had been able to live off the land to a large extent. The Finch-Smith family fortunes had looked up, though, when Edward had managed to gain paid employment working as a night watchman at the Crystal Palace. Dennis was fascinated by this information and asked her if she remembered what the old building was like in those days.

"Such a shame it was destroyed completely," he commented. "I would so love to have seen it, and you must still miss it, as it was such an important part of your childhood."

To our surprise, Peggy's face crumpled at that insight and she pulled out the old red scarf from her pocket, blew her nose and wiped her eyes on the tattered cloth.

"This is what Peggy has to tell before it's too late," she croaked, and pulled the tape recorder in Dennis's hand closer to her. "Us children played in the park, and we used to creep into Palace through hidey-holes. Nobody knew we was there, it were all run down then, not much happening and slowly falling to pieces. When some glass broke they boarded it up with wood, so it didn't look much of a palace no more. There were them television people working in South Tower and some big rooms in the glass house – didn't go near them, scared of their magic. Sometimes was horse-racing outside on a dirt track, sometimes people dress up and dance inside in the big hall. Last thing happen were smart ladies showing off fancy dogs in the big hall, month or so before ..." Peggy stopped for breath and put her skeletal hand on my arm. I poured her another cup of tea, which she sipped at then pushed away before continuing. It was as if she didn't want to be distracted from a task she had to get through before a deadline expired.

"Little Peggy and her friend Darklis, we used to go to Palace at night with Dada, when he let us. We played outside, went exploring in the glass-house and made cups of *chao* in the office. Had to be careful when Mr Buckland, the manager, was around. He didn't want no children round his Palace and turned out he was right."

Peggy turned and looked straight at me. Before I knew what she was doing, I was sucked into the vortex of her eyes and my mind went rushing down the tunnel to another place, another life. But this time she hadn't taken me to a new location; I was still in the park, in the same spot indeed, which was both completely familiar and disconcertingly different.

Mid-morning had darkened to a winter's evening and the view up to the ruined colonnade had changed and expanded. We were no longer sitting on concrete blocks with a car-park ahead of us, but crouching on a large semicircle of grass. Before us, the remaining flights of stone steps and balustrades had become complete, and at regular intervals ornate stone plinths bearing statues in multifarious national dress loomed pale through the dark. Most extraordinary of all was the building that stood on the previously empty grass of the top terrace: the Crystal Palace itself, far larger than twenty-first century imagination could conceive, its central, curved roof glinting in the moonlight, with the rushing clouds reflected in its glassy walls. I looked to the left and then right, where seconds ago the communications mast had stood. I saw instead the two round water towers, which I recognised from old photographs, again of surprisingly massive proportions, book-ending the long configuration. The whole structure had a lopsided look, though, with a gaping hole between the right-hand tower and the start of the glass edifice, through which I could see a thickly wooded hillside stretching back into the blue-black sky.

I was aware of a small figure at my side and realised that I too was in a child's body. A little hand gripped my arm and I turned to see a girl who was unmistakably Peggy, aged perhaps ten, with a red bandana tied over her long, dark hair, a shawl wrapped over an old-fashioned, thick wool dress, wrinkled stockings and ill-fitting button boots. She gave me a grin, so familiar and yet so different, with a full set of sharp white teeth.

"Now!" she hissed at me. "Run now, Darklis, follow Peggy." I had no choice but to follow the fleet figure as she darted from statue to statue, looking over her shoulder to check no one saw us. The Italian terraces were empty, though a few people were still promenading down the Central Walk, holding their overcoats around them, their hats to their heads, so as not to be blown off by the gusting wind. No one took any notice of two little girls zigzagging towards the gigantic building. When we reached the top of the main steps, Peggy took my hand and pulled me towards the central door. It seemed firmly closed, but my little friend dragged me to the right and, where some planks were fixed loosely in place to cover a hole in a shattered glass panel, she lifted one and squeezed in through the jagged gap, urging me to hurry.

Despite its transparent outer walls, it was pitch black inside the cavernous building, but Peggy knew her way by feel, and soon we were in the massive central transept running the full depth of the edifice, where I could just make out an endless stretch of dusty floorboards and the decaying ornate grandeur of the galleried walls. We tiptoed through to another room where the outlines of massive brooding figures made me pull back in fear.

"That's the 'gyptian Hall," hissed Peggy. "That's us, Ee-gypt is where us Gipsies come from. Come on, Peggy know where

Dada's office is." And she dragged me back through the transept and into a little side room where a single electric light bulb was burning, displaying a couple of battered wooden chairs, a desk with an old telephone that would be a collector's item today, a paraffin stove with a billycan standing on one of its rings and an old deep, square sink with one rusty tap. It was bitterly cold even in here and I shivered, pulling my thin coat around me. Whoever Darklis was, her dress-sense and personal hygiene left a lot to be desired.

"Peggy know where the matches are," she said with a sly smile, and opened a drawer in the desk. After some rummaging, the girl pulled out and shook a large box of Swan Vesta matches at me. "Want a cuppa *chao*? That'll warm us up good." Peggy filled the billycan at the sink and replaced it on the stove. She took out a long, thick match, struck it on the sandpaper side of the box and used this flame to light a wax taper with which she carefully ignited the paraffin. It flared into life under the billy-can. I held out my hands to the warmth and watched as Peggy took down from a shelf a metal canister, a box of lump sugar, two chipped, enamelled tin mugs and a greenish metal spoon. As she reached up her shawl fell from her shoulders to the floor. She kicked it over to where a pile of old newspapers lay, took the billycan off the ring, spooned in tea leaves from the canister and sugar from the box, stirred the mixture and replaced it on the stove.

We waited impatiently and in a few minutes the billy was boiling cheerfully. Peggy reached out to lift it, but burned her hand on the jet of steam that was shooting from its ill-fitting lid. She squealed and jumped back, accidentally knocking over the little stove. In an instant the flame had caught her shawl, which flared up with such a fierce heat that we leaped out of the way, letting the fire lick the edges of the newsprint which was now sodden with spilled paraffin. Peggy hurled the contents of the billycan at the blaze and I filled the two mugs with tap water and threw that at the flames, but to no effect, they licked along the floorboards and started to eat at a chair leg.

"Dada! Dada!" screamed Peggy, and we heard heavy footsteps outside. A swarthy man in his thirties ran in, followed by an older man.

"Darn, Peggy, what in hell you done now?" he cursed her, pulling off his worn overcoat and attempting to smother the flames with it. The other man rushed to the telephone and pulled the circular dial through its full circumference three times.

"Git out, you two *cheys*, run home now, Peggy!" shouted Edward, seeing his overcoat catch light. As we obeyed, we heard the other watchman shouting into the mouth-piece:

"Fire Brigade? Fire at the Crystal Palace, Anerley Hill. Send the engines now, if we can't put it out she'll go up like a tinder box!"

Outside on the terrace we could see the red glow pulsing in the heart of the building. Terrified, Peggy and I ran down the wide, central steps; as we reached the bottom a smartly dressed, middle-aged man started to run up, taking the steps two at a time.

"Stay back, Chrystal," he shouted to a young woman holding a dog on a leash, who was starting to follow him, "I'll find the night watchmen!" And he rushed on upwards.

"That's Mr Buckland, the manager," whispered little Peggy. "He'll kill Dada."

We heard the clang of the first fire engine's bell as it raced up the drive and firemen spilled out, pulling hoses off the vehicle and searching for the nearest water-hydrant. Another followed, then another, as the blaze grew, fanned by the strong North wind. We stood and watched the fire, helpless and horrified. People started to appear from all parts of the park and gather at a safe distance to watch the spectacle. When the flames reached the roof for the first time, there was a terrible cracking sound and molten glass fell to the ground. Peggy screamed.

"Dada, Dada, come out! It's all melting, falling down!"

A strange sense of dejá vu made me turn to look at her, and with a shudder I found myself back in daylight looking into the eyes of an old, old woman, not the little girl who had been standing beside me an instant ago.

"This is absolutely astounding!" gasped Dennis, who was by now scribbling notes as well as taping Peggy's words. "The mystery of what started the Crystal Palace fire could be finally solved. Is there anything else you can tell me that would back up your story, Miss Finch?"

Peggy reached into her pocket and pulled out the wad of yellow newspaper. She unwrapped the layers with her stiff fingers; I picked one up and saw it was a contemporary account of the fire. Peggy eventually retrieved from the centre a flattened, but unmistakeably authentic, box of Swan Vesta matches circa 1936.

"Don't know if that's proof, but it's the box of matches what started the glass house fire. Peggy put it in her pocket before she ran, so she could tell Mr Buckland it weren't Dada started it, but never did dare speak out. Can't go to meet Dada with the truth still hid. Promise Peggy you and lovely will tell the truth?" she croaked pathetically, and we both nodded. I took her cold hand in mine.

"Of course, Peggy, if that's what you want. You've given me all the proof I need," I assured her, knowing she would understand what I meant. She turned my hand over and smiled faintly.

"Love will win over fear," she whispered. "You use Peggy's gift to find the truth and there's family all around you. New blood, old and young, here and across the sea. Lovely by name and lovely by nature."

She was halted by a choking cough and I could hear the phlegm rattle in her chest. She held up the red bandana to her mouth and when she put it down I saw crimson blood had stained the faded pigment. Peggy exhaled judderingly and her head lolled backwards, her hand felt heavy in mine. It took a moment or two of silence before Dennis and I realised her strenuous breathing had stopped completely. He took out his phone and made the call he had suggested earlier. For the second time that day I heard the strident warning sound of an emergency vehicle speeding down the park from Anerley Hill.

"Mummy, Mummy," interrupted Lily insistently, as I was giving the manager of Morrisons my most persuasive spiel about good PR, community relations and being part of a historic tradition.

"Not now, Lily, I'm talking," I admonished her – and then instantly capitulated, realising that she was not going to give up. "Well, quickly, what do you want?"

"That's Cake Lady's trolley, she's left it behind now." Lily pointed at a single shopping trolley standing alone near the stack of identical ones by the door.

"Well, it's *like* Old Peggy's trolley," I said, smiling conspiratorially at the manager, hoping he would humour my daughter.

"Actually," he frowned, "your little girl's right, it was the one we lent to the old lady. It's just come back from having a disinfectant wash, see it's still got the tag on. How did it get out there, I've only just put it back with the rest? It's going to cause an accident in the doorway, there – " and he beckoned over a young sales-assistant badged as 'Vernon' and asked him to move the offending article.

"Well, that was a good guess, Lily," I told her.

"I didn't guess, Mummy. I saw her get it out. Cake Lady waved bye bye to us. She's gone home now, gone to see her Dada," she said, as if talking to an idiot. "You'll have to buy me doughnuts now, Mummy."

The manager grabbed Vernon on his way back from the trolley stack and asked him to bring a bag of jam doughnuts for the little girl. He also suddenly agreed to my request after having completely stonewalled me for the previous fifteen minutes.

"Well, seeing as she was a much-loved local character, and if we get signage at the buffet, I suppose, at the end of the day, we can dip into our budget for charitable donations and help out with the funeral costs," he conceded. "She should be laid to rest properly, we don't want any ... bad feeling from the other side."

Amazed, I sorted out the details with him while Lily munched on the doughnuts Vernon brought her. I wondered whether the manager was just jumpy about the possibility of an irritable revenant upsetting his customers, or Peggy had conceivably passed on some powers to the 'little princess'.

I felt more slivers of success come my way over the next couple of days. The arrangements for the Dulwich Association evening came together and slotted smoothly into place, and now Anthony was phoning to say he'd met Aurora, been madly impressed by her cool demeanour and creative professionalism, and offered her the job of getting his new East End gallery for young British artists off the ground and into the public eye.

Although I still felt shaken by my experience in the park and unexpectedly distressed by Peggy's death, I couldn't help wondering if her last prediction might have signalled the start of a new and more ordered phase in my life. Being surrounded by family seemed a forlorn hope when my own could be falling apart and my in-laws thought I'd betrayed them, but now that I could no longer bump into Peggy and be sucked into someone else's trauma, I might be able to focus on sorting out the more ordinary pressures I was facing.

"Thanks for putting me onto her, Mo," Anthony enthused, "and sorry I wasn't keener when you rang. I think I was a bit hung-over and I'd had a row with Sal about Mum forgetting a baby-sitting date she'd agreed ... or something."

"Did you talk to Sally about Mary Wilhelmina?" I ventured.

"Oh yes, that was the other thing. She's yours – in every sense. Sal's decided to redecorate the dining room to make the ancestors a retro feature: all Regency wallpaper and curtains, oak furniture, Masons china, period silver and glassware – the lot. The gipsy girl's a bit out of her element in that particular setting – a bit too Victorian kitsch. She'll be better off with you, which is where I think she belongs. I had another look at her and she really does have your eyes – and hair, before you miraculously went a few shades lighter, Sis!"

"That's just to cover the grey," I protested. We laughed and I felt the pull of our childhood drawing us together through the years. It was sad that Lily would have no one to share moments like this with when she was middle-aged. Mark and Jess would seem like another generation to her, though I knew they would always be there for their little sister.

I hoped it might be Jack when the phone broke its vow of silence again, but it was a secretary from PPR Lobbyists asking me if I was available to meet Nick and an associate in an hour's time in Westminster. No, she didn't know what it was about but assumed it was critical as he had wall-to-wall meetings and she would have to cancel an appointment with a client if I agreed to go. This was no social catch-up, then, which could only mean that Nick had picked up something about Maxwell Robards and didn't want to tell me on the phone. I asked the PA about the associate Nick wanted me to meet, but she had no information on that either. Her tone of voice urged me to make a decision so she could make the appropriate arrangements and get on with her life. I checked my watch – I would have to drive in to make the allotted time, pay the Congestion Charge and a fortune to park, but it might be worth it. I accepted and she gave me the exact time and rather unusual location of our meeting.

Despite my lack of recent communication with her, the Universal Spirit led me to a parking meter on Great Peter Street with an hour of unexpired payment. I put in an extra couple of pounds for luck and walked the short distance to Abingdon Street in search of the Jewel Tower. It turned out to be directly opposite the south end of the Houses of Parliament, with a sunken entrance that could have once been part of a moat. I must have walked past this remaindered piece of history many times without even noticing it. As I was five minutes early, I read the sign outside which told me that this ancient building, also known as the King's Privy Wardrobe, was built around 1365 to house the treasures of Edward III and was one of only two buildings of the original Palace of Westminster to survive the fire of 1834. I didn't read any further; I had had quite enough of fires in historic buildings for the present.

I walked down the steps to below pavement level, across a lawn and down into the little basement shop as I had been instructed. Surrounded by books, reproduction artefacts and memorabilia was a single table with four chairs, a small coffee-dispenser and a minibar-sized fridge. There was no sign of Nick and I was just wondering whether I had taken down his secretary's apparently precise directions completely wrongly, when a priest in cassock and dog collar entered, followed by my old boyfriend, Nick.

"Mo, sorry to keep you," he said, kissing me on the cheek. He had grown greyer and considerably fatter since I had last seen him; his tailor-made suit and hand-crafted shoes exuded success, but his smile still twinkled warmly. "May I introduce Father Colin O'Gorman. Father, this is Mary Mozart, the old friend I was telling you about." I shook hands with the gaunt, elderly priest, and tried to work out what possible reason Nick could have for bringing me right across London to meet him. *Peace and calm, I am always in the right place at the right time*, I repeated in my head as we served ourselves coffee in polystyrene cups and Nick paid the man behind the desk.

"Mo, you'll be wondering why on earth I've brought you here," began Nick, as if in answer to my musings. "I'm well known in every possible meeting place around Westminster, but there's never anyone here except tourists to interrupt a quiet conversation. My friend," he nodded towards the attendant, "sometimes keeps the table free for me by fair means or foul. Anyway, this is a very private matter. I know as a good journalist you'd never reveal your sources, and on that basis Father O'Gorman has some interesting information he is willing to share with you."

I nodded, unsure what a Catholic priest could offer me to

keep a sex education programme alive, and waited for Nick to continue.

"Father O'Gorman is advising me on … certain matters, and during a discussion, he happened to mention that he knew someone you're interested in, when they were younger."

I snapped to attention and followed Nick's gaze to the priest's face, which displayed some discomfort. I realised he needed some reassurance from me.

"Father O'Gorman," I started, feeling my way back into professional mode. "I am working on a project which I believe will reduce unwanted and unprotected sexual activity between young people, with all the suffering that brings in terms of unplanned pregnancy, abortion and sexually transmitted diseases. Maxwell Robards' current campaign has put that in jeopardy and, whilst I don't want to cause him or his family distress, anything you can tell me which might make him – change his attitude, would be incredibly helpful. It would be treated respectfully and with total confidence," I finished. Was that sufficiently reasonable to convince the priest to release his information? He hesitated, and then a flicker around his mouth told me he would take the plunge.

"Ms Mozart, what I have to say is of a very personal nature, but I want to assure you it was not told me in the privacy of the confessional, nor did I ever agree to keep it a secret." His rich, Dublin accent and intense, grey-eyed stare were compelling, and I willed him to go on.

"I have always leaned to the liberal side of my faith, and I do not believe that the Vatican's opposition to contraception is a Godly stance. When I took up my first position in London in the early 1960s there was anticipation that things were changing in the Catholic Church, but in 1968, Pope Paul the Sixth's encyclical, *Humanae Vitae,* dashed those hopes and set in motion some terrible consequences. However, even before this, life was hard for Catholic women who became pregnant out of wedlock, and I made it my business to offer sustenance to such unfortunates."

I nodded again to indicate my agreement with his position and for him to continue, which he did.

"In the mid-sixties – I forget which year exactly – a young woman started attending my church and after one mass, asked if I would pray with her. She confided to me that she was expecting a baby and that, though she wore a wedding ring, she was unmarried. We had a discussion about the morality of abortion, which was obtainable, though illegal, at that time—"

"So it must have been before the law changed in 1967," I interrupted.

"You may be correct, I don't recall exactly." Father O'Gorman seemed not to appreciate my knowledgeable intervention. "Anyway, the young lady came to only another couple of services and then I never saw her again. She was very attractive, though, and spirited, and had made enough of an impression on me that I recognised a photograph of her in the newspaper some twenty-five years later, when her husband became a member of parliament."

"Kathleen Robards?" I murmured, hardly daring to believe my luck.

"The same," he concurred. "I have no knowledge of whether she went through with a termination of her pregnancy, though I'm aware that she and her husband are often referred to by the media as 'childless.'"

I thanked the Father profusely, and assured him his information would be treated with the utmost sensitivity, whilst offering up a silent thank you to the Source and speculating on the impossibility of convincing Erica to take a tactful approach to such explosive material.

He stood up to leave; I stood too and held out my hand, which he shook briefly but firmly.

"I trust I will see you at our usual time tomorrow, Nicholas," said Father O'Gorman to Nick, who smiled and nodded, and the priest left us alone at the uncomfortable little table.

"What can I say? You've found exactly the information I needed, just as I'd pretty much given up." I smiled at Nick appreciatively.

"I can't take the credit for any detective work, it just came my way and not even from a professional connection," he admitted.

"So tell me about Father O'Gorman and what he's advising you on – if it doesn't require high level security clearance," I probed, curious about Nick's unusual contact.

He looked at me, made a slightly sheepish face, and then explained that although, or perhaps because, he was still the single workaholic he had been when we briefly went out together – I recalled the many cancelled dates due to work commitments, which had finally prompted me to end the relationship – he had started to feel a lack of purpose and spiritual content in his life of late. The intellectual tradition and formalised rituals of the Catholic Church had always attracted him and without quite knowing why he had started going to Mass. He had recently felt the need for a more in-depth understanding of the scriptural basis of the faith, and had made enquiries about a suitable spiritual director. Colin O'Gorman had been recommended to him; now Nick was seeing him on a weekly basis and felt he was gaining great insight into God's purpose for him. I was impressed and felt my recent drift from the Source more keenly.

"So you'd probably think that my yoga and meditation is all

New Age rubbish and the work of the devil," I said, thinking of Mel's reaction. Nick looked surprised.

"I respect anyone's spiritual path, Mo," he told me. "Father O'Gorman's just introduced me to Christian meditation and I can't believe it's very different from what you do. Do *you* think you're heading in the wrong direction?"

"No, not at all," I assured him hastily and, falling back into the easy relationship we had once enjoyed, poured out my insecurities about Jack's, Mark's and Mel's very different kinds of resistance to my beliefs in the Life Force and means of connection to it. When I had finished taking up Nick's valuable time, he looked quizzically at me for a moment.

"I can't speak for anyone else on this, Mo, and bear in mind that after clinging to atheism for the best part of thirty years I'm very much what they call a young Christian, but it seems to me you've made a fantastic personal journey since I last saw you. Think back to how you were living, what is it, ten years ago? And now you're settled, poised and perhaps ready to move into a new phase in your life. I no longer think we do these things by ourselves, and my recent experience tells me that if there are problems you can't fix, you just have to let go and trust whatever you feel is out there, connecting us all, to bring the right people and events together at the right time. I personally believe we all pray, talk, listen to the same God, whatever we call him – or her, and whatever routes we take to find him – or her! What kind of god would be so churlish as to reject any genuine attempt to reach her – or him? Organised religion is the way for some of us, but I don't discount the individual approach as any less valid."

I didn't trust myself to speak, feeling somewhat choked at the first support I'd encountered for the beliefs that Jack considered flaky and Mel downright dangerous. Nick reached into his breast pocket and brought out a tiny leather-backed Bible.

"Here's another quote for you, Mo, though I can't claim I was given it for you. It's one Father O'Gorman gave me to meditate on a couple of weeks ago." He opened the little book at a marked page. "'I know the plans I have for you, declares the Lord, plans to prosper you and not to harm you, plans to give you hope and a future.' Jeremiah: Chapter twenty-nine, for your info." He swigged down the last of his coffee and chucked the empty cup into the bin.

"And now, Mo, I have to meet the Chief Exec of a major telecommunications company. I'm still lobbying for my clients' interests and I certainly don't preach to them, but I try to persuade them to use their commercial power in positive ways as well these days." He leaned over and gave me another kiss on the cheek. "Keep me posted on the Robards case." And Nick was striding out of the door, polished leather briefcase in hand, before I even had time to thank him for everything he had done for me in the last hour.

Athene Mozart had never been the most maternal of mothers, but there were times when there was no one else I wanted to take my troubles to. The house in Pimlico still felt like home and I dreaded the day when she would feel the need to dismantle the trappings of my childhood and downsize. But for now she was marking a pile of papers at the kitchen table as she had always done, half-moon specs on the end of her nose and rogue strands of white hair falling over her face.

"Put the kettle on, darling, before you go up to Daddy's study. I think the old ones are stacked in the bottom cupboard," she said in answer to my request for her oldest edition of *Who's*

Who. When I came down with a 1986 version, the kettle was whistling shrilly for attention. I made tea for us both, refused Mum's offer of what looked like a rather decrepit fruit cake, and flipped through the pages until I found Maxwell Robards.

> **ROBARDS, Maxwell Peter;** OBE 1984, MBA (Harvard); Business Consultant, since 1972, Director, since 1982, Gilchrist Benton Parks Ltd (formerly Gilchrist and Parks Ltd); *b* 17 October 1942; *s* of Peter Charles Robards and Ellen Jane Robards (*née* Bourne); *m* 1970, Kathleen Mary, *d* of John and Mary Doyle. *Educ:* Manchester Grammar Sch.; Manchester Univ (BSc); Harvard Univ (MBA). Various posts in City Treasury, Manchester CC 1963-66; Associate, 1967 then Consultant, 1972, Gilchrist and Parks Ltd. *Recreations*: art, walking, cricket, tennis, squash. *Club*: Hurlingham.

This entry was much shorter than the current one, which featured his achievements as an MP and a later CBE for his charitable work with the Family Fellowship. There was, however, one piece of information that did not figure in more recent editions of *Who's Who*, which rang a discordant bell in my head and which I tucked figuratively behind my ear for later.

I recounted my visit to Julia and the fiasco of Betty turning up just as the full significance of her birth mother's letter imploded in Julia's head. I asked my mother's advice on how to set things straight with my in-laws. Simply leave well alone and wait for Jack to come home, she suggested. He had a way with his parents, particularly his mother, which soothed ruffled feathers and would allow rapprochement in time. Lily would also be a force for healing relationships, as Betty and Colin always had her best interests at heart.

"But shouldn't I encourage Julia to send a letter and photos of her and Danny via Niamh, the social worker?" I asked.

"I would keep your distance from Julia, too, for a while," advised my mother, "and if the social worker spells her name N-I-A-M-H, you pronounce it *Nea've*, not *Nee-am*. You're as bad as all these parents who give their little girls Irish names and don't even know how to say them. Not so romantic as they look written down, half of them ..."

Another neuron fired in my brain, sending out charges to some previously unrelated facts stored in my memory banks. I let my mother witter on a little longer about modern parents not knowing the meaning of classical names, the tiresome fashion of using surnames as forenames; the fads for misspelling traditional appellations and giving children inappropriate biblical monikers ...then took my leave as soon as I decently could. I had some urgent research to do.

Relieved to be home after the stress of negotiating the permanent South-East-London gridlock, I took out my yoga blocks and sat cross-legged. This was the most crucial act of meditation I had ever undertaken and now Peggy was gone, I was on my own with the "gift" she had released in me.

I took five minutes to ground myself with the three part breath; another five to distance the outside world by focusing on the high-pitched electrical noise within my head; and then I conjured up Peggy's face before my closed eyes, looked deep into hers and willed myself back to the riverbank where I, Caitlin, had just lost my soulmate.

Nothing happened.

I was all too aware of my bedroom around me and the sound of traffic bouncing across the speed bumps outside. I focused again on Peggy's eyes.

Still nothing – and then suddenly my head seemed to

expand and I was there, experiencing the full sunlit tragedy of that Irish afternoon.

I had no idea whether I could influence the actions of the person whose life I was sharing, or whether I would have to wait and see if she would behave as I needed her to. Peggy hadn't left me an instruction manual for the power she had passed on, but I now seemed able to experience directly the other person's feelings while at the same time observing as myself.

As Caitlin, I did those things she had written about in her letter to Julia; dragged Patrick's body onto the bank and heaved him into his clothes, then dressed myself, crying and panic-stricken. When there was no more to do but wait, and no one came, I did what any girl would; delved into my white, summer handbag and found a mirror, hairbrush and make-up.

I tried to slow down time as Caitlin held the small mirror to her face. I saw a creamy, lightly freckled complexion, large hazel eyes, red with crying and a wet tangle of long luxuriant, auburn curls. I tried to take a mental snapshot of those exquisite, eighteen-year-old features, and then returned to my own reality, as if from a long journey, with a slightly nauseous feeling.

Chapter Eleven

I stood at the back of the brightly painted room decorated with children's art, as Kathleen Robards stepped onto a small podium at the front and made an articulate, informed and heartfelt plea for the assembled company to donate, and get others to donate, funds to purchase specially-designed play equipment to help the young clients of the Early Childhood Centre improve their mental health and therefore chances in life.

She was slim, above average height and, though in her late fifties, wore her hair below her shoulders, pulled back at the sides in a pair of elegant combs. The colour had faded, not to grey, but a delicate strawberry blonde, almost matching her golden eyes, and her facial features were softened but fundamentally unchanged by the pull of gravity and a light network of wrinkles. After the warm round of applause she received, I watched Ros approach and engage her in earnest conversation. Mrs Robards drew out a Filofax from her diary and flicked through some pages. Some nodding and smiles indicated that she had agreed to the request. A few minutes later, Ros came over to me and confirmed that she had.

"Kathleen is happy to speak to Erica, or a researcher, between eleven and eleven-thirty tomorrow morning, if you can come to her house." Ros handed me a Filofax page with an address scribbled on it. "She'll answer questions about the clinic and her charity work, but not about anything personal or her husband's work. OK?"

"She can answer what she likes, but I just want to see her face when I present her with some information that's been brought to my attention," I agreed. "Thanks, Ros. I will explain why I needed you to ask, but not right now."

"Well, I assume you have your reasons, but I don't understand why you don't want to use your own name with Kathleen. She's not precious and I don't think Erica's reputation cut much ice with her."

Once more I asked Ros to trust me, promised she would understand when I could give her the full story, and turned to leave. It was a long journey back home and I didn't want to leave Lily at Mel's longer than I had to.

"And Mo?" Ros put her hand on my arm. "Joe told me you'd seen *As You Like It* – I wish you'd told me you were going."

"It wasn't planned," I said guiltily, "and I just forgot to mention it to you afterwards."

Ros looked disbelieving. "Don't bullshit me, Mo. I presume that means you've put two and two together and understand Joe's connection with the play? I hope you'll return today's favour and allow me to preserve my identity." She looked at me severely. I had no idea what she meant, and told her so.

"I think I saw something I wasn't supposed to backstage, but I didn't want to upset you, Ros," I added tentatively.

"Believe me, there's nothing I don't know about Joe, Mo. But I'd like to fill you in, given what's happened. Have you got five minutes?"

Without waiting for an answer, she took my arm and led me out of the room where potential donors were now tucking into a buffet lunch, down the corridor and into a little office. Ros sat at the desk and I took the only other chair, opposite, as if I were one of her clients. She fumbled in her bag and pulled out an envelope from which she took a photograph and an old passport with the corner cut off. She looked briefly at the photo then passed it across the desk to me. It was of Joe and a tall, dark-haired young man with a Freddie Mercury-style moustache, both in the height of early-eighties fashion. I looked up at her enquiringly.

She raised her eyebrows at my incomprehension and handed me the passport, open at the photograph. It was the same guy, but this time, without the moustache, his likeness to Ros was startling.

"I know you don't have a brother, so who's this? A cousin or something?" I asked, puzzled.

"Closer than that," Ros replied. "Surely you've guessed. That's me."

I gazed at her, then the photo and back to Ros again, unable to express the confusion I felt at this extraordinary revelation.

She began to explain in a detached tone, almost as if speaking about one of her patients, that she had been born with ambiguous genitalia due to an enzyme deficiency, which was not understood then as well as it is now. Her parents had been given the choice as to which gender they preferred for her and, as her macho father had very much wanted a son, she was designated male, named Lawrence, and underwent some operations to 'normalise' her as a boy. From a young age, though, she had felt herself to be a girl trapped in a boy's body, and as a teenager decided she must be gay. This, combined with her lack of interest in cars, sport and other masculine pursuits, had led to major disagreements with her father, and at university she took up a promiscuous, gay male lifestyle to distract her from her inner feelings, and rarely went home.

"Then two things happened," Ros continued, shaking off her objective standpoint and becoming animated. "I met Joe at a gay club and from a one-night stand, we fell madly in love. For both of us it was total commitment from the start. But I was also having psychotherapy as part of my post-grad training, and during that process I realised that I wasn't a gay man, but a heterosexual woman. I had tests and they showed that I had more female reproductive organs than male. I decided I had to reverse my childhood operations and become the woman I felt myself to be, or I would never be happy. It was painful, it took time and I still have to take daily hormones, but Joe cared for me enough to support me through all of it, and he learned to love the new me in every way. But the poor guy is gay. He was rehearsing another *As You Like It* when I started having the pre-op hormone treatment and became more physically female. The play helped him to come to terms with the bisexuality he had to develop to stay with me, and that's why we chose Rosalind as my new name. The play's still something of an obsession with him, and he picked it for his directing debut. I thought after what I'd told you, and then seeing the play in Stratford, you must have guessed our secret."

"So vitamins aren't the source of your fantastic figure!" was my first, fatuous response, as my brain started to process disparate pieces of data. It seemed obvious now I knew, "But no way could I have guessed that, Ros." I shook my head in disbelief. "I just thought Joe was … playing away in more ways than you knew."

Ros smiled and her body relaxed again. "You're the only person in nearly twenty years I've – we've – told. Joe realised you'd seen and he wanted you to know he wasn't cheating on me, that it was part of our relationship. He did try his best at the beginning to become totally straight, but it was driving him mad and we nearly split up. In the end we worked out a way that made it possible for Joe to get what he needed and what I could no longer give him. Jamie, the actor you met, reminds Joe of me as I used to be. He's a sweet boy who's just having fun, but for Joe he's a kind of necessary Ganymede until he comes back to Rosalind. There have been others I haven't minded so much, but I admit I was a little threatened when I first saw how gorgeous Jamie was. But I'm not any more because our way of dealing with it is that Joe tells me absolutely everything ... but you don't need to know the details."

There was silence for a while as I tried to take in what Ros had confided to me, and then couldn't help but make the correlation with my own situation.

"So do you think that if Jack's had an affair I should learn to live with it?" I asked Ros, thinking also of Peggy's last words.

"I'd just say that there are harder things to come to terms with and real commitment makes all things possible. Well, almost all things ..." Ros looked sad for a moment, then shrugged. "I had hoped, to begin with, that I had enough female reproductive organs to conceive, but I soon had to give up on that particular dream. I thought children might have helped Joe to stay straight. As it is, we're soulmates and lovers, and I get to sort out other people's messed up kids."

"I'm so sorry, Ros," I reached my hand out to hers. "When I asked before, I had no idea what I was digging into. You make me feel very petty after all you've been through. I promise I'll never tell another soul about you and I will explain the subterfuge with Kathleen Robards after tomorrow."

* * *

The number three bus took me straight from Crystal Palace Parade to Hanover Gardens, Kennington. Despite the convenient location, this time was far from ideal for me as Jack was due to arrive home from the airport sometime around midday. I wanted to be there to welcome him, but couldn't pass up this opportunity to meet Kathleen Robards. Lily and I had tidied the house and written welcome home cards in case I wasn't back when Jack arrived. I had texted his mobile for when he switched it back on after landing, left a bottle of champagne and some nibbles in the fridge, bought fragrant bath and massage oils from the chemist, and changed the sheets on our bed. Given Jack's attitude in our last phone-call, they would probably remain unused, like the two urine tests the chemist had recommended, which were still in their packs in the bathroom.

I didn't know whether I was more tense about the interview with Kathleen Robards or seeing Jack again afterwards. A half-empty bus was usually a soothing place to breathe and meditate, but I couldn't get air down into my diaphragm and the Universal Spirit gave no response to my pleas for help with my next task.

I walked up the steps and knocked on the front door of the Robards' freshly painted house in the pretty little Georgian square, a few minutes walk from the Oval cricket ground and tube station. Kathleen opened it, looking graceful in well-cut trousers and jacket, and invited me in. I smiled my thanks, hoping my mouth was steadier than the hand I put out to shake hers.

"Please take a seat, Erica," she offered as we entered the immaculate, double-aspect drawing room. "Would you like a tea or coffee?"

"A coffee would be very welcome, thank you, Mrs Robards," I replied like a well-mannered child as I sat down in a stiffly upholstered armchair. "I'm not Erica, though, I'm Mo, her researcher. I'm afraid she got tied up and couldn't make it herself. I hope that's alright."

"Of course, Mo. Excuse me a minute while I get the coffee."

As she went downstairs to the basement kitchen, I took a quick look around. The bookshelves on either side of the fireplace held a mixture of classic and modern novels, sociology and religious books. Maxwell Robards' interest in art was obvious from the walls, on which hung a range of contemporary paintings by visionary artists such as Roger Wagner and Charlie Mackesy, whose work I recognised from Anthony's gallery. Some Meissen china figurines and animals were positioned on the mantelpiece and occasional tables, and stiff arrangements of fresh flowers in cut-glass vases stood on the upright piano and the coffee table. Apart from an extensive tray of drinks on a cabinet at the far end of the room, there were no personal objects to give a clue about its occupants.

"Please do start asking your questions," said Kathleen as she re-entered the room holding a small tray with two steaming cups and saucers, sugar pot and milk jug. "I really have to finish at half past."

I pressed the record button and asked how she came to be involved with the Early Childhood Clinic, while I poured milk into my coffee. I took one gulp, as Kathleen started a cogent and well-prepared reply to my question, but couldn't swallow any more. As she spoke, I felt overwhelmed by her likeness to Jack and especially Julia, not only in looks, but her tone of voice and facial gestures, the way she twisted a strand of hair round her finger and tucked her legs up under her. I knew I couldn't play it cool any longer with my daughter's grandmother; all my plans for lulling her into a false sense of security before revealing my true identity at the last minute were thrown into confusion. As she finished talking, I leaned forward and my voice shook as I said, "Mrs Robards, Kathleen, I'm sorry to do this to you, but my name is Mo Mozart, Mary Mozart, I'm married to Jack Patterson, Julia's twin brother. I found out who you were almost by accident, but no one else knows yet. Please don't be upset, I know you're in a very delicate position with your husband's campaign, but I had to speak to you."

I stopped as Kathleen lost all colour in her face and put her hand to her mouth. In a panic about what I might have done to her, I went to the drinks table, poured a slug of brandy into a glass, brought it over and sat beside her on the sofa. She took a sip, shuddered and recovered a little. I wondered if I could slip inside her present-day head as I had experienced flashes of her past life, but put the thought aside as she started to speak in gasping breaths.

"Oh my God. I knew this would happen. Ever since I got your letter I've been waiting, dreading this moment. I've been screening my calls, screening my email, waiting for the post so I could check it before anyone else saw it. But I didn't suspect a journalist. Not Erica Beamish, especially – is she going to publish this?" Kathleen asked despairingly.

I saw my chance. "I am supposed to be working for her, but no, she doesn't have to know. We can do this another way. Just please listen to me." And I started to outline the plan that had instantly formed in my head.

Jack had been home for the best part of an hour when I came in. He was jet-lagged and irritated by arriving back to an empty house. I couldn't explain to him that I hadn't been able to leave

Kathleen until we had reached a way forward and she was calm enough to be on her own. I didn't envy her what she'd agree to do, but I knew she had iron in her soul – I had, after all, inhabited it, for a short time.

I needed to summon up some of that iron in myself to face what I was sure Jack was going to say. He looked grey with tiredness, but clearly wasn't going to let me down gently, refusing a relaxing glass of champagne, hot bath or massage to unwind before we talked. Strong coffee was all we had to fortify us when we sat down at the kitchen table to "sort things out".

I wanted to plunge in first and tell Jack that I had found his birth mother, that he should meet her for himself and find out about his genetic roots, think about what that and his ongoing presence meant to his daughter, but he asked me to let him speak first. Then seemed to find it hard to put what he needed to tell me into words. I waited, my heart pounding, for the death knell to fall on my family.

"Mo, this is hard for me to explain," he eventually started, falteringly. "I'm not the sort of person who deceives anyone easily, least of all you. I just want you to know that I haven't meant to hurt you over the last few weeks, but other people were involved and things happened that were beyond my control. I didn't know how to tell you, but it all has to come out in the open now, because the whole family has to know."

"Oh my God," I muttered. "Oh, Jack, no, please."

He was so focused on what he had to say next that he didn't seem to hear me, and went on, "You know I said I was going to Utah for the cardiac research conference?"

I nodded dumbly, tears welling in my eyes.

"Well that was only a small part of why I went and a bit of a lucky coincidence that it happened to be on then. I really went

to meet someone else, someone who's going to be very important in my life, and Lily's."

"Oh don't say that. Miranda will never be her mother," I
croaked.

"What? What's Miranda got to do with anything?" Jack
seemed genuinely irritated. "Please, just let me explain without
going off at a tangent. This isn't easy!"

There was no faint flush of embarrassment, no tiny twitch of
a muscle from having been caught out; none of the infinitesi-
mal, involuntary signals that flash like a beacon to a woman
who can read her man's face like a book. Could I have put two
and two together and made five? I concentrated on what he was
about to say with a tinge less apprehension than before.

"I was contacted a few weeks ago by – someone called
Francis Butler, from Ogden, Utah. He had taken some time and
effort to track me down and said he'd had to call quite a few
times before I actually picked up the phone myself. He said he
was my biological uncle, the twin brother of mine and Julia's
father, who, it turns out, died before we were born."

The search engine in my brain zipped into action and
accessed several facts: Caitlin had written that Patrick's twin was
called Frank; that he had emigrated; that he was the only one
she had told about her pregnancy. Knowing the dates, he could
have searched records and found details of Jack and Julia's births
and adoption, and easily tracked down Jack's whereabouts. The
silent, number-withheld phone calls I had picked up fitted in,
time-wise, with Jack's story and could have originated in the
States. But what would have prompted this man to get in touch
with his nephew and niece after all these years?

"Francis, Frank as everyone calls him," continued Jack,
"wasn't motivated by the idea of some happy family reunion,

but by pure duty. He made it clear he didn't consider me and Julia to be part of the Butler clan, and didn't want any personal involvement, but the family has recently discovered that they suffer from an inherited disease which has had fatal consequences down the generations. After a lot of soul-searching, he decided he had to find us and let us know."

"Oh my God," I said a second time. "Oh, Jack, no!"

"It's alright, hon," he said, putting his hand over mine. "I can tell you now, it's all going to be OK."

It was his touch, the first sign of affection for so long, and relief that he didn't want to leave me, that really started my tears flowing, but I let Jack think it was fear he might have a potentially fatal illness. I held tightly onto his hand while he talked me through the facts.

The Butlers had suffered a tragically high number of premature bereavements across branches and down generations of the family. The causes were always obscure, with no real symptoms other than occasional fainting or seizures preceding sudden, unexplained deaths, mainly in young children and teenagers. The family had just considered itself unlucky in its losses, until Frank's eldest grandson died eighteen months ago during a swimming gala. The Coroner had asked whether the family had been tested for a genetic heart condition called Long QT Syndrome. All the American Butlers, none of whom had heard of the illness before, had gone for genetic testing at the University of Utah's Eccles Institute of Human Genetics. A majority of them were found to carry Long QT, some with symptoms and some without, but all at risk from SADS, Sudden Arrhythmia Death Syndrome.

"So what exactly is this mystery disease?" I asked Jack. "Explain to me in layman's terms so I understand what you're on about."

"Put simply," he told me, "patients with Long QT Syndrome develop a very fast heart rhythm disturbance known as 'Torsade de pointes'. It's a form of ventricular tachycardia – meaning the rhythm is too fast for the heart to beat effectively, so the blood flow to the brain falls sharply causing the sudden loss of consciousness, often fatally."

"OK, I think I get that. And how do you inherit it?"

"If you have a parent with Long QT, they have an abnormal copy of one or more genes which they could pass on to you. If the other parent is normal, you have a fifty per cent chance of inheriting the abnormal gene. It's almost certain that mine and Julia's father had Long QT – he died aged twenty-one swimming in a lake, for no apparent reason. Frank thought it only fair that we should be informed and have the opportunity to be tested for the disease. That was all he wanted to do – tell me and leave us to it. But I insisted on going to meet him and the family."

I was astounded, suddenly angry too, that Jack should have resisted Julia's plea for support in searching for their mother, rejected me for helping her, then secretly gone to make contact with their father's family. I pulled my hand away from his, stood up and walked away from the table. *Peace and calm, peace and calm*, I inhaled. Don't let me blow things now, I begged the Source, but I couldn't contain my emotions.

"Why, Jack? Why was it OK for you to do that when you were so awful about me helping Julia look for your mother? And why the secrecy – couldn't you just have told me what was going on? Do you know what you've put me through these last weeks?"

Jack was on his feet instantly and held me close.

"I'm so sorry, hon," he stroked my head, which was buried in his shoulder, and kissed my hair. "I never wanted to keep things from you, and you were having such a bad time at work too. All those things I said about your work – I was just trying to show you it didn't matter to me, I was happy to support you, for you to be a full-time mum if that happened. But how could I tell Julia about Frank, when a) he didn't want to know us, and b) we might have a fatal genetic disease. You know how she would have reacted – and then there was Mum and Dad to consider. I had to get the medical side sorted out before sending the whole family into total panic. And I didn't want to frighten you either, honey."

I had to admit he had a point. For someone who hadn't even wanted to delve into his biological origins, he had taken on a huge responsibility in demanding recognition from a family who didn't even know of his existence, and facing a possible life-threatening condition. I felt a surge of emotion for my valiant, loyal, sincere husband, even if he had a curious, man's-eye view on how best to deal with complex emotional matters. I decided that however much I wanted to know all the details of his time away, and tell him my news, it was time to crack open the champagne.

"Hello, Mary … Mo. It's Kathleen Robards here."

My heart lurched. Had my plan worked, or had I ruined Julia's chance of meeting her birth mother and destroyed Kathleen's marriage?

"Hi, Kathleen. How are you?"

There was a brief silence at the other end of the phone during which I hoped she couldn't hear my heart thumping in my chest.

"This has been one of the hardest times of my life – and I've been through some very painful experiences, as you know."

"I'm so sorry," I muttered. "I hoped—"

"But now I feel a load has been lifted from my shoulders. I think

I actually feel happy for the first time, the first time since—"

There was a pause, so reminiscent of Julia's silences when emotion got the better of her.

"Since Patrick died. I can say that now. I haven't been able to say his name or talk about what happened to anyone for forty years. And now I'm free. Free of the guilt and free from my secret. I was angry at first, but now I have a lot to thank you for, Mo."

I was taken aback, relieved and touched in equal measure, and glad that Kathleen kept talking so I didn't have to try and express my own feelings. She told me how scared she had been after agreeing that the only option was to tell her husband about Jack and Julia and their adoption; how certain she had been that he would hate her, both for her history, and for deceiving him for so long. And how when, literally shaking with fear, she had sat him down that evening and told him the whole story up until my visit, he had responded first with blistering fury, then icy censure, followed by melting tears of sympathy and self-criticism.

They had spent the next twenty-four hours talking, shouting and crying until they had reached a point of exhaustion where all facts had been told, all questions answered and all feelings aired. Kathleen said they had finally fallen asleep together like children, and then woken to a new day, a new-found tenderness and a fresh determination to commit their lives to each other and the family they had acquired.

"That is," Kathleen hesitated, "if you want us in your lives. I don't wish to upset the twins' adoptive parents or try to take their place in any way. But if Julia and Jack would like to meet me, I would be so happy. And Maxwell and I would love to see Danny and Lily, and be a sort of extra aunt and uncle to them, if that was possible."

"I think everything will be possible, but give me time to talk to them all," I told her, wondering dubiously how Betty and Colin would react to Kathleen's offer.

"And Maxwell has asked me to organise a meeting with your sex education company. After all these years I've been able to tell him why I don't totally agree with the Family Fellowship's line on all this. It's such a relief to be able to be honest about that, as well as everything else. I know how you must feel about his views, but he is a good man and I think this has changed him."

The atmosphere was distinctly cool as Jack led me and Lily into Betty and Colin's spotless lounge. As usual, the newspapers and magazines were arranged as if with a set square on the coffee table and even the pot plants looked pruned to perfect symmetry. Unusually, neither of his parents got up to greet even Lily, as they sat in a row on the sofa with Julia and Danny, a very un-welcoming committee.

"Hi Dan!" Jack broke the ice by tousling his nephew's curly hair. "How's it going? Do you want to take Lily into the garden and feed the fish – she needs a stretch after the drive? Thanks, mate," he added as Danny got up wordlessly and took a slightly bemused Lily by the hand.

"Call me if you want me, Mum," he said over his shoulder to Julia, sounding more like an eighteen- than eight-year-old. Clearly he had been told that we were *persona non grata* with the rest of the family.

"How was the conference, son?" asked Colin, who looked uncomfortable with the way the battle lines had been drawn, but Betty wasn't going to allow any niceties to derail her terms of engagement.

"I think Jack and Mary have something to say to the family," she interjected. "Before you start, I'd just like to say that whatever excuses Jack may have for you, Mary, nothing but a full apology for your behaviour will cut any ice with me." A spot of red on either cheek broke through her smooth, beige foundation as she sat up even straighter to assess whatever it was we had to communicate.

For once I let Jack speak for me, recognizing, as my mother had advised, that Betty would take from him what she would dismiss out of hand if it came from me. I was expecting Jack to take a conciliatory tone and had prepared myself for a groveling apology if that was what it took to get the family back on speaking terms. But I had underestimated my husband's belief in me. He started on Julia first, gently but firmly taking her to task for putting me in an impossible position with her request for help to find Caitlin, and for not being brave enough to tell the whole family what she wanted to do. Betty nodded agreement at this last point, but Jack took no notice.

"Being the caring, supportive woman she is," he told Julia, "Mo tried her best to help you without upsetting anyone else. She asked my permission to look for our birth mother, and I don't feel proud of how I reacted, refusing to have anything to do with it. And it was you, Jules, who said you didn't want to tell Mum and Dad, and now you're blaming it on Mo. It wasn't her place to tell them, it was up to you to be honest and open, even if you didn't want them involved."

"Yes, it was silly of you, dear, to think I'd be upset." Betty adjusted her allegiance slightly so as to align herself more with her son. "I've always said I wouldn't mind if you wanted to look for—"

"And I'm really surprised at you, Mum," Jack broke in sternly. "I've always respected you for your fairness and open-mindedness, but you've judged Mo without even hearing her side of the story. You ostracised her while I was out of the country, made her feel awful about upsetting you, and worried her terribly about Lily being left out of the family."

"I told you, Betty, you weren't being reasonable with Mo," put in Colin.

"But you didn't phone Mo to say that, did you, Dad?" rounded Jack. "Not one of you called to see if she and Lily were alright while I was away, or ask for her version of events, or thank her for finding Caitlin, Julia. Because that's what Mo's done. At great cost to herself she's tracked down our birth mother and got her to agree to see us. Now what have you all got to say?"

There was a resounding silence and I wanted to fling my arms round Jack, thank him for his support and congratulate him on standing up to his mother and sister instead of forever playing the peace-maker. For once he was totally, unreservedly on my side and it felt wonderful. Julia was the first to break rank.

"I'm sorry Mo, I'm really, really sorry. I've behaved like a spoilt child and I hope you can forgive me." They were perhaps the most insightful words I'd ever heard from Julia's mouth. Her eyes were moist, but she didn't seem to be heading for an attention-seeking crying fit. "How did you find her? Will she really see us? When? What was she like?" she went on, unable to contain her excitement.

Before Betty and Colin could respond, Jack held up his hand for silence.

"That's not the only news, and what I've got to say is considerably more serious and affects Julia and Danny especially." And Jack explained to his parents and sister how he had met the other side of his biological family and been tested at LDS

Hospital in Salt Lake City for the genetic heart complaint that had killed his father. He had had an echocardiogram – an ultrasound transducer placed on his chest for about half an hour which built up a picture of his heart structure and blood flow through the heart chambers and across the heart valves. The immediate results showed that Jack did not suffer from Long QT, which also meant that Lily was safe as well.

"But, speaking professionally," he continued, "my guess, Jules, is that you have inherited the condition. It would explain your episodes of syncope – sorry, fainting fits – your inability to tolerate loud noises and even your emotional highs and lows. Long QT is often wrongly diagnosed as epilepsy, which happened to you at one point. And it looks to me as if Danny probably has it too."

Julia, Betty and Colin all started to speak at once, as the impact of what Jack had said hit home. Jules and Danny were suffering from a congenital heart disease that could kill them at any time. Once again Jack stopped them in their tracks.

"It's not something to panic about now we're aware of it. Julia and Danny need to have echocardiograms and I've booked them both in at the Royal Brompton Hospital on Tuesday. It's got one of the best adult congenital heart programmes in the world and I happen to have been at medical college with one of the consultants. If either of you have it, you will be put straight onto Beta blockers, which you'll then have to take for the rest of your life, but it regulates the heart rhythm and means you have minimal risk. If you just happen to be one of the few people who don't respond to Beta blockers, you could have a pacemaker fitted, but it's unlikely. In the meantime, don't swim or do any sport, stay calm, don't use noisy alarm clocks and stay away from other sudden loud noises if possible. "

By now, Betty was dabbing her eyes with a lace-edged hanky with Colin attempting to comfort her. Julia, though, looked remarkably cheerful.

"You know that's kind of a relief. I mean all these years I've thought I was, like, some kind of crazy, and everyone else just thought I was fainting and stuff to get attention, and now I know there's actually – well probably – something real wrong with me."

I left the four of them alone together and went to join Danny and Lily, who were listlessly kicking a ball around the garden. Danny frowned when he saw me coming.

"It's OK, Dan," I reassured him. "Everything's been sorted out and I think you'll find I'm not the big bad ogre everyone thought I was. Go and check with your mum, I'll stay with Lily."

He ran off with a happier face, pushing past Betty who was coming out of the kitchen door towards me. I looked at her warily as she put a hand on my arm.

"I hope you can forgive me too, dear; it was me that did a terrible thing, not you. It was just such a shock coming in and finding you there and Julia in such a state. I suppose we've been very lucky that all this upset hasn't, well, killed her."

"It's OK, Betty, I can understand how you felt," I said, not wanting to prolong her discomfort.

"But that's just it, Mo, you can't. You don't have to worry about whether blood is thicker than water; you've got three of your own children and there's never been anyone lurking in the background who's got any claim on them," persisted Betty.

I thought of Paul and the fear I'd had of him kidnapping Mark and Jess when he was at his craziest, but said nothing.

"You see, it was like suddenly finding your husband's been having an affair, that there's someone else taking your place in his life, and there's nothing you can do about it. And to discover that someone you trusted has been helping that to happen behind your back – well, that's how it felt and it was very upsetting."

I could suddenly identify with what Betty was saying. I bent over and hugged her diminutive frame.

"I'm sorry, too, Betty. I felt like I was being torn apart, but Jules seemed so desperate. Me and Jack really fell out over it as well. Caitlin – Kathleen you pronounce it – is a nice person, I think, but she's never going to take your place with your children. You're their mother, you brought them up and they adore you."

She stood on tiptoe and kissed me on the cheek, smoothed her blouse back into position and smiled brightly.

"Well that's alright then. How about a nice cup of tea?"

I sat with my hand on Jack's leg and my head on his shoulder as we drove home through the London suburbs from Surrey, something I hadn't done since Lily was born. He occasionally took his hand off the wheel and stroked mine; a smile playing round the corners of his mouth. I suddenly remembered something I hadn't yet confided in him.

"Jack, I think I'm menopausal. I've got a couple of tests from the chemist, but I haven't done them yet. Would it bother you? I mean apart from me getting even more grumpy, about not being able to have any more children?"

"My family's perfect as it is," he answered without hesitation. "Do the tests when we get home and you can go on HRT if you're feeling bad. Poor old Mo. Does it worry you?"

I shook my head.

"Not if I've got you to help me get through it. I love you, Jack Patterson."

"I love you too, hon. I don't know how you could have ever thought otherwise," he said disbelievingly.

"What was all that stuff with Miranda?" I asked. "Consultations, phone calls, going off to the States at the same time. She seemed to know more about what was going on with you than I did. Did you talk to her about Frank?"

"Of course I didn't!" Jack sounded miffed. "If I couldn't tell you, I certainly wouldn't tell anyone else. I wasn't talking to Miranda, she was talking to me. It was a medical matter … look, Mo, ask her yourself. She can tell you if she wants to. Let's not spoil a good day arguing about Miranda." And he slid his hand up to the top of my thigh.

Chapter Twelve

"Jack?"

I stuck my head out of the bathroom door and called the doctor for a professional opinion.

"Look." I pointed to the two tests I'd just done. "This one's negative, but this one's positive. That can't be right, can it?"

Jack glanced at them briefly and checked the boxes they'd come in.

"Looks pretty conclusive to me. You'd better make an appointment at the surgery tomorrow." He saw my face and put his arms round me. "Hey, it's alright, honey, everything'll be fine. There's nothing to worry about."

"But I'm forty-five," I said, and burst into tears.

Kathleen was as good as her word and, at exactly the appointed time, Maxwell Robards and his PA entered the offices of Generation Productions. They were shown into the goldfish bowl by an unusually subservient Ellie who even took orders for coffee without complaint, and closed the door quietly behind her. This left me, David, Jane and Peter Braithwaite with the MP and his note-taker around the board room table.

As I had brought everyone together, I made the introductions and suggested that Maxwell, as he asked us to call him, should open the discussion. As well-groomed as ever, he looked less confident and more haggard than when I'd last seen him on TV; a sadder, perhaps a wiser, man. So much so that I almost felt sorry for him facing the waves of hostility emanating from the Generation team.

Maxwell cleared his throat and gestured to his PA to put down her pen.

"May I start with some personal, off the record, observations?" he asked meekly. David, Jane and Peter exchanged glances and David spoke for them all.

"We're interested in hearing anything that could revive this project from its deathbed, where your campaign has consigned it," he said flatly. Robards flinched minutely, but took the hit without complaint.

"You must understand," he continued, "that any comments I've made in the past about your sex education project came from a position of deeply held conviction, which in theory I still adhere to. But I confess I had no personal experience of the effects that ignorance and lack of support could have on young people."

Maxwell stopped, ran a hand through his thick, white hair, mopped his brow with his starched, breast-pocket handkerchief and poured himself a glass of water from the carafe on the table. After a couple of mouthfuls he took a breath and returned to his topic. "I have recently discovered that someone very close to me, raised with a strong faith, became an unmarried, teenage mother. My first instinct was to condemn, but as she talked to me about her experience, and the impact it has had on our – I mean her life, I began to understand and to realise that compassion was a more appropriate response. Not only did she have to deal with the situation she found herself in completely alone, but until now has felt unable to tell anyone what she went through. What happened to her has left her vulnerable to mental and physical illness through-out her life and affected others in her family."

Maxwell Robards broke off, and blew his nose noisily. I doubted that I was the only one who had seen his eyes water.

No one moved or spoke.

Maxwell composed himself, cleared his throat and pressed on. "Although this all took place many years ago, I have come to realise that there must still be many young people who find themselves in the same position, or something similar. I see now that when children can't talk to people close to them because they fear their judgement and disparagement, they need other sources of adult support. So in the light of this new understanding, and with apologies for the damage my dogmatic approach has caused your project, I would like to see if we can come to some agreement on the style and content of the programme which would allow me to support its funding through the Department of Education."

This time the team exchanged looks of cautious exhilaration. Jane couldn't suppress a smile and Peter Braithwaite checked his reflection in the glass wall with apparent satisfaction.

David's response was measured and generous.

"Thank you, Maxwell, for that statement which, I'm sure we all realise, took guts to make. I think I speak for us all when I say we would be pleased to take you up on your offer, your support would be very welcome, and I hope we can convince you of the integrity of our project."

For once Ellie chose a timely moment to barge in without knocking, carrying a tray of coffee mugs and, with uncharacteristic consideration, a plate of chocolate Hobnobs. Robards' PA, Amanda, passed them round, glad to have found a useful function. When we had settled down and a more convivial atmosphere had asserted itself, David pulled out from the pile of papers in front of him a set of bound and laminated documents, which he passed round.

"While the project's been on hold, Jane and I have taken the time to re-formulate the whole concept, in terms of both content and delivery. Jane, would you like to explain what we've done?"

Jane opened her copy of the new proposal at the contents page and glanced down at it.

"Following your question in the House, Maxwell," she smiled coolly at him, "we realised that if the Department of Education was going to commit funds to the project, they were going to be under pressure to justify every aspect to politicians of all shades, the media, tax-payers, parents, teachers – the lot. So what we did was sit down and try to answer every possible question in advance. We've also introduced a new element which we think will have better take-up by young people and may be less confrontational to some adults. This document is the result – perhaps we could take a few minutes while you look through it."

Maxwell Robards, Peter Braithwaite and I all started scanning the professional-looking brochure that David and Jane had obviously put a great deal of work into. I saw instantly what they done: come up with a brilliant new idea that would be perfect for today's teenagers, making the video and schools-based part of the programme an optional back-up. I read David's introduction to the service they had called TXT M8:

> Using virtually unique "intelligent database" technology, the TXT M8 service allows young people to text any question on sexual health to TXT M8 ('Text Mate' in text speak) and receive an accurate, up-to-date and appropriate answer from a trained sexual health, relationships, or other professional in minutes. It's that simple – 100% responsive and available 24/7/365.

> TXT M8 is aimed at the UK's 12-20 year-olds. They make up approximately 12% of the total UK population, some 7.2 million, and are a notoriously difficult demographic group to target. Engaging with young people rather than preaching to them, TXT M8 communicates with them in the way they want, and has been designed as a 'joined-up service' forming partnerships and relationships with every agency and charity that works with children, young people and sexual health.

I speed-read a few more pages, which included much of the background research I had done, full sets of financial projections, details of the technology to be used and the intensive training process for the phone operators. There were signed endorsements from all major charities dealing with relationships and family-planning, organisations working with young people, even NHS practitioners.

David asked me for my feedback.

"I think this is a brilliant concept, David, better than anything we were working on before. And having recently brought up young teenagers, I know this could have been of use to them, and certainly for some of their friends with less approachable parents than me!"

He turned to Peter Braithwaite, who was still shuffling through the back pages.

"Yes, I agree, I think it's a strong idea, but … you haven't mentioned a high-profile expert in relation to TXT M8 …"

"Sorry, Peter," replied David smoothly. "It's not really that kind of service. Kids don't want a celebrity signing a text telling them their penis is an acceptable length or that they won't get pregnant from giving their boyfriend a blow job. We'd still like you to be involved with the education package, but that will take a back seat for the moment."

Peter looked as if he wanted to protest, but closed his mouth and settled for a disgruntled expression. David turned to Maxwell Robards for his response.

"So this service would tell young people about relationships as well as just sex?" Robards asked tentatively.

"It certainly would," replied Jane. "Our objective has always been to inform kids about the benefits of waiting until they're ready, and committed relationships rather than casual sex, but through factual information rather than moralistic preaching. They have to be able to make their own decisions, based on real knowledge. We know from other countries that preaching total abstinence from sex, any more than alcohol or drugs, simply doesn't work. Did you know the American virginity programme, The Ring Thing, has an eighty-eight per cent failure rate, Maxwell?"

"Does it really? No, I didn't know that." Maxwell indicated for Amanda to note it down.

"But if a young person contacted this T X T M Eight service to ask about Christian values or support, they would be given the phone number of organisations like the Family Fellowship, for instance?"

"If that's what they asked for," said David. "TXT M8 is conceived as a conduit through which young people can access the information they want without having to front up to adults and ask embarrassing questions, or rely on erroneous information from their peers in the playground."

Maxwell visibly relaxed and smiled warmly for the first time. He turned to his PA, who was following the conversation with an open mouth and motionless pen.

"I hope you're getting all this down, Amanda, especially what I'm going to say next. Given those reassurances, I would be happy to supply a written endorsement from the Family Fellowship and write a letter to the Education Secretary urging him to fund the

T X T M Eight proposal. I could also make myself available to attend any meetings you might have with the Department of Education if you found it helpful."

I left the office an hour later. Maxwell had shaken my hand and said he hoped we'd be meeting again soon, Peter had stormed out in a huff and Jane had hugged me and said she wanted me to take on a more executive role in co-ordinating the TXT M8 service.

"My choice of days and hours?" I asked. Jane nodded. "Working from home unless I'm needed in the office, and plenty of notice for meetings, which will always be at reasonable times?" I hoped I wasn't pushing my luck.

"And a decent salary, rather than just a temporary contract," she added.

David walked me to the door and thanked me for the magic I'd performed in getting Maxwell Robards to perform such an unprecedented U-turn.

"If you could just use your powers to line up a mobile phone company to sponsor us," he joked, "we'd be sorted!"

I had a lot to tell the group when we met at the French café the next day, and they were suitably impressed with my news.

"We got the results of Julia and Danny's echocardiograms straight away – Jack went with them to the Brompton while Betty and Colin waited at home with me and Lily. Everything's fine between us again now, in fact everyone seems much happier since all this has come out in the open."

"So, what were the results? Are they alright?" asked Suzy impatiently. I guessed she was remembering the stress she'd been through with Olly's heart operation at the Royal Brompton Hospital when he was young.

"Sorry, I missed out the vital information. Both Jules and Danny have inherited Long QT Syndrome. They were started on Beta blockers straight away and seem to be responding well. Funnily enough, Julia seems to have grown up a lot since she's been diagnosed; I don't know whether it was finding out about her roots, or just knowing there was something tangible that explains her health problems, but it's like she can move on. Danny was a bit upset by it all, but he's looking much better and playing sport again now."

"They'll be fine, believe me," Miranda assured me. "We may have developed some more specific medication in a few years, but Beta blockers are tried and tested on this kind of cardiac malfunction. Tell me, have Jack and Julia met their biological mother yet?"

"Yes. They were invited round to Kathleen and Maxwell's house and had a long session with her."

"And how was it?" Miranda was insistent, and I felt uncomfortable sharing the very private responses Jack and Jules had had to meeting the woman who had given birth to them.

"It was quite emotional. Julia said it was weird, but nice, meeting someone who looked so like her and seemed so familiar."

I decided to keep Jack's confused response to meeting a second mother private; it had been one of the few times I'd seen him cry in all our years together. Nor did I mention how I'd felt for Kathleen herself. Finding you had a solid, dependable adult son, and a grown-up daughter whose emotional needs still seemed unmet, was a position I could identify with – and I had at least seen it develop. How must she have felt coming to this situation after all she had been through?

"Jack told her about the Long QT and that it wasn't in any

way her fault that Patrick had died – his genes meant it was an accident waiting to happen. Kathleen said she'd lived with the guilt all her life and it had led to bouts of severe depression. Also, she had complications after the twins' birth which meant she couldn't have any more children. She'd been relieved when she got ill with fibroids and had to have a hysterectomy, because it stopped Maxwell pushing her to have fertility treatment. She knew it would be useless, but couldn't tell him why, and it nearly sent her over the edge. Sad, isn't it?"

Everyone agreed and there was a quiet moment – as quiet as it was possible to be with the bus station opposite and continual traffic roaring past – while we sipped our coffee and counted our blessings.

At least that was what I was doing.

Miranda broke the silence.

"I want to update you guys on my visit home. Not the wedding stuff, that all went smoothly and only took a day. There was another reason for going and Simon agreed I could tell you all. He said Venetia knew too much about him to bother hiding anything and Mo deserved an explanation for his miserable behaviour when he bumped into you the other day."

"Oh, right." I hadn't dared to confront Miranda directly, as Jack had suggested, and wondered what was coming.

Venetia was smirking, but I guessed she had no more idea than I did. Suzy looked avid for potential gossip and Ros had assumed her professional, expressionless mask.

"I have to go back to when Simon and I first met at Idaho State Uni when he was teaching theatre, and I was doing my Masters and dancing in a student production." Miranda sounded as if she had prepared a statement.

"I think we can remember the fairy-tale romance you both

regaled us with at such length, even if we didn't witness it in person," Venetia remarked drily.

"I know you think you know it all," responded Miranda defensively, "but the point is you don't. You all met me for the first time when we arrived back in the UK as a couple with two small children. You heard about how we fell in love and assumed we'd married, conceived and had the babies like everyone does. Well it didn't happen quite like that."

"Si got you pregnant and your Catholic parents made you marry him against your will?" suggested Venetia.

"Sometimes, Venetia, you don't know how hurtful your jokes can be!" Miranda spat, suddenly. We rarely saw her claws come out, but this time her back was up and her hackles raised. "We did fall in love and we did get married, in our own good time, but Simon could not get me pregnant. He is infertile."

Shock waves ran around our table. Ros put her hand on Miranda's; Suzy produced tissues from her bag in case of tears, but Miranda was inscrutable. Venetia flushed slightly, but said nothing. My heart was beating fast.

Miranda looked at each of us in turn, finishing on Venetia, and addressed her directly.

"It might be my Catholic upbringing, but a marriage without children couldn't work for me. So after trying unsuccessfully to boost Simon's sperm count, we decided on AID – artificial insemination by donor."

Venetia looked away from Miranda's insistent stare and stirred her espresso.

The rest of us sat motionless.

"We chose a donor whose records said he looked reasonably like Simon, had a college education and even had similar interests. The clinic was efficient and when I became pregnant with

Naomi, we reserved more of the same donor's sperm and used that to conceive Lola. We always planned to tell the girls when they were old enough to understand, and that's exactly what we did just after this New Year's."

"Oh, Miranda," said Suzy, sitting on the edge of her chair. "How did they take it?"

"They were shocked, of course" answered Miranda. "Naomi dealt with it and got on with her life. Lola raged at us both, hated Simon and did all the rebellious stuff I told you about. Then she kept demanding to meet the man who was responsible for her big nose and dyslexia, as she saw it. Simon felt threatened and said no way. He didn't want his problem made public so I couldn't talk to you girls; in the end I consulted Jack, as my GP, so he couldn't tell anyone else. Though knowing how close you are, Mo, I worried that he might drop a hint to you. I kept fishing to see if you knew anything, but I guess he's a complete professional."

"I would never want Jack to break patient confidentiality," I affirmed forcefully, "even with me, Miranda."

"So what did he suggest?" asked Ros.

"He found me and Simon a counsellor and after a couple of sessions, Simon saw that we needed to show Lola that he was still her dad, that we were on her side and agree to try and find her biological father. So when I was invited to my friend's wedding, I booked an appointment at the clinic we had used and they gave me the information I needed. Luckily our donor was still living in Montpelier so he was easy to track down, and he met me for a no-strings-attached discussion. Because Jack was at his conference down the road in Utah at the same time, he'd offered to come with me if I needed support, but in the end I thought I should go on my own."

"Oh, I see," I uttered involuntarily. "I mean, I see why you've been so stressed lately. What was he like?"

"Oh, pleasant enough. He told me about himself and his two little daughters – he's divorced from their mother and has a new girlfriend. He showed me a photo; one of them looks a little like Lola. He let me take a shot of him for the girls, but said he wasn't prepared to have any contact with them until his children were old enough to understand. When I got home, Lola and Simon seemed to have made up – he'd helped her through a difficult period at school which she appreciated, he'd actually finished his thesis and they'd all had a fine time without me. The house was a total mess, but it was worth it. Lola looked at the photo of her bio-dad, said he was a geek and Simon was better looking. That's the last we've heard of it. For now, anyway."

"Well done, Miranda," Ros declared approvingly. "You've handled a tricky situation with sense and courage. I hope Simon appreciates what you've done for him."

"Sure he does," smiled Miranda, unbending a little. "We're taking a little break, just the two of us, leaving the girls with his mom, in a couple of weeks."

"Snap!" Ros smiled at her. "Joe and I have booked that holiday in Prague now the season's ended, and I'm really looking forward to it."

"Well good for all you happy couples," snarled Venetia. "Enjoy yourselves while it lasts."

"Vee?" asked Suzy, eyebrows raised.

"I know this is all very trivial compared to what you've been up to, but the Latin American art exhibition was a disaster. Charlie was furious with me for wearing that dress and for nearly causing a diplomatic incident by arguing politics with the Chilean ambassador. He got into major hot water and he's decided I'm too much of a liability."

Venetia's mouth trembled.

"He's finished with me," she sobbed.

Jess's email was all for me – short and very sweet, she'd copied-in no one else this time.

Hi Mumma

What amazing news! I'm so happy for you and Jack and Lil sister. Your such a star you know. I'm still loving it here but now I cant wait to come home and be part of the buzz. You always work things out for everyone! My friends all say your the coolest mother and its true. Our familys the best even if its crazy and now its getting even better. Do I get to meet Kathleen and Maxwell? What about Jacks American relations – I can see a family holiday in the States coming on. Congrats on the new job too, its all happening at once.

Hugs for Mark and Zo, Lily and Jack and Aurora too if you see her around.

Luvyasomuch
Jess xxxx

Absence seemed to be making Jess's heart grow fonder and I was staggered by her admission that I was the coolest mother. She might not think so if she could see how much weight I'd put on recently. I was still wondering what I could squeeze into for the Dulwich Association party tonight, when Mark and Zoe arrived home with Jack, bearing a big bunch of flowers and a bottle of champagne.

"Hey, Ma, how ya doing?" Mark hugged me with his usual gusto, and Zoe remonstrated with him.

"Careful, babe, don't squash the flowers, or your mum for that matter. Hi, Mo, it's good to see you. How are you? You look really well."

"Thanks, Zoe, I am," I said, kissing her with affection, and smiling at Jack over her shoulder as he closed the front door. "Hello, darling. What have you got there?" I asked, seeing an expensive-looking carrier bag dangling from his hand.

"I thought you might need something – special, to wear tonight, so I kidnapped these two on their way here to help me choose an outfit. Hope you like it," he said, handing me the bag.

The three of them watched as I pulled out a stylish pair of wide, black jersey trousers and a sparkling black top. I was touched, but hoped the disappointment didn't show on my face. Something a little less tight and a little more concealing would have been more tactful on Zoe's part, I thought, guessing Jack and Mark would have relied on her fashion sense.

"They're beautiful, but I'm not sure they're quite – me, at the moment …" I faltered.

"Just try them, Mo, you might be surprised. They're really well cut," said Zoe. "Come down and show us, if you like them."

When I returned to the kitchen, the flowers were arranged in a vase on the table and Mark was standing ready to pop the champagne cork. They all exclaimed at how good I looked, and indeed Zoe had been right. The designer separates fitted perfectly and even managed to flatter my curves into an elegant line.

"Here's to a beautiful woman and a brilliant evening," Jack toasted me as they raised their glasses. I sipped the sparkling water he'd poured into my glass and sent out a request to the Universal Spirit that I could keep all the arrangements for Suzy and Duncan's evening perfectly on track until the end of the night.

While the others were getting into the car, I rang Mel's door-bell and popped in to say good night to Lily, as I'd promised. She was already in her pyjamas, earlier than she'd ever consent to at home, and excited to be having her first sleepover. They were both impressed with my eveningwear; Lily especially with my shimmering top, which she ran her fingers over.

"Looking good, girl," approved Mel. "You have a real fine time tonight. We'll be having fun here, won't we Lily?"

"I know you will be. Thanks Mel. And you're sure you're OK with doing some extra over the next few months?"

"Girl, looks like you asked and you received. I'm here to do what God asks me and help you do what He's got planned for you. What's more, a few more hours will just bring that holiday we're planning back home a little closer. Say night night to Mummy, now Lily."

My daughter planted a smacking kiss on my cheek and waved goodbye as we drove up the hill. While Mark, Zoe and Jack chatted animatedly on the ten-minute drive to Dulwich, I breathed deeply to contact the Source and did some discreet shoulder-lifts to release my tension. In spite of the distractions, the Spirit buzzed around my head and I felt my body tune in to the Energy Flow. As we drove up Anerley Hill in the dusk, I could have sworn I caught a glimpse of Old Peggy, silhouetted by the park gates and her words flicked into my head: "*Love will win over fear*".

If Suzy's house looked inviting from the outside, with chandeliers and candles glowing through the tall ground-floor windows, its promise was more than met within. She had excelled herself with glorious flower-arrangements in all the rooms, each of which had been rearranged to accommodate different elements of the evening.

I whipped around the house, ensuring that everything was going to plan. The caterers had turned one end of the kitchen into a well-stocked bar and at the other were assembling the first, delicious-looking dishes of the buffet, which would be served in the dining room where the table had been pushed to the wall. The jazz quartet had arrived and were setting up at one end of the playroom in which the carpet had already been rolled back for dancing. Duncan's capacious study held rows of chairs for those who needed to sit for Dennis's talk, and the massive drawing-room looked magical with its low lights, a fire blazing in the grate and chairs and sofas arranged in intimate groups for easy conversation.

We were admiring the set-up when Suzy swept in, magnificent in full-length maroon velvet, followed by Duncan in an ample dinner jacket with matching maroon velvet bow tie. He kissed me on both cheeks and gave me a warm hug.

"Mo, my dear, you look utterly blooming and you've worked miracles getting us organised tonight. You're a lucky man, Jack, nearly as lucky as I am." He shook Jack's hand, clapped him on the shoulder and smiled round at Mark and Zoe. "And now the next generation are on our heels – good to see you, Mark, and to meet you, my dear. Come and get something to drink."

Suzy put a hand on my arm as the others followed Duncan to the kitchen.

"You've done a fabulous job, Mo, thanks so much. My only worry about tonight is Venetia. You don't think she'll drink too much and make a scene or get upset, do you?" she asked.

"Don't worry, I'll keep an eye on her and I'll brief Jack and Mark to pay her attention so she doesn't miss Charlie too much," I reassured Suzy, smiling as Olly and Martin appeared, also in dinner jackets with matching dickie bows. They, Naomi and Lola and a dozen of Martin's friends were earning pocket money as waiters, sous-chefs and cloakroom attendants. Out in the hall I could hear the first arrivals having their coats taken and the clink of drinks trays as my little team sprang into action.

As the rooms filled with people, conversation and bon-homie, I checked to see whether my plans for certain guests, who I'd managed to slip onto the invitation list, were material-ising. In one corner of the drawing room, David was in ani-mated conversation with Erica. She had resigned herself to there being no scandal in Maxwell Robards' background, and was warming to the idea of her tabloid newspaper running a cam-paign promoting TXT M8. As I was attempting to lip-read their discussion, Aurora came up to me, unusually pink-cheeked, with a beaming smile.

"Mo, how can I thank you enough? You've changed my life since that lunch at the Picture Gallery," she said, kissing me.

"I'm so glad about the job with Anthony – he thinks you're brilliant. Well done, sweetheart," I congratulated my surrogate niece.

"It's really cool, but I have you to thank for Dennis too. You knew I fancied him at the lecture and it was so sweet of you to write Anthony's number on Dennis's card. You doing that gave me the courage to ring him. We went on a first date a few days ago and we haven't been apart since." Aurora flung her arms round me. "You've always been a second mum to me, Mo. I re-member you and Paul being such fun when I was small. It's great to see Mark, and Zoe's cool isn't she?"

"And Jess sends you her love from Thailand," I remembered. "I'm happy for you and Dennis, he's a really nice guy."

"Must go, he's starting his talk in a minute – " and Aurora floated off towards the study.

I caught sight of Nick chatting to Duncan and waved to him. He excused himself to his host and came over.

"Thanks for sending me an invite for this evening," Nick greeted me. "There's a few people here I've been wanting to make contact with for some time. I gather you made use of Father O'Gorman's information?"

"With results I couldn't begin to have imagined. I'll fill you in, but not tonight. In the meantime, though, there's someone I'd like you to meet."

I led Nick over to David, who was beginning to look a little trapped by Erica's insistent manner, and introduced them.

"Nick, last time we met, you were off to meet a client who was head of a telecommunications company. Would that include a mobile phone business, by any chance?" I asked, disingenuously.

"Well, yes, actually," he replied.

"And you said you tried to persuade your clients to use their commercial power in positive ways?"

"I do my best," Nick said modestly.

"Well, I think David may have a way to help you do that," I said, and left them to discuss a sponsorship deal for TXT M8, as I spied Venetia, in her dangerous dress, taking yet another glass of champagne from a proffered tray.

"Are you OK, Vee?" I asked her, as she took a gulp.

"Couldn't be better," she replied, her words only slightly slurred. "Charlie dumping me's the best thing that could have happened. I'm free and easy again, just the way I like it. Look at the lovebirds, makes you sick, doesn't it?"

I followed her gaze and saw Si with his arm round Miranda, sitting together on a sofa looking very contented.

"That was a bit of a revelation about Si," I remarked to Venetia, while smiling at Miranda who had noticed us looking at them. "It put paid to one of my theories about who Aurora's father was."

"You idiot," she scoffed. "I never slept with Si, he was much too straight for me. I'm amazed you never guessed, but then that's one of the reasons I've kept it quiet all this time. I was protecting you and your kids, as well as Aurora."

I looked at her, dismayed, as what she was suggesting slowly dawned on me.

"You don't mean—"

"Yes, I think it must have been your Paul," she mumbled. "Just one of those evenings in my room before graduation. You were there, but everyone had fallen asleep except me and him. We were pissed, stoned – it meant nothing. I had no idea I was pregnant until you two had gone off on your travels. When you came back Mark was on the way and I didn't want to make waves, and then Paul turned out to be such a crap father that I was glad I'd never told anyone. Aurora's definitely better off without him, and don't you dare tell her, ever. Well, hello, and who are you?" Venetia suddenly went into siren mode as Nick approached us.

"This is Nick; my friend Venetia," I introduced them.

"Thanks, Mo, useful conversation with David. I think we may get somewhere," Nick told me, before turning his attention to Venetia. "Haven't we met before; I'm sure I've seen you around the Westminster village?"

"I'm sure you have," Venetia purred. "Mo, shouldn't you be circulating?"

I took the hint and left them to it. I was somewhat shaken by what Venetia had told me, but decided that if she wasn't just winding me up, it was too long ago to be important now. It wasn't my business to interfere in Aurora's life, even though she might be Mark and Jess' half sister. I stepped into the study, where Dennis was finishing his talk to another appreciative audience.

" ... so it's perfectly possible that Peggy Finch did start the Crystal Palace fire as a child. The box of matches she gave me was certainly authentic, and her story tallies with the account we have from Henry Buckland, the manager. He recorded that at about 7 pm he and his daughter Chrystal, who was named after his beloved palace, left their house 'Rockhills' on the northern corner of Crystal Palace Parade, to walk their dog. As they walked towards it, Buckland noticed a red glow in the building and ran inside to find two night-watchmen attempting to extinguish a small fire in the office in the central transept. It soon became obvious that the situation was very serious. The first fire-brigade call was received by Penge Fire Station at 7.59 p.m. and the first fire-engine arrived at three minutes past eight. By the next morning, 88 fire engines, 438 firemen from four fire brigades and 749 police officers had been on duty and failed to stop the building disintegrating. The cause of the fire has never yet been established, but there have been theories of arson and electrical faults. It was certainly spread by the quantity of dry old timber flooring, broken glass panels in the roof that had been replaced with boarding and a strong northerly wind.

"Anyway, almost as soon as she had told us her story, old Peggy Finch passed away, and she is buried in Beckenham, next to her ancestor, Margaret Finch. Just as the Gipsy Queen's funeral was funded by local traders, my enterprising colleague, Mary Mozart, organised a collection around shops in the Triangle, for the funeral and a headstone for Old Peggy, as most people knew her.

"And now, ladies and gentlemen, please enjoy the rest of

your evening. A buffet supper is served in the dining room, and there will be music and dancing."

There was enthusiastic applause and I moved out of the way as the audience began to filter out of the study. Ros and Joe were among them, and stopped when they saw me.

"Wonderful evening, Mo, well done," said Ros, kissing me lightly.

"Are we still friends?" asked Joe. I hugged him.

"Very good friends. It was a fantastic production, and I never meant to come backstage anyway. Did you get stuck with the theatre bore for long?"

"Hours!" chuckled Joe. "I had to pretend I was due on stage to get rid of him!"

As they wandered off to the buffet, I went in search of Jack, and found him talking to Olly on the stairs. I sat down on his other side and he put his arm round me.

"Auntie Mo's going to marry me," said Olly, getting up and heading down to the hall.

"Is this true?" asked Jack "Are you leaving me for another man?"

"You won't get rid of me that easily," I laughed. "Especially when I'm carrying your baby." Jack put his other hand on my belly.

"How's he doing? Has he been kicking tonight? He's going to be a footballer, this boy." He stroked the small bump beneath my maternity top and stretch-fronted trousers. "Has anyone guessed?"

"If they have, nobody's said anything. When shall we go public?" I asked, nuzzling my face into Jack's neck.

"Let's keep it in the family for a little bit longer," he requested. I smiled up at him as I heard an echo in my head:

"*There's family all around you. New blood, old and young, here and across the sea.*"

I shut my eyes and let the Life Force flow over me in waves of peace and contentment.

Or was it just my pregnancy hormones kicking in?